PRAISE FOR LARA BERNHARDT

"Lara Bernhardt writes with ferocious honesty and tenderness, laying open the world of the trafficking of young girls with a bright spear of hope."

— JACQUELYN MITCHARD, *NEW YORK TIMES* BEST-SELLING AUTHOR OF *THE DEEP END OF THE OCEAN*

"This is entertainment with a punch, an exotic setting with a dark side that tourists rarely see. We come away with admiration for those who refuse to look the other way when confronted with evil, and perhaps with a little more courage to do the same."

— MARCIA PRESTON, MARY HIGGINS CLARK AWARD-WINNING AUTHOR OF *THE SPIDERLING*

"Written with skill, compassion, and sensitivity, this is a story that will break your heart and restore your soul.

— TAYLOR JONES, BOOK REVIEWER

SHADOW OF THE TAJ

LARA BERNHARDT

ADMISSION
PRESS

SHADOW OF THE TAJ

Copyright © 2019 by Lara Bernhardt

Cover Design by BEAUTeBOOK

All cover art copyright © 2019

Paperback ISBN: 9781955836913

eBook ISBN: 9781955836906

Hardcover ISBN: 9781955836920

LARA BERNHARDT

Shadow
of the Taj

A Novel

Marilyn,

"In a gentle way, you can shake the world." —Mahatma Gandhi

Thank you for being a reader!

Lara Bernhardt

ADMISSION PRESS

www.admissionpress.com

*For everyone who has ever intervened to improve the life of a child,
whether through teaching, adoption, fostering, mentoring, volunteering
—or any other way.*

No act of kindness, no matter how small, is ever wasted.

— AESOP

The Taj is the very best of India. The light strikes the face of the Taj and sends up her lovely image for all to enjoy. But she is to be enjoyed from the front, in the light. In her shadow is the Yamuna River, one of the most polluted rivers in the entire world. This is the worst of India. Stay where tourists are intended, madam. Do not enter the shadow of the Taj.

CHAPTER 1

*L*eslie Matthews hated the frenzied chaos of New Delhi's streets. Almost as much as she hated her husband's silence.

Outside her window, auto rickshaws beeped, weaving between lanes of vehicles spewing exhaust into the grimy air. She gritted her teeth as a rickshaw squeezed by, so close she expected to hear metal scraping.

She shifted in her seat, the cracked vinyl scratching her legs.

Her husband, Tom, stared out the opposite window, arms crossed. She wished he would say something.

When the battered taxi shuddered to a stop at a red light, an elderly man rose from the curb and pressed against her window, brandishing a stump of an arm. Dirty fingers tapped the glass. Though she couldn't understand the words he formed with his toothless mouth, she knew he wanted money. Everyone wanted money. She turned away, but his image joined countless other memories of poverty and suffering.

The light turned green. The taxi left the man behind, his wild hair and ragged clothing blowing in the breeze. The memory, she knew, was not so easily left behind. She wanted to help him—she wanted to help them all—but that was impossible.

She missed home. Most of all, she missed the class of third-graders she would be teaching had she turned down the trip to India with Tom. She could help her students.

The taxi driver slammed on his brakes and swerved sharply to avoid a truck that veered halfway into their lane as if the taxi didn't exist. Tossed in the back seat, she tried to steady herself while the driver lurched around vehicles and returned to their lane. She should be used to this by now, she thought, as she straightened back up and unclenched her teeth. Nearly six months in India and the frenetic activity of the streets still shocked her.

She took a deep breath and made an attempt at conversation. "The lane lines mean nothing. I don't know how anyone gets anywhere without crashing."

"We didn't have to leave the hotel," Tom answered, not looking at her. "You insisted we 'go do something.'" He was still annoyed. He didn't even try to hide it.

"How many days can I sit by the hotel pool? I don't like swimming."

"Or anything else I enjoy," he muttered.

She decided to pretend she hadn't heard and turned back to the window.

A group of young women draped in jewel-tone saris—gems in the dull, hazy street—clustered on the sidewalk, each clutching a frozen confection. Laughing, they fought to keep their dark hair out of the sticky, sweet mess as they licked the dripping rivulets that ran down their bangle-adorned arms.

At her elementary school in Kansas, she and the other teachers chatted over cups of coffee every morning before the first bell rang, laughing like the Indian woman she was watching out the window.

When was the last time she laughed?

A bright orange and green truck swerved into their lane

and barreled straight toward them.

The driver didn't move over. He seemed oblivious to the impending danger. She wanted to say something, but the words didn't make it out of her mouth. She almost reached for Tom, but knew he would offer no comfort.

The driver eased the taxi sideways, squeezing into a space that had not existed moments earlier. A horn blasted behind them. The truck blew past in a rush of garish color and jangling chains.

She gasped, sinking back into her seat.

The driver glanced in his mirror. His dark eyes crinkled, crow's feet deepening in his dusky, brown skin. "Okay, lady?" he asked in his musical Indian accent.

She nodded and returned the smile while her pulse pounded. Another near miss like that and her hair would be as gray as the driver's.

"Still can't handle the traffic? Relax. He does this all day, every day. He knows what he's doing."

She decided she liked Tom better silent after all.

"Zoo. Zoo." The driver announced their arrival as he turned into the parking lot.

She clenched her teeth, dreading the coming onslaught their fair skin always attracted. Everywhere they went, men pressed in on them, hands out, anxious for rupees, offering to give tours, pressing trinkets and T-shirts into their faces, relentlessly begging for money.

Tom made arrangements for the driver to wait for them, then stepped out and stood near the taxi.

She hoped he would open the door for her and shield her from the crowd. He didn't.

The driver, settling in for his wait, glanced back and forth between the two of them then jumped out of the car and opened the door for her. "Memsaab." He offered her a hand.

She remembered how Tom hurried to help her when they first arrived in India. Her stomach tensed. They thought this trip would be a refreshing change of scenery, a break from teaching, time alone. Something to recharge their marriage, like a honeymoon. It hadn't worked out that way.

Now he was mad about not getting his way and would be distant all day. She almost asked to go back.

But the driver spoke again. "Memsaab?" His well-worn, gray *shalwar kameez* hung limply from his gangly frame. He nodded, gesturing her out.

She took his hand and stepped from the taxi, straightening her own *kameez*, the more form-fitting, feminine version of the traditional clothing. It tapered at the middle, hinting at her narrow waist and slight hips, with elaborate designs embroidered in golden thread about the neckline and hem. She'd purchased several outfits shortly after their arrival in India, eager to fit in and experience a new culture. The clothing did not help her blend in, however, as nothing camouflaged her green eyes, fair skin, and russet hair.

Why should she go back and give up what she wanted to do? One day's activity wasn't much to ask for.

She followed Tom through the zoo parking lot, choked with taxis and rickshaws and scooters, as well as merchants, beggars, would-be tour guides, and pickpockets.

Voices called out, hands waved wildly, enticing them to purchase cold, sweet lassis, sodas, bags of snacks, souvenirs.

An elderly man hunched on his heels held a cluster of peacock feathers. He waved to her. She couldn't understand his words but imagined him pleading for rupees to buy food.

A man with a wild black beard and busy eyes stood suddenly at her left. "Madam, would you like a tour of the zoo today?"

She shook her head and tried to continue on but was stopped by a younger man—this one in jeans and a T-shirt—offering "Souvenir T-shirts, madam?" while pushing several styles in her face.

She kept moving toward the entrance gate, the men trailing

after her doggedly, growing louder and louder, as if they believed she simply hadn't heard them.

Something snagged her right pant leg. A man with crooked teeth, wispy white hair, and a patch over one eye sat on the sidewalk, clutching her loose-fitting cuff with one hand, thrusting his other hand at her insistently, palm up.

A woman emerged from the crowd, hair drawn back tightly in a bun at the base of her neck, an infant at her exposed breast, nursing. Head cocked to the side, she drew close, pointing at the infant, brown eyes pleading. "Madam, please."

"You like?" interrupted the T-shirt salesman.

"Sir, for your wife?" suggested the man clutching peacock feathers.

"…memsaab…" The tour guide again.

"…rupees," pleaded the nursing mother.

"Hello? Best prices." A man with carved wooden camels joined the throng.

She held up her hands to ward off the endless requests. She couldn't take any more plucking and pleading. But still they came, pressing ever closer.

Tom appeared beside her. He enveloped her and drew her out of the crowd. His strong voice quieted the swelling cacophony, one arm curled around her, holding fast, the other arm out, fisted, a battering ram clearing the path.

He didn't touch anyone. It wasn't necessary. His demeanor told them everything they needed to know. He flicked his eyes at the hawks like someone might brush away pesky flies. They backed away, realizing this one wouldn't budge. And now that she was enveloped solidly within his protective hold, she too enjoyed immunity.

She leaned against him gratefully. He squeezed her gently and led her to the entrance gate.

Two boys—not more than twelve years old—chased each other near the front of the zoo, up and down the steps that led to the entrance gates. They laughed, tagging each other and reversing roles. Reminded of recess, Leslie missed her classroom of kids back home.

The boys noticed the foreigners. They halted the game and shuffled to stand in front of her. Listing to the side, heads hanging, jaws slack, each held out a hand, mumbling words she couldn't understand. They reminded her of zombies as they droned tonelessly.

Tom pulled at her, but she shrugged him off. She ignored the poverty and the pleading as much as she could. But these boys should be in school, learning. Not on the streets.

"Please, Tom?"

His jaw clenched. After a moment, he gave her an eye roll from hell and thrust a hand into his pocket.

"It won't help them," he said, dropping a few coins into her hand and stomping away.

She split the coins into the boys' hands. They nodded, but that was all. What had she expected? Beaming faces? Hugs?

She hurried after Tom. "It might help them," she insisted.

He didn't answer. Instead, he stopped, grabbed her by the shoulders, and spun her around. "Dammit. Look." She followed his pointing finger.

A man stood by the boys, scowling, hand out. They surrendered the rupees she'd given them. He drifted back into the crowd and took up a position some distance away.

Leaning against a fence, he lit a cigarette as the boys resumed their game of chase.

"An adult always watches them, far enough away not to be noticed, but close enough to make sure the kids don't run off with the money. It's a scam. Dr. Hameed warned me months ago. You just fell for it."

She didn't regret it, despite Tom's renewed bad mood. Maybe the boys would eat better tonight. She hoped so.

She wanted to make a difference in someone's life.

She knew how easily one moment could change a life forever.

CHAPTER 2

*E*ven halfway around the world, Leslie recognized a field trip when she saw one. Several groups of children lined up, holding hands, waiting impatiently while their teachers arranged their tickets. Couples and families waited in line, too. She and Tom joined a queue.

A chalkboard sign listed hours of operation, forbade "eatables" within the park, and detailed entry fees.

"Indian citizens pay less than foreigners," Tom noticed.

"It was the same at the Taj Mahal. Don't you remember?"

"It doesn't seem fair. Indian adults pay ten rupees, Indian children pay five rupees. But foreign adults and children pay fifty rupees each. No child discount even."

"It's less than a dollar for each of us. That's nothing."

"I don't think it's fair that they have different prices."

She opted not to argue. She wanted to have fun today. Once, when they were in college, Tom had taken her to the zoo in Omaha—an impromptu weekend road trip. They'd had so much fun, laughing, holding hands. She remembered the warm, fuzzy feeling he inflamed in her every time he turned those gorgeous eyes on her. He'd picked her up and swung her in a circle at one point, and she'd squealed with laughter in a way she never had. Perhaps now that they were both in their thirties, she should be mature enough not to want to be swung like a child. But she did. She wanted to feel that happy again.

Tom paid their entry fees and took a map, which he passed to her.

The zoo sprawled before her, a tangle of sidewalks waiting to be explored. She unfolded the map to calculate the best route to see as much as possible. "They have a pair of white tigers here. We should make sure we see them. Very rare. We're not likely to ever have this opportunity again."

"Obviously, I don't care. We're only here at your insistence."

She gave up hope that he'd remember their zoo trip all those years ago and resigned herself to making the most of the day.

A little girl, just inside the gates, caught her attention. She wore a sari, stomach bare. A long, heavily sequined veil hung down her back, almost to the ground. Although she couldn't be more than ten years old, she wore bright red lipstick and heavy blush.

She danced, though no music played, hips swaying provocatively. Bangles on her wrists and ankles jangled as she stomped her feet and undulated her arms suggestively at passersby.

As she watched the child, her mother's voice echoed through her mind. *'The Good Lord created you perfect in His image, and you are beautiful in His eyes. Do not cover His work with adornment.'* She heard this lesson from a very early age. As she grew older, her mother expanded the lesson to include, *'Such adornment is meant to excite men's hearts and lure them into the way of sin.'*

She was never allowed to wear makeup growing up. She still didn't wear much, even though she'd distanced herself from her parents years ago. In her experience, no adornment was necessary to entice men. Some of them were just inclined to sin.

A group of men clustered around the child, pointing at her, watching her dance. They pressed closer and closer, nodding and clapping as her hips gyrated.

One man held out a paper bill. When the girl accepted the rupees, he curled an arm around her waist and caressed her bare stomach. The girl stopped dancing, her eyes staring resolutely at the ground. The other men jeered and cackled as he leaned closer and nuzzled her neck.

The memory of groping hands and hot breath against her skin crashed over Leslie like a tidal wave. Heart pounding, she scanned the vicinity, searching for the girl's keeper, hoping he would put a stop to this.

Among the couples and families, she spotted a lone, lanky man leaning against a tree, one foot propped behind him.

Absorbed with a cell phone, one hand texted frantically, his thumb flying across the keys, while the other hand pinched a smoldering cigarette. He glanced toward the girl periodically. No concern crossed his face. In fact, he looked amused.

The men continued to harass and tease the child, touching her inappropriately and running their hands over her exposed skin. People walked by as if she didn't exist. The girl's expressionless face indicated that this treatment was all too common. And that she was helpless to stop it.

One man dropped to his knees behind her, grabbed her hips, and ground against her, contorting his face in feigned orgasmic delight while his buddies laughed and snapped pictures with their phones.

"Excuse me," she said, stepping closer to the girl, unable to watch another moment.

"What are you doing?" Tom said, grabbing her arm.

"Those men are molesting that girl. If no one else is going to stop them, I will."

"It's none of your business. Don't make a scene."

None of her business? Wasn't that the attitude that allowed this sort of thing to happen in the first place? She felt her face harden as she returned her attention to the girl, scowling at the men.

The groping man dropped his hands and stood. She wedged herself between the men and the girl, daring them with her eyes to try anything more. They drew away, leering at her and making a few comments she didn't understand before drifting to the exit.

The man under the tree straightened. He pulled deeply on his cigarette, squinting. Something about him made her skin crawl.

The little girl resumed her dance, hands out, pleading for rupees. Her deep brown eyes flicked up, holding Leslie's stare before returning to the ground. Those eyes. They reminded her of someone else's. A little girl from long ago.

"Tom?"

"No. You already gave all my change to those boys outside. Forget it."

"But —"

"Do you want to see the zoo or not?" He pulled her in the direction of the nearest cages.

Their usual roles reversed. Tom tried unsuccessfully to interest her in the animals. She couldn't focus. She'd been so excited to get away from the hotel, hoping to recapture the excitement from long ago, but now she walked past the cages without seeing what was inside.

The little girl churned up a memory. Far worse than the armless man, the crowds of groping men, the begging children, the poverty and suffering. Worse than anything else she'd seen or experienced in her life. Something she couldn't forget no matter how hard she tried.

CHAPTER 3

*L*eslie watched for the girl in the crowds. Several times, she spotted her—and the lanky, smoking man was always within sight.

A jarring ride on an ornately-painted elephant could not distract her or drive the girl from her thoughts. When she remained sullen during the plodding ride, Tom fell into his own frustrated silence. One cage after another, they stood silently, not speaking.

They watched the white tigers romp about their enclosure, pouncing on one another and rolling through the grass, when a cacophony of chatter announced the arrival of a group of children. One of the groups she had noticed at the entrance gate surrounded them.

The children whispered and pointed at the foreigners. Apparently the white people were more fascinating to them than the white tigers.

One crept forward and asked, "You are from America?" His English was quite good, if heavily accented.

"Yes," she answered.

The children giggled and chanced moving closer. They all

carried notebooks and pencils. Some of them thrust paper and pencil toward her.

"Please, American Auntie," they said. "Autograph, please."

"You want my autograph?"

She took the nearest notebook and pencil and quickly scratched her name across the top of the child's page of zoo notes. Below her signature, she wrote, "America." The boy accepted the notebook almost reverently, and though she was baffled as to why he appeared so happy with it, she enjoyed his smile. She missed crayons and glue, construction paper and stick figures, recess and story time. She signed every proffered notebook.

"Look at you. You're famous," Tom teased as the children continued requesting autographs. He looked relieved that she'd finally responded positively to something. "They're more interested in you than the animals."

The children drifted away, continuing their tour of the zoo, clutching their notebooks. She realized she'd never seen a teacher with the group and scanned the vicinity for an authority figure. When she felt a tug at her sleeve, she turned, expecting one last straggler requesting an autograph.

The little dancing girl stood beside her. Dark, chocolate-brown eyes gazed up at her. She couldn't read the child's expression and wasn't sure what she wanted. But those eyes. The resemblance was remarkable.

She glanced about, searching for the lanky man, but didn't see him anywhere.

She turned to Tom. This time he dug several bills out of his pocket and pressed the paper rupees into the girl's hand.

The little girl tilted her face toward Tom, examining him shyly. The veil shifted on her head.

That's when Leslie noticed a bruise on the girl's face. Without thinking, she raised a hand, lifting the heavy veil to reveal the purple marks across the child's cheek. The girl jumped at her touch, dropped her eyes, and adjusted her veil to once again cover most of the bruising.

Bile rose in the back of her throat. So the girl was physically abused and molested. What else did this child have to endure?

Small, grubby fingers rested tentatively on her forearm — a familiar touch she missed.

"Please, Auntie, help me," the girl whispered.

The words punctured her heart, draining away everything else. The zoo melted into the background. She heard nothing but the quiet desperation in the words.

"Please help me."

Leslie squatted down and peered into the girl's dark eyes. Big and round, with dark circles beneath, accentuated by high cheekbones, these weary eyes didn't belong in a child's face.

She recognized the hollow emptiness, as if nothing ever made her smile, as if she had given up on life. Filled with a desire to see a smile on the child's face and hope in those empty eyes, she placed her own hand over the little one still resting on her forearm. "How can I help you?" she asked.

The dark, brown eyes dropped to the ground again. The little hand trembled. "Please, help, Auntie."

She tried to make eye contact. "What's your name?"

Silence. Then, quietly, "Raveena."

Progress. But Raveena still stared at the ground, her entire body trembling.

"Leslie." Tom tried to intervene, tapping her shoulder.

She shrugged him off, took the hand from her forearm, and clasped it between her own. "We will help you, Raveena. Just tell us how."

"You stopped those men —" The girl stopped, as if frightened by her own voice, and her eyes scanned the area, searching perhaps for the lanky man.

Dark suspicions clouded Leslie's mind. But she didn't want to push the girl too hard. She'd worked with a few child abuse cases as a teacher, enough to learn from counselors that children were often afraid to ask for help. Children, completely at the mercy of caregivers, suffered terrible repercussions if discovered seeking assistance. This girl was taking a huge risk reaching out to her.

"No one has the right to hurt or mistreat you, Raveena," she whispered.

Raveena's gaze shifted, and her demeanor changed completely. The girl resembled a hunted rabbit watching a predator approach, caught in the open with no place to dash.

Leslie turned and saw the lanky man storming toward them. A small knot of fear balled in her stomach. She clutched Raveena's hand tightly.

The man scowled as he strode toward them. Clean-shaven and nicely dressed, his eyes darted constantly, glancing about as if expecting trouble at any moment. As he drew near, he ran a hand through his slick, black hair and forced a wide smile. A crooked red scar slashed across one cheek, turning the smile into a grimace.

His eyes raked up and down her. "Hello," he began with a nod.

Tom stepped in front of Leslie and answered the stranger. "Hello."

The man shifted his attention to Tom, smiling wider still, the red scar twisting along his cheek. "Hello, sir. American?"

"Yes, we're American. Can I help you?"

The man cocked his head and held his hands out to his sides. "No, sir. Not at all. I am only collecting the girl. I am sorry if she has disturbed you."

He smiled again and held his hand out to Raveena, who shrank away from him.

Leslie pulled Raveena to her side and curled an arm around the girl's shoulders. Raveena trembled.

"What do you want with the girl?" Leslie asked.

"What?" The forced smile melted from the stranger's face.

"Who gave her these bruises?" She pushed the girl's veil away to reveal her cheek.

She met the man's hostile eyes, waiting for his answer. Raveena quivered beside her, one hand clutching the loose fabric of her kameez.

"Raveena, come," the man insisted.

Leslie pulled the girl closer. "I don't think she wants to go with you."

"She belongs to me," the man replied.

"What does that mean? She's your daughter?"

She sensed he wasn't accustomed to being questioned.

"Come, Raveena." He spoke quietly, extending his hand to her, staring intently into the girl's eyes.

Leslie suspected more was being communicated than she was able to comprehend.

"Raveena," she said, keeping her arm around the trembling girl. "Is this man your father?"

Raveena turned her wide eyes upward. She didn't answer.

"Do you want to go with this man?" she pressed.

"No," the girl finally said.

"Raveena. Come." The man's voice took on a harsh tone.

Raveena jumped. He snatched her wrist and jerked the girl to his side.

"Just a minute," Leslie demanded as the man dragged Raveena away, the girl's quick little steps no match for his long strides. Raveena turned back, eyes imploring.

Leslie knew they would soon be lost in the mass of people. She couldn't let that happen.

Tom restrained her with a hand on her arm.

She pulled away from him. "We can't let him take her."

"What right do we have to stop him?"

"What right does he have to her? She was pleading for help. You didn't feel her shaking."

"We have no right to interfere. I didn't like the looks of the guy either, but that doesn't mean we have any business getting involved in something that's none of our concern."

"She asked for help. She was terrified of him. She's obviously being abused—you saw those men molesting her. If we do nothing, that makes us partially responsible. She asked me to help her."

"There's nothing you can—"

"That's what everyone always says." Her eyes blazed. He didn't understand. No one ever understood. They couldn't. "'There's nothing more we can do.' 'It's not our concern.' 'We just have to accept that little girls disappear—'"

"Hey, come here." Tom looped his arms around her and drew her close. "I get it. But what can we realistically do? I suppose we could report it to the police, but what would we tell them? That we were at the zoo and saw a creepy guy with a little girl and we think he might be mistreating her? We don't know that for sure, and we don't know how to find her. What could they do?"

She allowed him to rock her while the words sunk in. *Be realistic.* The same thing she'd been hearing all her life. *Accept it. No matter how much you wish or pray or regret, terrible things happen and no one can change it.*

She lifted her head from his shoulder and looked at the crowd around them.

The lanky man and the little girl were lost in a sea of people, long gone. Raveena was one of the many abused children in the world that went without help. One more girl Leslie couldn't help.

"Let's go back to the hotel. You still have plenty of time to swim." She pulled away from him and headed to the front gates.

Tom fell in step beside her. He twined his fingers between hers. She let him.

They discovered their taxi driver with his bare feet propped on the dash, snoozing through the afternoon. Startled by their early return, he sat up quickly, smiling sheepishly, and slid his plastic flip-flops back onto his dusty feet. "Memsaab okay?" he asked Tom.

"Yeah, she's fine." Tom released her hand and helped her into the taxi before following her in. "We want to go back to the hotel now."

"Back to hotel? Yes, sir."

She slumped in the back seat, anything but fine. There were so many things she wanted to change, so many people who suffered. How did other people ignore it? How did they push aside all the pain in the world?

As their driver steered the taxi into the clogged streets, she thought of Raveena. Where had that man taken her? Was he the cause of her bruises? Why was she so hungry? Didn't he feed her? Leslie envied people who simply looked the other way. She wished she could put the little girl's face out of her mind. Especially the look in her eyes as the man dragged her away. She'd seen that pleading look before, in another set of eyes that belonged to another little girl. The encounter with Raveena dredged it from her childhood memories.

Leslie closed her eyes and tried to press that memory back into the little corner of her mind where it lurked constantly, waiting to pounce, to remind her how she failed. She needed to relegate the memory of Raveena there too. She shouldn't have let the man take her. But she did, and now she had no way to find her. And once taken, little girls never came back, no matter how much anyone searched.

Her mother would instruct her to trust God in all things. That was a pretty worthless bit of advice, like most of the words of wisdom her mother had planted in her psyche as a child. She could trust God all she wanted, but Raveena would still be hungry and bruised. Who was that little girl supposed to trust?

CHAPTER 4

$\mathcal{L}$eslie settled into a wooden lounge chair beside the pool, warm sun on her bare arms and legs. Tom draped his towel over the back of another lounge chair and went straight for the water.

The pool wasn't crowded. Two hotel groundskeepers planted flowers in the mulched beds surrounding the pool area. A young woman in a pale pink sari sat on a chair, keeping an eye on two boys swimming.

Leslie watched Tom swim a few laps before leaning back and closing her eyes.

At least the hotel was modern and clean, a far more comfortable place to spend time than the dismal guesthouse she'd spent the last four months stuck in while Tom conducted his research.

She couldn't believe she'd agreed to give up half her school year to come along. He'd promised romantic palaces and time together. Instead, she was left alone all day while he went into the fields with professors to collect samples, visit farmers, and inspect crops. She knew his research excited him, knew he felt strongly about reducing pesticide usage and improving the environment while maintaining an abundant crop. And she knew advancing from his postdoctoral fellowship to a faculty position depended on publications and grant money. This research could be the stepping-stone forward. But when she asked to help, eager for something to do, he said no, it wasn't possible, that she would make the other professors uncomfortable. "Women don't work in these rural areas."

He came back in the evenings, eager to share his experiences with her. But after a day alone in a stifling room with no one to talk to, nothing to do, a toilet that barely flushed, and often with no electricity, she didn't want to listen. Maybe he had expected it to be different, but he offered no sympathy.

One night he snapped, "Just go do something tomorrow."

"Like what?"

The tiny town, about an hour from the lake resort city Nainital in the foothills of the Himalayas, sat in the middle of nowhere and offered nothing to do.

"I don't know. Walk to the market. Have you been there?"

She hadn't. The guesthouse employees did all the shopping. And the cooking. And the laundry. They had no television, no radio, no magazines, or newspapers. Nothing to occupy her mind or her time. So she walked to the market the next day, past smoldering trash piles, cattle, fields of rapeseed, and curious eyes.

When she reached the strip of concrete stalls selling local fruits and vegetables, men surrounded her. She wasn't sure where they all came from. They crowded and jostled her, pressing against her, talking rapidly. She tried to break free, but they blocked her path. She couldn't understand what they said, but she could tell it wasn't complimentary. They leered at her. She heard the word "American" at least once.

She turned to the vendors for help, but they all looked the other way. Before she could do anything, she was completely walled in by a blur of faces.

The men reached out, touching her, groping. Fingers caressed her arms, searched out her hips, slid up her body. She tried to push the hands away but there were too many. Her whimpered pleas to stop brought only jeers.

A rickshaw pulled up beside the crowd. The nearest men pushed her toward the puttering vehicle. She called for help, but no one answered. She was certain she was about to be kidnapped. And she didn't want to think about what these men intended to do with her.

Heart racing, she shoved one of her would-be captors, knocking him backward. She wriggled through the crowd, hands still pawing her, and ran. Feet pounding the pavement, lungs burning from the acrid smoke in the air, she didn't stop until safely back inside the crumbling guesthouse, the door to their tiny room locked behind her. Ghost hands slithered over her body. She slid down the door, curled into a ball, and tried to forget the fingers of a dozen strange men on her skin.

The tears came a moment later and streamed down her cheeks.

Tom found her still shaken hours later and scooped her into his arms. "What happened?"

She related the horrifying experience, breaking down all over again as she described the men attacking her.

"In this little university town? Where did all these men come from? Who were they?"

"I don't know. I wondered the same thing."

"Everyone has been really nice to me. I'm sure no one was trying to kidnap you." His skeptical tone stunned the tears from her eyes.

"They tried to push me into a rickshaw. What do you think they were doing?"

"They were probably excited to see an American. Maybe they wanted to take you on a tour of the city. Out in the fields, the farmers' wives bring me tea and all the villagers want to talk to me. I'm sure you misunderstood."

"A tour and tea? They groped me. Do the farmer's wives and the villagers grope you?"

"Maybe they wanted to shake your hand. Or touch your hair. A lot of villagers want to touch my hair. The lighter color fascinates them."

"I was lucky I escaped without being kidnapped or raped. You are being completely insensitive right now." Tears spilled from her eyes, this time from frustration.

Tom sighed. "I'm sorry. I'm sorry they scared you. And I'm sorry you're bored here. I didn't know it would be like this. I wasn't prepared."

He was right. They weren't prepared for how different India would be. She'd never been outside the United States before this trip. And the culture shock had hit her hard. She'd learned lots, and the culture and history were fascinating. But very different.

The extreme poverty and hunger disturbed her most. Sure, people suffered from poverty and hunger in the United States. But the people of India dealt with these problems on a much greater magnitude. The begging children were a perfect example. Where were their parents? Or were they all orphans?

What about Raveena? What happened to her after that man dragged her away? Did he punish her for attempting to ask for help? She imagined the man inflicting more bruises on the girl's tiny frame, the girl cowering, whimpering, but with no place to go.

Leslie flinched at the imagined blows and jumped to her feet, unable to sit still. She wrapped her arms about her, fending off the sudden chill that overtook her.

Tom noticed and called out, "Want to get in with me for a bit now?"

She walked to the side of the pool. He swam to meet her. Wiping the water out of his eyes and blinking in the bright sun, he gazed up at her.

"I'm going up to the room to get dressed," she said. "Then I'm going back to the zoo."

Tom stared at her, uncomprehending. "Why?"

"I need to go back." She wasn't sure how to put this into words. How could she explain to him? "I can't stop thinking about Raveena. I'm worried about her."

"Wait. You're going back to the zoo to look for the little girl? Leslie, that makes no sense. The odds of finding her there again are statistically improbable."

"I realize that. But I have to try."

She could see the thoughts racing through Tom's mind as he tried to understand her. His day at the pool had once again been spoiled. "You're wasting your time."

"I have to do this."

"What if she isn't there? We can't hunt all over New Delhi for one little girl."

"If she isn't there, I'll accept it. At least I'll know that I tried—that I did everything I could. I wish I hadn't let that man take her away." Another little girl ripped from her life as she watched, helpless. She couldn't stand by and let it happen. Not again.

Tom sighed. He half-swam, half-walked to the side of the pool, placed his hands on the concrete deck, and hopped out, dripping a puddle of water as he snatched up his towel, making sure she saw how disappointed he was.

"You don't have to come," she told him.

He dried himself quickly. "You don't honestly think I'd let you go alone, do you?"

Her heart swelled with gratitude, pleased for the support. There was the man she'd married, the man who wanted to make the world a better place, like she did. He was once the sun that dawned her days, warming her with his smile. She wasn't sure when the clouds developed.

She offered him a smile. "Thank you. This means a lot to me."

"Not like I have any choice. You'd just come back complaining someone tried to kidnap you again. I'd never hear the end of it."

CHAPTER 5

By late afternoon, Leslie was sweaty and discouraged. The zoo would close soon, and she hadn't seen Raveena anywhere. Her tired eyes watered as she scanned the dense crowds choking the sidewalks, inundating the animals' enclosures and food vendors.

When she'd hopped from the taxi and hurried to the zoo entrance, images of the little girl running to her open arms played vividly in her mind while Tom paid their entrance fees for the second time that day, shaking his head, still incredulous of her wild scheme.

After hours of walking around the zoo, jostled by crowds, she felt foolish. She ignored Tom's sighs and glances at his watch.

She rounded through the entire zoo and retraced her steps repeatedly near the white tigers' enclosure, where Raveena had approached her earlier.

Finally Tom spoke. "Well, I'm getting hungry. How about you?"

"No. But I guess we're not going to find her."

She half-listened as Tom debated which of their favorite restaurants they should eat at that evening. He picked up his pace and headed for the zoo exit. She almost missed the soft voice.

"Hello, Auntie."

She whipped around. There stood Raveena, just inside the zoo entrance, collecting change from anyone willing to part with it.

If the girl hadn't spoken, Leslie doubted she would have recognized her. Raveena no longer wore the bright red sari with the long veil. Instead, a threadbare *shalwar kameez* draped her gaunt frame. Her hair hung loose about her face, and the gaudy makeup had been removed. Someone had intentionally smeared the girl's face and arms with dirt and tangled her hair. Show girl in the morning, beggar in the afternoon. This girl had to be the victim of exploitation.

Leslie hurried to the girl, knelt, and hugged her, appalled by the thin frame. Raveena threw her arms around her.

"I came back to find you, Raveena."

Raveena's searching eyes gazed at her, then drifted to Tom.

"He's my husband," she explained. "He wants to help you, too."

Raveena hesitated, casting glances left and right.

"Shall we go?" She held a hand out to the girl.

No reply.

Leslie wondered how much English the girl understood. Perhaps she'd misunderstood and overreacted.

"Is your mommy here at the zoo?" she asked, just to be certain.

Raveena shook her head slowly.

"Where's your mommy?"

The same slow shake of the head. "No mama." She pointed up, toward the sky.

"I'm so sorry. Your daddy?"

Raveena simply shook her head, then said, "I'm so hungry, Auntie."

"Well, then, come with us, and we'll get something to eat."

Raveena continued to stand quietly, staring at the ground.

Leslie turned to Tom, who shook his head and raised his hands in an I-have-no-idea gesture. "Maybe she's afraid to run off with strangers?"

Small, grimy fingers gingerly gripped her still-outstretched hand. Like an anchor catching on solid ground, the touch jarred her, grinding the entire world to a halt.

"Help me, Auntie."

She looked down at the weary girl. "I will. I promise."

"They will find me, Auntie. They will never let me go."

"Let you go? Raveena, is someone holding you against your will?"

"Raveena!" a deep voice called loudly from behind them.

The nervous little hand pulled quickly away. Raveena backed off. Her eyes went wild with fear. She held her collected rupees out in front of her.

The lanky man stormed at them. He snatched the money from her then glared at the Americans.

"What are you doing?" he demanded, looking back and forth between them.

"We're just talking to her," Leslie told him, eyes drawn to the angry scar no matter how hard she tried to ignore it. "Who are you?"

"What do you mean?"

"Raveena says she has no father. So who are you?"

The man's jaw clenched as he glared at the girl. "She belongs to me."

"She 'belongs' to you? What does that mean?" The hair stood up on the back of her neck.

The man stepped toward her. Leslie pulled Raveena close. The girl trembled against her.

"This child is not your concern. You will leave her alone. Raveena, we go now."

The child clung to her, and Leslie did not relax her hold. Though terrified, she tried to appear far surer of herself than she was. She couldn't stand by and watch him drag her away again. She knew it would haunt her forever.

"Raveena, now!" he growled.

When the child still didn't move, he grabbed her arm and yanked her forward.

"Stop that." Startled by the scene the man was making, Leslie glanced around.

No one appeared to care. She kept her arm firmly around the girl, refusing to budge.

All at once, the man rushed her, his stale breath in her face. He grabbed her upper arms and shook her violently, fingers digging into her skin. She cried out.

Tom interceded. He grabbed the man's wrist, twisting until he released his grip. "Don't touch my wife again."

She stared at this angry man, stunned he would lash out at her. In public. "I just want to take her to dinner," she finally said, when no one else spoke. "You don't object to me giving her something to eat do you?"

The man scowled deeply at Raveena. He reached into his pants pocket and pulled out a cell phone. He flipped it open and punched in a number then turned his back to them. He spoke into the phone rapidly, but quietly.

"He doesn't need to whisper," Tom muttered. "We can't understand him anyway. What is that? Hindi?"

She didn't know. But she was certain she knew how Raveena's face came to be bruised. What else did this man do to the helpless child? Breathing heavily, Leslie tried to compose herself. Thank goodness Tom was there.

When the man clicked his cell phone closed and turned to face them once more, he scowled but wobbled his head in a figure eight. "You can take," he told her, "but you pay."

"Yes, of course we'll pay for her dinner," she answered, smiling down at Raveena, still pressed against her side.

"Pay for dinner, yes," he agreed. He held out a hand. "And you pay me now."

Tom put his hand into his pocket. "How much?"

"As you wish, sir."

Tom handed him the equivalent of about ten dollars in rupees. "Okay?"

The man thrust the rupees into his pocket. "I come," he informed the Americans.

"Did you just pay him to be allowed to feed this little girl?" Leslie whispered to Tom.

"I believe I did, yes." As he spoke, he grabbed her by the elbow and led her toward the zoo exit. "But he looks appeased, so if you want to take her to dinner, let's go now while he's happy."

Raveena clung to her hand, the girl's bare feet slapping the concrete as she hurried along beside her. No shoes. Her teeth ground together as she wondered if the man forced her to go without shoes for sympathy or if she truly owned no shoes.

They clambered into the back seat of the taxi, Raveena between Leslie and Tom. Raveena's disgruntled guardian slid into the front seat beside the driver.

The startled driver turned to Tom for instructions. "Sir?" he asked, looking at the newcomers.

"Back to the hotel, I guess," Tom suggested, looking to her for further instruction. "One of the restaurants there? Or did you have something else in mind?"

"I didn't have anything in mind," Leslie admitted. "Sure, back to the hotel."

"I was thinking of the jungle-themed restaurant. Do you think that's a good option?" he asked as the taxi driver eased the vehicle into the clogged street.

She nodded at him. She didn't have a plan. The only thought on her mind had been to keep the child close. She'd hoped perhaps they could even get her alone, but the surly man obviously wasn't going to let that happen. Tom was right —the jungle-themed restaurant should delight anyone.

Normally. This was anything but normal. What had she been thinking?

Silence settled over the taxi. She glanced at Tom. He offered a watery smile and went back to fidgeting, his fingers drumming against his legs.

Raveena nestled close beside her.

"What do you like to eat, Raveena?" Leslie asked when the silence became unbearable.

The man in the front seat turned at the sound of the girl's name and glared at her again. He ranted at her in another language, causing the taxi driver to glance into his rearview mirror. She saw concern in his eyes and thought he wanted to tell her something.

Raveena shrank even closer to her. Though Leslie could not understand the words, she knew the man intimidated her. And she didn't like that at all.

"Maybe some rice and chicken?" Leslie suggested, determined not to allow this man to ruin their dinner.

Still the girl remained quiet.

"I know you'll like something there," Leslie assured Raveena, combing fingers through the girl's tangled hair.

They continued in silence until the driver hesitantly spoke to the man beside him. Again, she could not understand the language, but the barked reply conveyed plenty. She patted Raveena's arm, not sure if she was comforting the child or herself. What had she gotten herself into?

CHAPTER 6

$\mathcal{L}$eslie watched as the doorman scurried from the hotel lobby to open the taxi for her. The driver hopped out to get Tom's door. Their angry visitor let himself out, lit a cigarette, and stood nearby watching while Tom paid the driver and tipped him a bit extra because he had waited for them at the zoo.

The driver leaned very close to Tom, speaking in a low voice. He then bowed, shook hands, and turned to wave good-bye to her.

"What was that about?" she asked Tom quietly.

"All he said was, 'Very bad man.' I don't know what exactly is going on here, but I don't like it. You may be right—the girl may be in trouble." He took her hand and spoke aloud, "Who's ready for dinner?"

He patted Raveena gently on the back. His timid show of affection surprised Leslie. A warm flush ran through her—something she hadn't felt in a long time.

As they crossed the white marble floor of the lobby, the staff—eager to assist in any way possible—smiled and waved or nodded. One woman cocked her head at the sight of the young Indian girl accompanying them. She had seen them come and go enough times to know this was a new development. The attention unnerved Leslie, but she tightened her grip on Raveena's hand.

They passed numerous shops offering jewelry, handicrafts, souvenirs, and toiletry items. The woman working the jewelry store, clad in a silky royal blue outfit this evening, beckoned to her and gestured to her wrist with a huge smile. The woman had commented before on her lack of accessories and regularly cajoled her to come inside and fix that.

As the group passed, the woman reached out and clasped Raveena's wrist, gently lifting it in the air. "Another empty wrist! You must come see me." She pinched Raveena's cheeks.

They passed the bakery. Raveena's brown eyes widened at the glass cases full of sweets. The girl gripped her hand even more tightly.

"Maybe after dinner?" Leslie suggested.

They had eaten at almost all the various hotel restaurants at some point during their stay. They had not yet sampled the Taj Palace, and briefly contemplated taking their young guest there, since it supposedly offered the most authentic Indian fare.

But after further discussion, they led Raveena and her surly guard to the outdoor restaurant Tom had originally suggested, Bandipur, named for one of India's national forests and designed to give the illusion of eating in a jungle.

Bamboo railings lined the walkways that led to candle-lit tables under thatched roof huts. Exotic bird song played over the sound system, periodically punctuated by the screech of a large cat. Potted bromeliads hung from the thatched roofs of the huts, while vines curled around the railings and posts. She hoped the whimsical décor would amuse the girl.

A host met them eagerly with a smile, lifting menus as he asked, "Four tonight, sir?"

"Just three," Tom corrected.

"Yes, sir," replied the host. "If you please, come this way."

He gestured them forward and led them to an intimate table, where he pulled a seat back for Leslie, then for Raveena, who stared about the restaurant with large eyes. "For you, little memsaab," he told her with a smile, encouraging the girl to sit.

Once settled, Leslie pulled her menu close. Raveena mimicked her, pulling her menu close and staring down at it.

The lanky man settled into a chair at the end of the table and flipped open his phone.

The waiter returned with bottles of water, filling their glasses.

Watching Raveena, Leslie noticed the girl dwelled on the photos of food as opposed to the list of available options. "Do you know what you want?" she asked.

With a glance at the man, now smoking and occupied with his phone, Raveena shook her head. "I cannot read, Auntie," she whispered.

The admission stunned Leslie, but then she realized how naïve she was. "You don't go to school, do you?" Raveena shook her head. Leslie suppressed the rage bubbling within her. Regardless of the fact that she'd just met the girl, she felt protective of her. Perhaps that made no sense, but she wanted better for the child. "Well, then, let's just order lots of different dishes and you can try them all. Tom, what sounds good to you?"

The waiter hurried forward to take their order—cucumber and tomato salad, tandoori chicken, vegetable biriyani, curry vegetables, dhal, and naan. They chose from the more traditional Indian offerings, hoping the little girl would find them familiar.

"Anything else you would like?"

The little girl grinned and shook her head. It was the first smile Leslie had seen on her face.

The waiter took the menus and hurried away.

She tried to encourage conversation. "Have you ever gone to school?"

Raveena shook her head.

"But you speak English. Who taught you?"

"Mama," Raveena replied quietly after a short pause and another glance at the man.

He had returned his cell phone to his pocket. He leaned back in his chair, arms crossed, and stared at them.

"Who is that man?" Leslie asked. She had a feeling she did not want to know.

Raveena dropped her gaze once again and did not speak.

"I know he is not your father."

"No, Auntie."

"An uncle? Or another relative?"

A slight headshake was the only response.

"Who then?"

"Shardul," came the quiet reply.

At this, the man sat up straight and spoke harshly. "Raveena!" When she looked at him, he shook his head.

Leslie continued to press, determined to draw out more information.

"Is that his name? How do you know him?"

Raveena only sat in silence, staring down until the food arrived.

'They will never let me go.' Chilling words from a child. The way Shardul remained close and vigilant, Leslie suspected he was one of "they." She wanted to ask so much more but knew silence would be the only answer under Shardul's brooding gaze.

The waiter brought many platters of food, arranging them in the center of the table. The tandoori chicken sizzled. He cautioned the patrons, "Please, be most careful. The dish is quite hot." He lifted their plates one by one, scooping food from the platters onto their individual dishes. "Can I bring anything else?"

"No, thank you. This looks great," Tom answered.

The waiter left.

Raveena stared down at the plate of food before her then looked up at Leslie. "This is for me?"

"Yes, of course," Leslie replied. "And more if you want it."

Raveena looked to Shardul. He wobbled his consent then lifted his hand to his mouth, giving her permission to eat.

Finally, Raveena picked up her naan, tore a piece from it, and scooped a mouthful of rice with it.

"Is it good?" Leslie asked.

Raveena beamed and wobbled her head, picking up a piece of chicken and trying that as well.

They joined their young guest in relishing the spicy dishes. As much as she enjoyed the food, Leslie took greater delight in watching Raveena. Though the girl started slowly, her pace quickened, and she soon cleared her plate.

Leslie refilled Raveena's plate, amused by how much food the child tucked away, glad she could eat until satiated. Though the girl initially ate only by using pieces of naan to pinch up bites of food, Raveena watched Leslie using a fork and spoon then tried to imitate her. The girl gripped the fork as a toddler might, and Leslie found it the most endearing thing she'd seen in a long time.

She took no more after finishing her first helpings, wanting to leave as much for Raveena to eat as possible.

Leslie had seen plenty of underprivileged children who didn't wear the latest fashions, the cool shoes, the designer backpacks. Often they had nothing to eat at snack time. She kept assorted snacks at her desk and allowed no one in her class to go without. But nothing back home prepared her for this. Raveena appeared to be fed only enough to keep her alive so that someone could use her in whatever way they desired. She remembered the men pawing her and grinding on her at the zoo—for a few rupees.

The plight of this little girl brought back the memory of another little girl, a hand clamped over her mouth, eyes filled with terror. She imagined that girl locked away, starving, scared, and alone. Perhaps pawed and groped by strangers. Shuddering, Leslie pushed the thoughts away.

When Raveena sighed contentedly and sank back into her chair, Tom picked at the remaining chicken and rice.

"Good thing we ate it all," he remarked. "You know I don't like to see food go to waste."

"And there's no point trying to keep leftovers when we'll be returning home in a week," Leslie agreed.

Raveena looked stricken at these words.

The waiter returned to remove empty platters and plates, teasing Raveena, "Little memsaab was hungry tonight!" He winked at Tom. "And now for dessert?"

"What do you like?" Leslie asked Raveena. "Rice pudding? Mango pudding? Some ice cream?"

Raveena, looking dazed and overwhelmed, finally responded, "As you wish, Auntie."

Tom ordered mango pudding for all three of them. "Okay?" he asked Raveena after the waiter bustled away. "Do you like mango pudding?"

She shrugged. "I have never eaten it."

It was the first time she spoke directly to him.

He smiled at her. "I think you will enjoy it."

When the dessert arrived, Raveena watched the two adults pick up spoons then lifted her own, taking a small taste. Her face lit up at the flavor, and she devoured the entire dish. Afterward, she leaned back in her chair and clasped her hands to her stomach. "Auntie, I am so full!"

"But you don't feel sick, do you?"

"No, Auntie. It is good." For one moment, the cloudy pall lifted from her eyes.

Tom called for the check.

Shardul took his cell phone and made another call.

"GB Road, Auntie," Raveena murmured, her eyes frantic.

The words meant nothing. "What was that?"

"Raveena!" Shardul snapped his phone closed, stood, and beckoned her to come. "You have eaten. Come now."

The girl obediently pushed back her chair and stood, shoulders slumped, eyes downcast.

"Wait...give us a minute." Leslie scrambled from her chair. Bending down, she pulled Raveena close and hugged her.

"Thank you, Auntie," Raveena whispered.

"It was my pleasure. In fact, maybe tomorrow—" Leslie turned her eyes to Shardul, who cut her off quickly.

"No." He stepped closer to Raveena.

She automatically drew her again into a protective hug.

The little girl pressed her cheek against hers, whispering, "GB Road, Auntie," before Shardul grasped her by the shoulder and yanked her away.

Leslie saw the desperation settle back into those warm, brown eyes.

She rose from the ground and fell against Tom's shoulder, watching the child dragged farther and farther from her.

"He's taking her away," she said, gesturing helplessly.

"I know," Tom answered. "But she isn't ours. We did what we could to help. At least tonight she'll fall asleep with a full stomach and maybe know that two people actually care about her."

She was glad to hear him say he cared. Neither of them spoke as Tom led her through the lobby to the bank of elevators that deposited them on their floor. After swiping the key card, he opened the door and ushered her inside. She sat on the edge of the bed, the room silent and empty.

"Will we ever see her again?" she asked eventually.

Tom sank onto the bed beside her. "I...don't think so," he responded. "We're leaving soon. Let's focus on the positive. You found her today and got to see her. That was very unlikely."

"I thought I would feel better but...it isn't enough. Do you think he takes her to the zoo every day?"

"I don't know, but he was quite clear that he did not intend to let you see her again tomorrow. I just don't know what else to do. I'm sorry." He rubbed her back. "Put her out of your mind. You did what you could."

Those words again.

"I know this may sound silly, but I feel empty without her. I feel like something is missing."

He leaned in, nuzzling her neck. "Why don't we focus on something else? I know what I'm missing." His hands slid up her back.

She pulled away. "Not now. Please."

He dropped his hands. "Not now. Not ever."

"I'm sorry. I can't just forget about the little girl. It's really upsetting me."

She met his eyes and recognized the all-too-familiar sympathy plain on his face. That look had reflected back at her from countless eyes. As always she fought the urge to snap, "Quit feeling sorry for me." She knew his thoughts before he opened his mouth. And she didn't want to hear them.

"Leslie, I think I know why you're so drawn to this girl —"

"Don't, Tom. Please. I can't. I don't want to hear it."

"I'm not being mean, I just think you need to try to forget it —"

"I said I don't want to hear it."

"Okay." He stood quickly. "I'm going to shower and get ready for bed. And I hope you'll come join me." He brushed a quick kiss against her cheek.

Was it any wonder she couldn't forget? No one let her.

CHAPTER 7

$\mathcal{L}$eslie gritted her teeth while Tom cried out. He collapsed on her, panting for breath. She enveloped him in an embrace, pleased she'd satiated him, while the usual mixture of guilt and satisfaction settled over her.

Tom crushed her cheek with a long kiss. "Now what about you?" He pressed his pelvis against her, still erect, straining farther inside her enticingly. "I can go another round."

She heard desire rough in his voice and knew he wanted her to climax, wanted her to cry out in pleasure with him. For a moment she joined him, rocking against him, straining to find just the right spot.

Until the guilt of desire overshadowed the urge to commune, the longing to join with him completely in ecstasy drowned out by shame.

She pushed his hips away, disengaging his throbbing member.

"What?" he gasped. "Something wrong? Am I hurting you?"

"No. No, I'm fine." She kissed his cheek and caressed his hair, knowing he'd take it personally. He always did.

"I can do something different. Want to be on top? Or I can use my hand."

Thankfully, the dark hid the crimson blush that blossomed over her face. "No. Let's sleep. I'm tired."

She snuggled against him, but he rolled away.

She ran a finger over his shoulder. "Oh, come on. Hold me. Please?"

"After you shut me out? No, thanks."

"I didn't. I let you...I mean, you came."

"Yes, you allowed me to ejaculate inside you, fulfilling your duty as a wife. But I wish you wanted me in return."

"I do. It's just—"

"I know. I've heard it before. Good night."

"Please. Don't be mad."

"I'm not. At least, not at you." He sighed, and she heard the frustration simmering just beneath the surface. "It's just...you left all the other religious brainwashing behind. I wish you'd jettison that damned purity pledge garbage. We're married. We're allowed to have sex. Good night."

She rolled away and curled up in a ball, hugging the pillow as silent tears wet it. If only it was that easy. She wanted to leave it behind, wanted to enjoy intimacy with her husband. And she hated the distance this wedged between them.

And yet knowing something to be true didn't necessarily make it any easier to change.

He could have had anyone he wanted. They both knew that. She still wondered why he pursued her. Sometimes she thought they both chose the other just to spite their parents. Did he regret that stubborn pursuit now? Did she?

When she first caught Tom's eye, he knew nothing of her upbringing. He had no idea that her father, Pastor Bill, and his wife, Peggy, had taught their two daughters to be living examples of good Christians in a polluted world—shining beacons in a dark night. That did not include dating or hanging out with friends. The only parties she attended growing up were heavily supervised church functions. At the age of twelve, her parents pressured her into taking a purity pledge.

"You're the pastor's daughter, Leslie Lynn," her mother reminded her. "The congregation looks to you as an example. Think of all the other girls you'll inspire when they witness you taking the purity pledge. Christ's daughters should remain pure. Pledge yourself to Him."

Leslie stood before the crowd not long after, before she even completely understood sex, or hormones, or even gave much thought to boys, and vowed to remain chaste until marriage. In exchange for her purity and commitment, God would bless her with a beautiful, perfect marriage. And then, with God's blessing, she could enjoy her body completely with her husband.

Neither part of the pledge came to pass. Was it because she wasn't a virgin when she married that she now couldn't enjoy sex at all? Why did she continue to feel dirty when Tom touched her? She was supposed to enjoy sex now that she was married.

If only she'd been better prepared to cope with the world when she left for college, refusing the Christian university her parents selected for her and choosing instead a state school, tired of their suffocating hovering and ready to make her own life.

She greeted her new roomie enthusiastically the day they moved into their dorm but realized thirty minutes later they were as unalike as two people could be. Karen turned out to be a single-minded party girl with no interest in studying, a vapid, silly thing who could spend hours straightening—or curling— her hair and painting her nails but could not be bothered to spend ten minutes reading their English assignment. She drove a brand new, bright-red, two-seater convertible, though she never put the top down because that would have ruined her carefully coiffed hair.

Karen tried to interest Leslie in extracurricular activities—

which for Karen meant boys. Leslie refused, reminding herself of her purity pledge and her promise to her parents that she'd remember her beliefs. Several weeks into the semester, however, Karen finally convinced her to attend a Friday night party at one of the fraternity houses. She knew her parents wouldn't approve, but after all she was an adult now and exhausted by her mother's smothering phone calls. She accompanied Karen—though she still refused the makeover and the offer to borrow one of Karen's form-fitting blouses.

The party shocked her. Every reveler clutched a plastic cup of "spirits," as her mother referred to alcohol. "The Good Lord gave you a spirit, and we have no need of imbibing spirits not created by Him." Couples clutched and groped, some under the pretense of dancing, some just making out on the sofa.

She'd never seen anything like it and realized she didn't want to see it. She headed for the door, but a young man intercepted her. He stood about an inch taller than her, with worn jeans, an untucked shirt, and hair carefully gelled to appear unkempt. Hands thrust in his front pockets, he ducked his head—almost shyly it seemed—as he greeted her. "Hey."

He talked her into staying, pressed a cup of something he called "innocuous" into her hand, and led her away to "someplace a little quieter," which turned out to be his bedroom in the frat house.

Her heart thudded in protest as he closed the door behind them. She'd never been alone with a boy. She sipped nervously at her drink, unsure what to do with herself. The beverage was fruity and sweet. She thought he'd given her some punch.

A lava lamp glowed softly, shapeless lumps drifting aimlessly up and down.

She tried to relax as he chatted amicably about classes, inquired about her major and where she was from. Then she began to feel dizzy. The boy's face swam alarmingly out of focus. The edges of her vision frayed.

After that she had only vague snatches of memories—the

boy moving closer, being unable to move away, hands groping her, hot breath against her neck, hands on her stomach, fingers fumbling with the snap of her jeans.

She wasn't sure how much time had passed before she woke and was once again aware of her surroundings. That stupid lava lamp still glowed, throwing hideous shadows on the walls. The boy—she didn't even know his name—snored beside her, naked, everything God had given him right there in the dim light. She was undressed from the waist down. A painful ache and an unfamiliar throbbing and sticky ooze between her legs nauseated her.

What had she done? Her first time with a boy—a total stranger—and she couldn't even remember what happened. She hadn't even dated, hadn't relished a first kiss. The realization that she was no longer a virgin horrified her as she struggled back into her panties and jeans with trembling fingers. She'd broken her purity pledge.

She stumbled back to her dorm in a mental fog, berating herself for going to such a disgusting party. What had she been thinking? She fell into her own bed, shame blanketing her, unable to sleep, determined no one would ever touch her again.

If only she'd known the worst was yet to come.

Tom snored loudly, startling her from the dismal memories. Normally, she pushed him onto his side to quiet the noise. Tonight, she let him drone on. She couldn't sleep anyway. A tendency to snore was one of the many things you didn't learn about someone until after you were married—at least if you didn't live together prior to the wedding because your mother pitched a fit when she found out you were engaged to a man she despised and chastened you with stern reminders of your upbringing. Her mother's disapproval only made Tom more desirable. She wondered now if perhaps he enjoyed how her religious background annoyed his father.

She twirled her wedding band about her finger, remembering the happiness and hope that filled her the day it replaced the purity ring. *'Do you, Leslie Lynn Martin, take this man, Thomas Reginald Matthews III...'*

She lay perfectly still with her eyes pinched closed, slowly breathing in and out in carefully measured breaths. Raveena's deep brown eyes stared back at her. She shifted to her side and tried counting to one hundred and back again. Somewhere around eighty-three, Raveena's voice whispered, "I'm so hungry." Leslie opened her eyes and watched the minutes tick by on the clock. Raveena's voice pleaded over and over again. "Help me, Auntie."

Leslie reached over the edge of the bed, groping about the floor until she recovered her clothing. Clad in crumpled sweats, she padded softly into the bathroom, quietly closing the door before flicking on the lights.

Her reflection stared back from the mirror, cheeks flushed from sex. She splashed cold water on her face.

Objectively studying her face, she couldn't call herself ugly. Certainly she was plainer than women who painted and highlighted their features. Was that what Tom wanted? Did he now wish he had avoided, rather than pursued, her? He definitely wanted someone more eager in bed.

Back in college, when he prodded her to go out with him, he claimed to appreciate her plainness. Of course, he never called her "plain." His words were kinder euphemisms like "no-nonsense" and "straight-up."

He'd first approached her in the library, her favorite haunt after the frat party, thanks to the silent, solitary nature of the building. By that point, she had withdrawn from study groups, couldn't talk to anyone, barely ate. She only picked at food when she ventured into the cafeteria. She had no appetite. Nausea frequently made her leave in a hurry. She loathed herself for the stupid, sinful mistake she'd made. She cried until there were no tears left and avoided people. In the library, no one questioned that desire to be alone.

Except Tom. He walked right up to her table—that was

how she thought of it, "her table," where she always studied far away from everyone else. He stood there, not saying anything. He was close enough that his cologne or aftershave or deodorant—something very masculine—penetrated her invisible wall.

She ignored him. But he didn't leave.

"Yes?" she asked, when she couldn't stand the awkward silence another moment.

"Are you expecting others? Or can I join you?" His voice was deep and resonant and genuine. She couldn't detect a bit of sarcasm or any undercurrent of maliciousness. But she still didn't want company.

She looked around pointedly at the numerous completely empty tables nearby—and then she noticed his eyes.

Wow, were they blue. Not slate or hazy, or muddy, or pale, or watery. His eyes were crystal-clear, vibrant. They glowed, so striking they startled the rude reply right out of her.

With a quick shake of the head, she turned her flushing face back to her book. "I'm not expecting anyone else," she mumbled. She reached up to smooth her hair then realized it was pointless. Nothing would improve her puffy, bloodshot eyes and plain face. She tried to return to her reading but lost her place.

He settled into the chair directly beside her. She edged away from his distracting nearness—mostly, but not entirely, unwelcome.

"Oh, good. You're working on biology," he said, pulling a book from his backpack. "We can help each other study."

"Oh," was all she could manage.

He had the same textbook her class used. Maybe they had the same professor.

"I saw you aced Paulson's first exam. Good job. You always study alone? Or do you have a group?"

She stared at him blankly. Dr. Paulson was her biology

professor. How did this boy know that? Or that she managed an A on her exam?

"Tom Matthews." He introduced himself, extending a hand, which she shook tentatively. "I'm in your biology class. Guess you hadn't noticed."

Running his fingers through his shaggy hair, he grinned. His chin came to a rather sharp point, she noticed, which shouldn't work with his prominent cheekbones. Somehow it all blended together in a very pleasing fashion, though. How had she not noticed him before?

She wasn't thrilled with the sudden heart palpitations this boy prompted. But his blue eyes were so warm, and he seemed truly interested in studying. She quietly agreed to work with him. Two hours flew by. After an hour or so reviewing biology notes and completing their assignment for the week, he asked her if she happened to also be taking Gen Chem I and whether she was equally brilliant at that subject. Out came the chemistry books, and they studied for another hour.

Not once did he comment on her appearance or ask personal questions. He never asked for her phone number. He didn't inquire into her plans for the weekend. They only studied. And she had to admit, she didn't mind his company.

She did, however, panic when he asked her to lunch. She shook her head and gathered her books.

His uninvited appearances at her study table continued. Frustrated by her calculus class—math never was her best subject—she finally asked if he was taking that. He wasn't— he'd taken AP Calculus in high school and tested out of it—but he quickly offered to help with her homework. They spent hours together during the week prior to mid-terms, then both gloated over their matching A's in Biology and Chemistry.

Tom suggested coffee to celebrate. "Unless you need to study for Calc?"

"No, the mid-term was this morning. No homework."

"How do you think you did?"

"I feel pretty good about it."

"So...coffee?"

His eyes glowed that beautiful vibrant blue. He wasn't like anyone she'd known before. He didn't subscribe to a rigid set of condemning rules that suffocated the life out of a person. He never called her a "big nerd" like kids had always done in school. And he definitely didn't behave like the frat boy who had taken advantage of her. She nodded and accepted the hand he offered, wondering how he would feel about her if he knew she was pregnant.

CHAPTER 8

*L*eslie didn't respond to the small talk Tom attempted the next morning. They ordered breakfast from room service, neither of them in a hurry to get cleaned up. Raveena dominated her thoughts. What happened to her after dinner last night? Where was she? Who was she with?

When she wouldn't talk, Tom gave up and flipped on the television. He passed a Bollywood musical, a cooking show, a dance program, the local news, an Indian soap opera, a decades-old American soap opera, and news.

Something caught her attention.

"Wait, can you go back one channel?" She sat forward on the edge of her chair. Tom did as she requested. The program was a British international news program.

"...and the aid workers reported dramatic deterioration in public health conditions in all red light districts. Calcutta, Mumbai, and New Delhi prostitutes suffer not only from malnutrition but also an alarming rise in venereal diseases, particularly HIV/AIDS. Often trafficked against their wills, these women are kept as sex slaves in dismal conditions by the brothel owners. On Falkland Road in Mumbai, Sonagachi in

Calcutta, and GB Road in New Delhi, aid workers attempt to reach out—"

"Did she just say 'GB Road'?"

"I think she did," Tom replied. "Why?"

"Raveena whispered that to me at dinner. She muttered it while Shardul was distracted with a phone call then repeated it when I hugged her, right before he yanked her away." She watched the images of dingy buildings, busy streets, and women's faces. Children stared out of the screen, their clothing ragged, faces smudged. The reporter continued, but Leslie no longer heard the woman's voice.

Something clicked into place. "There must be a reason why she said it. I think she was telling us where to find her."

"On GB Road? The red light district? Where you go to find a prostitute?"

"Why else would she say that? How else would she even know about it?"

"Is there anything else around there?"

"I have no idea." She returned her attention to the television. If Raveena was there, and if she could find her... "I want to go look for her."

"Leslie, that's—"

"I want to find Raveena."

"On that street? You? The woman who's been constantly complaining about the lack of sanitation?"

"I know, but—"

"Did she give you an address? A building name?"

"No, but—"

"And for Pete's sake, Leslie, what would we do if we found her? What if we disturb her family?"

"She doesn't have a family. Her mother passed away."

"Someone takes care of her, and we can't just barge in on them."

"Someone sort of takes care of her, maybe, if it qualifies as care. Shardul isn't family. She said so."

"And he made it clear he doesn't want us to see her again."

"Why? What true guardian would object to anyone offering assistance? Who would refuse food for a child so clearly in need of it?"

"He doesn't want your charity. That isn't so unusual."

"That's not it. I felt that little girl quaking in fear of him. Guardian or not, she needs help. I want to help her."

"No. We've done everything we could. We need to just mind our own business now."

"What if she—"

"What, Leslie?" Tom stood. "What if we go searching, and we find her, and she's an orphaned child living on the streets? Begging with a handler? Then what? What are you planning to do?"

"I don't know."

"Exactly. And what can we do? We leave for home in a week."

"So we do nothing? We just ignore the plea for help?"

"If I thought we could do anything, I would try. But we can't. Now, I'm going downstairs to swim. Are you coming or not?"

"No, thanks."

He stared at her, his eyes burning with increasing heat. Then he simply shrugged. "Okay." He grabbed a towel. "Maybe come down and meet me for lunch?"

He didn't wait for a reply. The door closed behind him. She turned back to the television. The camera panned over a small group of ragged children in the street, hands outstretched, faces gaunt and filthy.

"The children of the brothel workers begin working at a young age," the reporter continued. "These children are sent into the streets to beg or to search for odd jobs such as shining shoes or carrying bags for tourists. Like their mothers, they receive little or no education, no health care, and often suffer from malnutrition. Some of these brothel babies, particularly the boys, eventually resort to thievery and crime. The girls, sadly, often have no other options but to follow their mothers into prostitution."

A hideous image surfaced in her mind: Raveena at the mercy of a man, his hands reaching for her, pinning her down. In Leslie's mind, Raveena struggled and screamed for help. But no one helped her.

She turned off the television, slid her feet into her sandals, and left the room. Her pulse quickened as the door clicked shut behind her. She knew Tom would be furious if she didn't show up for lunch. More so if he discovered she'd left the hotel without telling him.

She crossed the lobby quickly, afraid her resolve might fail. The doorman, with his red turban and crisp white uniform, saluted as he opened the door for her.

"Taxi, madam?"

"Yes, please," she replied, still feeling like a fugitive.

He called out and waved to the line of waiting taxis. Stepping from under the protective awning into the bright sun, she tried to calm the butterflies in her stomach. She had not ventured out alone since the nightmare in Pantnagar. She was relieved to see that the same man who had taken them to and from the zoo yesterday drove the summoned taxi. His gentle, familiar face comforted her.

The doorman opened the car door for her and bade her good-bye with another small salute. She slid in, palms sweaty.

"Memsaab!" The taxi driver recognized her. "Lady go zoo, yes?"

"No. GB Road, please," she directed.

"Memsaab?" he questioned.

"GB Road," she repeated.

The driver shook his head. "Not good for lady. American lady not go...GB Road—" He raised his hand. "Lady stay."

He got out.

She watched him carefully, alarmed that he may be going to find Tom.

He returned momentarily with the doorman, who stuck his head in the taxi. "Where is it that you wish to go, madam?"

"GB Road, please," she informed him.

He frowned, retracted his upper torso, and spoke with the driver. They chatted quickly in Hindi, and though she could not understand a word, she knew they were concerned by this request. The doorman reappeared.

"Madam, is there some shopping you wish to do? Something you wish to buy? Perhaps your husband could run this errand for you? Or Prajit here can take you to an excellent shopping center."

"Thank you, but I want to go to GB Road. I'm...looking for someone."

The two men spoke again in Hindi. And again, the doorman attempted to dissuade her.

"Madam, Prajit says that is a very bad man that was with you last night. He says you must not go looking for this girl. They went to a very bad part of town after dinner last night. Perhaps you do not know what sort of place GB Road is, madam."

"I think I do." That was the problem, and she couldn't leave the girl there. Her mind turned the words over again. "Wait. He knows where they went last night?" She leaned forward, looking up at Prajit. "Did you take them home last night after we ate dinner? Do you know where he took the girl?"

The doorman spoke with the driver again. "Please, madam, this is most unsafe. There are thieves and thugs on GB Road at all times of the day. Prajit would not feel good about taking you there."

"If it's that bad, then it's not a good place for a little girl either. I'm scared for her."

"That man with her can protect her from others. You have not even got your husband with you, madam. There would be no one to protect you." The doorman was all but pleading with her now.

"I really want to see where Prajit took her. Can he just show me where? If I stay in the taxi?"

"You will stay? With the doors locked?"

She nodded. If it was truly that dangerous, that was probably a good plan.

The doorman turned and spoke with the driver, who still looked skeptical but eventually wobbled his head in a figure eight.

"Okay, he will take you. Be most careful, madam."

Prajit climbed back into the vehicle. "Memsaab, please." He gestured to the lock on her door before he even started the engine. Muttering and shaking his head, Prajit left the hotel behind them, guiding the taxi into traffic on Aurangzeb Road.

She remained silent during the drive and could not help noticing Prajit's periodic glances in his rearview mirror. She suspected that he hoped she would come to her senses and direct him to return to the hotel rather than continue in what she knew he considered a foolhardy and risky mission. Her pulse pounded, hands sweating and stomach quivering.

But she remained determined to see where Raveena was. She had to know. Dangerous or not, she had to try to help.

CHAPTER 9

*L*eslie stared out the window as they passed the National Museum, its gardens tended by groundskeepers taking advantage of the morning's cooler temperatures. The palaces and monuments, the beautiful garden oases in the sea of smog and people, normally astounded and delighted her.

But at this moment, all she could think about was Raveena. Leslie understood why the doorman and Prajit didn't want her to go to GB Road. Even if she stayed in the taxi with the door locked, she was still intentionally driving into the worst part of town, still putting herself in a dangerous situation. Prajit probably didn't want to go there himself.

Was this reckless of her? Should she go back?

Thoughts raced through her mind while Prajit raced through the streets, entering another traffic circle and exiting on Indira Chowk.

Somehow, all the logical arguments didn't make any difference. She knew this was foolhardy, but she had to do it. She couldn't put Raveena out of her mind, couldn't pretend she'd never met her and leave the girl to whatever may come.

Prajit turned his taxi onto Vivekananda Road, continuing on to Bhavbhuti Marg. They passed the New Delhi Train Station, central hive of the city, abuzz with people as always. He slowed the taxi in response to the increased traffic.

"Almost there, lady."

He turned again, onto Shradhanand Road according to the sign, and cruised slowly. She leaned forward for a closer look at the buildings lining both sides of the street. Cramped and claustrophobic, several stories high, the pale yellow, blue, and brown buildings pressed together as tightly as a crowd of people, shoulder to shoulder. Dilapidated and crumbling, the structures sagged under the weight of years. Looking up, she saw balconies on almost all the buildings, some partially screened.

Signs plastered the buildings, but she couldn't read many of them. The signs she could read were store names, she supposed: "General Power Supply" and "Quality Tools." She spotted other closed shops that appeared to be grocery stores. Power lines or perhaps phone lines—or both, she wasn't sure—hung limply, strung from building to building. Garbage littered the gutters. She saw a squatting man crouched beside the curb, his loose dhoti trousers lowered as he peed into the street.

"Not good place for lady," Prajit reiterated. "We go now?" A gaunt, bony dog raised its head when he pulled the taxi to the curb. "Memsaab? Back to hotel now?" he asked again.

The stench was nauseating. Her resolve wavered. "It's filthy here. Quiet, though."

A few parked cars rested along the curbs, mingling with yellow-and-black-striped auto rickshaws. This wasn't what she expected. She noticed a few dark, narrow alleyways leading off the main street, and shuddered at what might lurk down those corridors. The entrances were cluttered with piles of garbage, smoldering as always, black smoke curling into the air.

Men lounged on the street. Some of them smoked, some chewed. She assumed they were chewing betel nut. They confirmed that suspicion by spattering the sidewalk with the red discharge.

"Quiet, now, yes," Prajit told her. "Morning. Many people come night. Soon people wake up. All people fill the streets. Thieves and thugs. We go back hotel?"

"Where is Raveena? Which building?"

Prajit sighed and wiped his face, shaking his head and muttering. She knew he would do as she asked. She could see he didn't like it, though. He pulled away from the curb and wound the taxi further down the street. He stopped in front of a six-story building and pointed. She rolled her window down despite Prajit's clucks and complaints.

No sign hung on this building. Drooping and weary, the pale yellow concrete structure, streaked gray where rain had washed down the front, appeared to weep, reminding her of mascara running down a crying woman's face. A dreary alley, reeking and dismal, ran along the side of the building. Bars covered all the ground floor windows. Above, on the upper floors, several windows along the length of each floor opened onto balconies. Broken bricks framed the edges of the windows. This building seemed the worst possible place for a child.

And then she saw her. One of the windows at the far end on the second floor opened, and Raveena leaned out onto the balcony. She wore the same tattered outfit she had worn at the zoo yesterday, and she looked very sleepy.

The girl appeared to be alone.

Without thinking, she called out to her. "Raveena!"

Prajit realized too late that she had spotted the girl. He turned and shushed her, shaking his head vehemently. "No! Memsaab, no!"

Raveena heard too, and stared for a moment at the scene below her, as if afraid to believe what her eyes saw. "Auntie!

American Auntie!" the girl called, reaching out toward the taxi before turning and disappearing into the building.

Just seeing her, just knowing where she lived, was not enough. Leslie fumbled with the door handle, forgetting she had locked herself in.

Prajit continued objecting, reaching for her, grabbing her shoulder, and raising his voice to chide her in a language she could not understand. She didn't care. She had found Raveena. She pulled the lock, opened the taxi door, and jumped out.

She stepped over garbage and picked her way between globs of red spit.

A man sitting on the sidewalk near the door raised his head and leered at her as she approached. She edged around him, trying to decide if she should knock or wait. He reached out and placed his hand on her ankle, moving slowly up her leg beneath her skirt.

"Hey!" she protested, kicking her leg to shake him off.

Prajit jumped from the taxi and hurried forward, still pleading for her to return to the hotel.

The door opened. A scowling woman glared at her. She looked very tired, as if she'd been roused from bed.

Raveena appeared on the stairway behind the woman, raced forward, and threw herself into her arms. Leslie clutched Raveena tightly, until the woman pulled the girl away from her, scolding her angrily in Hindi.

The taxi driver stood beside them, plucking at her elbow, cajoling her to leave. The angry woman turned on him. He became defensive, shrugging his shoulders, shaking his head, holding his hands out. They squabbled back and forth until the woman suddenly shushed them all and listened intently. She looked up and down the street, glared, grabbed Leslie's arm, and pulled her inside. With a few final harsh words to Prajit, the woman shooed him back to the taxi then closed the door.

Leslie's eyes adjusted to the dim light in the cramped room. One drooping couch, cushions stained and unraveling, pressed against a bare wall. A tiny table in front of the couch held a burning stick of incense. The sweet odor did nothing to mask the smell of the building, a mixture of sweat, urine, unbathed bodies, and smoke. She suppressed a gag and ventured a few steps away from the door, sandals clacking on the bare concrete.

Raveena clung to her arm, beaming even as the other woman glared. "American Auntie!" the girl told the woman.

The woman asked, "You speak Hindi?"

Leslie shook her head. The woman muttered something. She suspected it was a curse word.

"You should not be here," the woman told her.

"I'm sorry," Leslie replied. The horrible smell burned her throat. She breathed as quickly as possible in short bursts. "I was worried about Raveena."

The woman shook her head. "Why?"

"I saw a man with her yesterday. I thought he might be holding her against her will." Her stomach knotted. Was she wrong? The man wasn't here and this woman seemed to be caring for Raveena.

"I sent the driver to hide the taxi. You will get us all in trouble."

"I'm sorry I disturbed you. I only wanted to help."

"You must go quickly."

"I am glad to see you, Auntie," Raveena interjected. "I knew you would come!"

"Of course. I promised I would help you. Any way I can."

"Sanjana knows I told you how to find me, Auntie. But where is Uncle?"

"Uncle? You mean my husband? He stayed at the hotel."

Raveena's eyes opened wide, fear replacing the delight. "You should not be here alone, Auntie."

A car in the street outside screeched to a stop in front of their building. Sanjana and Raveena exchanged a quick look.

Sanjana peered around a sheer, dingy curtain and gasped.

"No taxi! Shardul! Shardul!" She pushed them both to the stairs.

"Go, Auntie! Go! Hurry!" Raveena pleaded, tugging her arm as Leslie clambered up the steep, narrow staircase. Sanjana hurried up the stairs as well, right on their heels.

The steps continued, but Raveena pulled her down the hall at the first landing.

Some of the doorways were covered only with blankets, hung as thin partitions. The blanket curtains hung askew. Though Leslie averted her eyes, she saw the occupants of a few small rooms. In one, a naked man sprawled across the floor. Beside him, a young woman lay flat on her back. Eyes open, she stared blankly at the ceiling. A young woman in another room curled on a cot, sleeping, her face and arms bruised.

Raveena led her to the end of the hallway and wrenched open a door. The three of them hustled inside. Raveena closed the door quietly behind them. A woman dozed on a cot, covered by a thin, stained blanket.

"What are you doing, Raveena?" she murmured. Then she noticed the newcomer. "Is this your American Auntie?"

Sanjana shushed the woman, grabbed Leslie by the arm, and shoved her into a draped-off portion of the room where a second cot sat.

"This is my bed, Auntie. You hide here," Raveena instructed. "You must be quiet now."

Sanjana urged quiet, too, before hurrying from the room.

Behind the drape, Leslie could no longer see what was happening, but she heard Raveena speaking softly and thought she heard her climb into bed with the other young woman. Leslie shrank into the corner, wishing she had a better hiding place. The room had no closet. The cot was too low for her to crawl under. She had only felt so vulnerable once before, in another unfamiliar bedroom, when the boy closed the door on the party downstairs.

What would she do if she were discovered? What could she

do here, unprotected and undefended on GB Road? Shardul could do anything he wanted to her, and no one would be there to stop him.

Breathing heavily, ears straining for sounds, she waited to see what would happen next.

CHAPTER 10

a moment later, she heard heated discussion from below. She recognized Shardul's angry voice and heard Sanjana's fevered replies. Silence ensued, followed by heavy footsteps on the stairs. The bedroom door opened. Leslie clamped her fingers over her mouth, her ragged gasps sounding like an air horn to her ears. She pinched her eyes shut and held her breath. *Please, God, don't let him find me here.* It was the first time she'd prayed in years.

After what seemed a very long time, she heard Shardul's voice again, calmer than it had been before. "Raveena," he called softly. His voice was still harsh, but quiet this time.

Leslie wondered if he was trying to not disturb the other woman. She heard mumbling and rustling sounds and guessed Raveena was pretending to wake. They spoke quietly, but Leslie could not understand what they said. She heard footsteps. The door closed.

Several minutes later, she heard the car start and drive away. The other woman finally broke the silence.

"Okay, they are gone. You can come," the woman said.

Afraid to move, Leslie peeped around the curtain, half-expecting to see the angry man waiting for her. Instead, she was alone with the strange woman who had just hidden and protected her. "Where did they go?"

"I do not know. All he said was, 'Not the zoo today. I have a new place for you.' What is your name?"

"Leslie," she replied, holding out her hand.

The woman clasped her hand, staring openly. Her brown eyes were heavily painted with make-up—thick, black eyeliner, blue shadow. "Tarla. My name is Tarla."

"I'm sorry we burst in here and woke you. I don't really understand what happened." Leslie was suddenly aware how little the woman wore—just a sheer nightgown. She looked away, embarrassed, feeling completely out of place.

A bowl of water rested on a tiny table near the door, dead bugs floating in it. Pictures of scantily clad, buxom women taped to the walls made her squirm. She had no experience with pornography but thought some of these images might qualify.

Certainly her mother would scowl and shame her for looking upon such trash.

She turned back to Tarla, focusing on her face to avoid staring at her nearly bare body. "Who is that man?"

"Shardul," Tarla told her. "He watches us."

"But who is he?" What kind of man terrorized women so completely? How did he hold such power over them?

Tarla stared closely, as if memorizing her features. "You are just like Raveena described. She told me all about you, how you stopped the men at the zoo, how you talked to Shardul, and she chattered on and on like a little monkey about how much food she ate. So much food."

"You speak very good English. Raveena said her mother taught her English."

"Yes." Tarla said.

"She also told me her mother was dead?"

"Yes."

"You knew her mother?"

"We were like sisters. When she died, she asked me to watch over Raveena for her."

"So you adopted her?"

"Oh, no," Tarla shook her head. "She is Bikram's child."

"Whose child? She said she didn't have a dad."

"Bikram," Tarla repeated. "Not her father. He is the owner of us all."

She stared at her, at a loss for words, her mind struggling to comprehend the idea of owning a person.

"He bought us, and now we owe him money. We work for him until the money is paid back," Tarla explained. "But I have paid back all my debt. I am free adhiya. I pay rent and food to him." She looked proud of her accomplishment.

Leslie remembered the news report: '*Often trafficked against their wills, these women are kept as sex slaves in dismal conditions by the brothel owners…*'

"I'm so sorry," she mumbled, not sure what to say, feeling foolish.

The door opened, and Sanjana returned with a tray of tea. She held the tray out and they each took a cup. Sanjana took the last cup herself and sat on the cot, setting the tray on the floor. She spoke to Tarla, who chuckled at the shared joke.

"The *chaiwallah* was surprised to see her so early. We normally sleep all morning." Tarla giggled.

"I can't sleep now, after all the excitement," Sanjana said. She nudged Tarla. "Should we open early to catch some of the men on their way to work?" The two women laughed again, but Leslie could not. Sanjana gestured for her to drink her tea.

"I'm so sorry," Leslie repeated, at a loss for words. She didn't see how these women could laugh.

Tarla wobbled her head. "Enjoy your tea."

When Leslie sipped it, both women smiled. Sanjana spoke again. "I am sorry I was angry before. You must be a good woman to take Raveena to eat and to want to see for yourself how the child lives. I was scared because you surprised me, and I knew Shardul was coming to get Raveena. He would beat us all if he found you here."

"Why?"

"He is afraid you will try to take Raveena away. He told us all last night that she is not allowed to see you anymore. He is not taking her to the zoo today in case you look for her again."

"Where did he take her?" Leslie asked.

"We never know until she comes back," Tarla answered. "She was so excited yesterday. She told me you wanted to help her." Tarla still smiled at her.

Leslie couldn't think clearly. Everything here was so wrong. These women spoke casually of being beaten and of an orphan kept in a brothel. "I'm going to the police."

Tarla spoke with Sanjana. The two women shared a look then chuckled softly. "The police will not help us," Tarla told her.

Sanjana made a disgusted sound, a cross between a grunt and a laugh.

"Why not? They should."

"No, ma'am. The police would not come even if we call them."

"But why?"

"Bikram pays them," Tarla explained.

Sanjana launched into an explanation, speaking rapidly. "The police are as bad as the thugs in this neighborhood. Bikram pays them to buy their silence. They do not come to protect us or to check on us. They come only to harass us and extort money. Bikram pays them every month, but sometimes they sniff around for more. Or swagger in and make sex with the prime women, taking up so much time that could be spent with paying customers. And sometimes they make raids, bursting in and taking all the minors. Then they hold them until I come with money to buy them back."

Sanjana drew in her breath. "Two times the police take Raveena when she was so small. Sunita cried and cried, 'Do not take my child,' but still the police take her. Sunita cried so much, no man wanted to make sex with her. I go and buy her back. How can we make money to eat this way?"

Leslie could not drink any more of her tea. She knew something about the hopeless plight of these women, but nothing close to the full extent of their problems. What could you do when the people who were supposed to protect you didn't? When they actually made the problem worse?

She wondered what her mother would say if she knew about forced prostitution. Where was God in this? How could He allow women to be treated so?

"Sunita? Is that Raveena's mother?"

"Yes," Tarla confirmed.

"And the police would take Raveena from her mother?"

Sanjana's voice dripped with contempt. "The police decide which laws they will enforce. And then I must go buy back the child for my weeping girl. Bikram expects so much money from my girls every day. He will not accept any excuses if I have to use the money to pay bribes. The police laugh at us and ask who we will complain to. So I go. I pay for Raveena. Make Sunita happy. I good gharwali." She smiled at Tarla, who leaned against her shoulder.

"Yes, she is good gharwali."

"What is that? Gharwali?"

"Gharwali...umm. She lives here with us. She watches us for Bikram. He pays her to watch over girls, make sure we are healthy, make sure we all work. She was a worker too, but now she is gharwali."

"That sounds like a madam." Just speaking the word made Leslie feel dirty. "If Bikram is the brothel owner, and Sanjana is the madam and lives here, what is Shardul?"

"Shardul is our dog," Tarla said, and she and Sanjana laughed.

The meaning was lost on Leslie. "I'm sorry, I don't understand."

"Dog. Teeth and claws." Tarla looked at Sanjana, trying to decide how to make herself clear. "Bikram is very busy man. He owns this house and four more. He has many workers. Also he has boys selling opium on the streets. He is busy every day, so he does not come. Sanjana is like mother to all the girls. Shardul is..." She made her hands into fists, scowling and mimicking his angry attitude.

"The hired muscle," Leslie finished for her, remembering the earlier comment about Shardul beating them all. "So he hurts you if you don't work?"

Tarla nodded. "But also, if some bad man is here, if he refuses to pay for sex or if someone tries to steal from us, Sanjana calls Shardul and he will make them pay."

"He protects you and he beats you?"

"He protects Bikram's money. He also pays the police the monthly bribe. And he takes Raveena during the day. He comes back at night to check on us. Or if we call him for help."

A new idea occurred to Leslie. "You said Raveena is Bikram's child now," she began hesitantly. "Does she...also... work here?" She was afraid to know the answer.

"No, he makes her go to the streets to beg," Tarla answered. Relief washed over Leslie, until Tarla continued, "He is saving his 'Cherry Girl' and lets no man touch her. He says she is so beautiful that any man would be glad to pay for her any price. But first he will sell her as a virgin. She will bring so much money the first time she has to make sex with a man."

"Oh, my God." Leslie thought she might vomit. She covered her mouth and closed her eyes. All she could think of were Raveena's big, brown eyes gazing up at her. The thought of a man touching her, forcing himself on her...

She knew the disgust of a stranger's hands groping her, the indignity of a body forced upon her, the sickening helplessness of not being able to stop it. "But isn't there anything...I mean —how old is she?"

"She has twelve years now."

"And the police would do nothing?"

"No, ma'am, they would only tell you to mind your own business. She belongs to Bikram."

"She's an orphan! How can she belong to anyone?"

"Sunita owed Bikram money when she died. Now the money must be paid back by Raveena."

"She's just a little girl. How is she responsible?"

"The children must take the parents' debt."

"So he's going to sell her to men for sex? That isn't right. I know that's illegal. When will he do this? How much time does she have?"

Sanjana spoke in a quiet voice. "When I was first sold, I was fourteen-year-old virgin. Now, men want younger and younger virgins. The younger the girl, the more the owner can charge for her. With twelve years, men will pay so much money. Sometimes very wealthy men will buy a cherry girl for week, maybe two weeks. That is what he is hoping for Raveena. This would make so much money for Bikram."

"One or two weeks? A man will keep her for weeks? Doing God knows what to her. And this could happen any day now?" Leslie turned to Sanjana. "This was done to you? What happened? Will you tell me?"

Sanjana lowered her head. "Yes, ma'am, this is common. My family was very poor. Six children, four boys and two girls. All the time the family is hungry. Then one summer, there was no rain. There was no food. My father had to go look for work. One day, a man came to our village. He said if any of the girls in the village could sew, he could take them to work in Agra. The Taj Mahal attracts so many tourists, and the tourists buy so many clothes, and there were not enough hands sewing to keep up with the demand. The man told us he could offer a small down payment for any girls that would go with him, and then he would send money each month from the girls' earnings. My mother did not want to send her daughter so far away. But this man told her that he could guarantee good working wages, and the amount of money he offered was too much to resist. Rather than watch her children all starve to death, my mother took this man's money and sent me away with the man."

"How far away from Agra was your village?"

"I think it is maybe around eight hours away, but I am not sure as I have never been there. The man put the seven of us into a van. He told us all to smile and wave goodbye and told the parents what good hands the girls would be in. But we did not go to Agra. He drove us to Varanasi."

"Let me guess. You weren't being hired to sew either, were you?"

"No, ma'am. As soon as we were outside the village, the man told us that he had spent so much money on us, giving our parents so much money. And now he had to pay the petrol for the van to drive us, and he would have to buy our food and pay for our lodging. So he told us that we must do whatever he told us to do to pay back the money we owed him."

Leslie listened, stunned that Sanjana could recount this story with so little emotion. She tried to imagine being taken from her family. Tried to imagine desperation so severe a mother would send a young daughter away with a strange man.

"One of the other girls read a sign as we passed and realized we were going the wrong way. She told the man he made a mistake, that we were going the wrong way. He reached back and slapped her and told her to close her mouth. The rest of us girls knew then that something was wrong. We all cried until he said, 'Let me buy some ice cream for all of you to make you happy again.' He left us in the van and returned some time later with dishes of ice cream for everyone. He passed them out, telling us, 'There we go. Everyone eat. All happy, all smiling. Good girls.' I remember thinking perhaps things would not be so bad after all."

Leslie's stomach tightened. Some part of her didn't want to

hear any more. She sensed that Sanjana had never shared this story before—with anyone.

"The ice cream was drugged. Probably opium. That is a common method used to subdue young girls. I woke up the next day. We were in a filthy little house. When the man returned, he brought other men with him. He instructed us to take off our clothes to be inspected for health. We were very shy and very uncomfortable with this. The man screamed at us to undress. We cried but most of us obeyed. Some still refused. One older girl crossed her arms and said she wanted to go back home. The man grabbed her roughly by the arm, shaking her violently. He said, 'This one will not do a thing she is told. Take care of her.' He threw her to the other men, who ripped her clothing from her, laughing and jeering. When she was naked, they dragged her to the back room where we could hear her screaming for help, begging them to stop, promising to obey. The men all took turns raping her, one after the other, laughing and joking. Some of the men mimicked her when she cried out for her mother."

Leslie wiped tears from her eyes. She reached out and placed a hand on Sanjana's arm.

"You good heart." Sanjana smiled. "I wish someone like you had come to check on us as you have come to see about Raveena. After the screaming stopped, the men returned without the girl they had just raped, tying their britches and smiling. The man who took us from the village told us we could see what would happen if we did not do as we were told, so we might as well cooperate. We were so scared. One of the girls said that if they let a man make sex to them, no one would ever marry them. The man laughed and said, 'You will all be used goods soon enough, one way or another, so you might as well give it up. You can open your legs willingly, or they will be forced open.' After that, we all did as we were told."

CHAPTER 11

*L*eslie wiped the tears from her cheeks. She tried to stop crying, but the story was just too horrifying.

Sanjana continued. "Eventually that man sold me to Bikram. After many years, Bikram made me gharwali. I good gharwali."

"Yes, she is good to her girls," Tarla agreed. "She never beats us," she teased.

Sanjana hugged the girl and patted her cheek.

"And Raveena." Sanjana lowered her voice, her eyes sparkling, as if sharing a secret.

Smiling a mischievous smile, Tarla said, "Sanjana allowed Sunita to have Raveena."

"You mean, instead of giving her up for adoption?"

"No, instead of forcing abortion," Tarla corrected her.

Another shock. Not just an abortion, but a forced abortion. Her hands covered her abdomen, as if protecting her uterus even though it was empty.

"Some gharwalis cause abortions when their girls become pregnant. Sunita came to me when she realized she carried a child. She cried on my lap, 'Please, let me have it. I will never be married, never have my own little house, please let me have a baby.' And I allowed it."

"She was pregnant by one of her...clients?" The words felt awkward in Leslie's mouth. "Does she know who the father is?"

The two of them laughed. Face pinking with embarrassment, Leslie realized what a foolish question this was.

"No, ma'am, not possible," Tarla told her. "Yes, she became pregnant from a man she serviced. Most brothel owners do not like their girls to become pregnant or have children, but it does happen. When Shardul noticed her bulging stomach, he told Bikram, but Sanjana and Sunita pretended they did not realize she was pregnant until it was too late to bring on abortion. Bikram yelled at them and called them stupid and complained about how much money a baby would cost him. But Sunita got her baby." Sharing a conspiratorial smile, the two women hugged again.

"What happened to Sunita?" Leslie asked, although she was afraid to hear the answer. She had heard enough horrors for one day.

"Sunita got very sick. So sick. Then one morning she did not wake up," Tarla told her.

Leslie's father's sermons of heaven and hell—rewards and punishment—were buried in her childhood memories. Like fairy tales and myths of Santa and the tooth fairy, she'd outgrown these and left them behind when she no longer believed.

Now she questioned her complete dismissal of hell and the demons her parents believed inhabited it. The stories she'd just heard were hell incarnate.

The women's stories stirred her most horrific memory. The darkest day of her life, when she witnessed the abduction of a little girl from her neighborhood. Her twelve-year-old mind experienced insomnia for the first time that night, imagining all the dreadful things that could be happening to that girl while her stomach churned and she wondered over and over again why that girl and not her. But her wildest imaginings could not create such horrors as she'd just heard these women share.

I was only twelve. So was Raveena, and so were these women when hell came to call and demons carried them away.

Leslie remembered her mother's prayers for the missing girl, her assurances she was now in a better place. Not true, not if that girl experienced anything remotely similar to what these women just described. For the first time since that terrible day, she took relief in the assumption the girl was dead shortly after the abduction. Perhaps her suffering had been short-lived.

Unlike the plight of the women sitting beside her, sharing their terrible sufferings at the hands of men. '*We are the hands of Jesus on this earth,*' her mother would say. Regardless of how Leslie felt about that, there was no questioning the right decision here. How could anyone walk away, unaffected?

"How can I help you?" she asked. "All of you. What can I do?"

A knock at the front door interrupted them. She had been so involved with the conversation, she was startled to notice the sun was quite high in the sky. The rays shining through the window warmed the room. Her clothing stuck to her damp skin, and a bead of sweat trickled from her brow. Sanjana muttered.

Tarla explained. "It will be the trash sweeper, come to collect his weekly bribe."

"What bribe?"

"He demands money each week. If Sanjana refuses to pay him, he takes the garbage he sweeps from the streets and dumps it in front of our building."

"Unbelievable." Leslie jumped up and followed Sanjana downstairs. In the hallway, Sanjana bumped into the man Leslie had noticed sprawled in one of the rooms earlier. He had woken enough to put on his britches and held his head in both hands as he meandered slowly down the hall.

Sanjana spoke as she pushed past him then translated for Leslie. "I told him this is a brothel, not a hotel, and to hurry along home before I charge him rent for the night on top of what he paid for the woman."

Back in the tiny lobby, Sanjana opened the door with money in her hand. Sure enough, a man stood there with his hand out, clad in dishwater-brown dhoti britches and a stained gray shirt, shuffling idly on grimy bare feet. His white hair and beard twisted in matted clumps. Watching him, fury filled Leslie. No one offered these women a shred of understanding or compassion. They were abused at every turn, on every level. No one helped them.

"How can you do this to these women?" she demanded, watching the man greedily pocket the rupees. He turned his dark eyes on her and surveyed her carefully.

"Kya?" he asked.

Tarla spoke to him. He grinned in reply, revealing his few remaining teeth were stained and broken. Leslie could not understand what he said.

"I told him you are upset that he is taking bribe money from us to do a job he is paid to do. He says what business is it of yours and why do you care? He takes money from us because he can. Who will stop him? He says go ahead and call the police—he knows they will not come. And he says you should stop being so rude to an old man or he may tell Shardul that his girls are entertaining foreign women instead of resting up for tonight."

Last night's client came clumping down the stairs, appearing very hung over, buttoning his threadbare shirt. The smell of alcohol surrounded him. Without even looking at the street sweeper, he pushed past him. The street sweeper spoke to him but was only waved off. The sweeper and the man lounging in the street laughed again.

Tarla said, "He asked that man if he had a good time here last night. Then he said maybe they can all come tonight for a taste of this white skin."

Leslie clenched her teeth. The thought of these repulsive men touching her—

All at once, her knees felt so weak she wasn't sure she could continue standing.

The trash sweeper grinned openly at her, knowing he was right, knowing no one would help these women. And she realized she gave him further ammunition for extorting money by being seen here. The old man sitting in the street said something, and the two of them enjoyed another laugh at her expense. She slammed the door in the sweeper's face and turned to Sanjana and Tarla, her whole body shaking.

"Do you think he will say anything to Shardul about my being here?" she asked.

Tarla shrugged. "If he does, Sanjana and I will just tell Shardul that he was stoned. He probably is anyway."

"Is there any way I can help you? Can you run away?"

Again Tarla shrugged. "Where would we go? Sanjana is an older woman now. She has no family. No man will marry her. I cannot go back to my family. If I could find them after all these years, I would only bring shame on them. And no man would take me for wife after so many have shared my bed. Sanjana was free to leave many years ago, but she stayed all this time. I was free to leave last year, but I stay as a free woman. Here, I make money. Sanjana is good to me. I do not make trouble. I live on the first floor now."

"Is the first floor nicer?"

"The new girls go to the top floor, when they are first brought here. They stay upstairs so they cannot escape. The longer we are here, the better our service, the more Sanjana likes us, we move down."

"What about Raveena? What can we do for her? Can we take her to an orphanage?"

"No, ma'am," Tarla answered very quickly. "She is Bikram's child until Sunita's debt is repaid. Bikram has dreams of much money from Raveena. He will never allow someone to take her."

"He'll make that money by allowing filthy pedophiles to rape her. How can he expect her to fulfill Sunita's debt? He doesn't even feel sorry for a young girl who lost her mother. He's going to use her for money and then just throw her away. She's had her childhood stolen from her. All of you have." Indignant tears swam in her eyes, and Leslie found herself hugged and consoled by the other two.

"You are good woman," Tarla assured her, "but there is nothing we can do. This is our fate."

Leslie drew back to look Tarla in the eye. There was a hollow look there, a vacancy left by the life she could have led, the house she could have lived in, the family she could have raised.

Leslie knew that vacancy.

The memory of a smiling freckled face edged with pigtails swam to the surface of her thoughts—a little girl ripped from her life.

She thought of something Tom sometimes said as he analyzed data, running statistical equations: "The slightest deviation changes the trajectory; the path is altered forever."

Certainly that was the case here. Had these women not fallen prey to vicious, greedy men, they would still be living in their original communities, leading radically different lives. What if someone had stepped in and intervened for them? If only somewhere along the way someone had stopped this endless cycle of horrifying events that brought them here.

The time had come for someone to break the cycle.

Leslie would not allow Raveena to fall victim as these women had. As the little girl in her childhood neighborhood had. As she herself had. Somehow, she would find a way out.

"If fate brought you here, then it is fate that brought me

here as well," she told Tarla. And maybe, maybe, this was her chance to make up for the mistakes in her past.

Before she could answer, they heard a rumbling car pull to a stop in front of the building. It sounded very much like the car Shardul had driven off in.

CHAPTER 12

I hope that is my nervous taxi driver," Leslie whispered as a car door slammed.

Loud voices outside told her otherwise.

"Oh, God," Tarla whispered. "The idiot outside is asking Shardul when he hired a white American woman. There is no hiding you now."

Heart pounding, Leslie turned to Sanjana for instructions. "Why is he back? Didn't you say he only comes at night?"

"There is no way of knowing," Sanjana replied. "I do not know what to do now. We can try to hide you again but —"

The door swung open. Shardul yanked off his sunglasses and squinted into the dark brothel, the sunlight glaring behind him like a starburst, throwing his body into shadow. He stepped inside, eyes locked on her. Raveena trailed behind him, face stricken.

Leslie froze instantly. Her limbs went ice cold. Her hands shook. She couldn't think.

"Why are you here?" Shardul's angry growl sent her heart into palpitations.

Mouth dry, she swallowed hard, hoping her voice would not betray how terribly frightened she felt. "I was looking for

Raveena," she managed to answer, trying to scrape up some of the defiance she brandished at the zoo. She didn't want the little girl to see her fear.

"You have no business with her. Stay away from her." He turned on Sanjana and Tarla, berating them for allowing her into the building. "I told you this morning. I do not want her around Raveena!"

"Raveena was gone," Tarla stammered out. "We were just telling her to leave and never come back."

Leslie feared he would beat the two women mercilessly. No telling what he would do to Raveena. They were all prisoners.

"They told me there was no little girl here," she lied.

"How did you know where she lives?" Shardul breathed heavily, his hands clenched as he turned on Raveena. "Did you tell her?"

Not Raveena. Don't hurt the girl. "She didn't tell me anything. I've been searching all the brothels. I was just leaving when you came in." Leslie prayed the story would protect them all, at least a little.

"The man in the street says you came early and have been here all morning," Shardul contradicted her.

Damn him, she cursed silently, hoping her eyes did not reveal the truth.

"He is stoned on opium," Tarla responded before she could say another word. "What does he know?"

"You have no business here." Shardul raised his voice and advanced on Leslie.

Raveena gasped.

"Okay, I'll go," Leslie assured him. She tried to move toward the door, but he stepped in front of her.

"Stay away from Raveena." He spoke each word distinctly. His eyes bored into her as though he were able to peer into her mind, as if somehow this man knew she was devising a plan to rescue the girl. "You hear me?" He stepped closer.

Shardul steered her where he wanted her to go just as the

college boy steered her into his bedroom all those years ago—
the last time she'd been so completely unequipped to deal with
a guy. How had she let this happen again?

He stood directly in front of her, looming over her, glaring
down into her eyes. She backed away from him, placing herself
farther from the door that was her only hope of exit. She
bumped against the wall, sending strips of peeling paint
floating to the floor. Pressed against the wall, she scarcely
breathed.

He was so close. She could feel the warmth emanating from
his body and smell his masculine musk. What was he going to
do to her? Her mind raced and yet produced nothing, clouded
by fear. He was bigger, stronger. What would she do if he
dragged her into one of the rooms upstairs? She imagined him
pinning her down, his rough hands on her body, her pants
yanked down, hot breath against her neck...

She shuddered. *God, please, not again...*

She sent up a silent prayer for the second time that day.

He struck like a cobra. Mesmerized by his dark brooding
eyes, and distracted with thoughts of what he intended to do,
she didn't see him move until it was too late. He raised his arm
and whipped the back of his hand across her face.

"Auntie!" Raveena cried.

Leslie had never been struck before. Her parents did not
follow the adage "spare the rod and spoil the child." She may
not have approved of their beliefs or how they chose to raise
her, but they never hit their children.

The complete and utter shock stunned her before she even
registered the staccato sound of the backhanded slap or the
pain that exploded across the right side of her face. She stag-
gered sideways from the force of the impact.

"Stay away from Raveena!" he screamed, though she could
scarcely hear anything but the ringing in her ears.

Her face throbbed with heat. Whether the pulsing warmth
spread from the blow itself or the sheer embarrassment of

being struck, she wasn't sure. She turned to face him, but a second slap sent her spinning again. This time, a knuckle caught her lip with enough force that she tasted blood.

Cold fear ran through her. She was at a loss what to do, how to extricate herself from this situation that had so quickly gone horribly wrong. She stood absolutely still, staring down at the concrete floor, afraid any movement might provoke him. She tried to devise an escape plan, but the only thought in her mind was, "My face hurts." Was he going to continue assaulting her?

As if in reply, he grabbed her by her upper arms, shaking her violently. He shoved her backward, her head banging against the wall. He leaned down close, pelvis grinding into her. He was aroused, completely enjoying terrorizing her.

She whimpered and struggled, tears leaking from the corners of her eyes. He only ground against her harder. He let go of one of her arms and lowered his hand, fumbling with her skirt until he found her inner thigh, and ran his fingers over the sensitive skin. He breathed against her neck, trailing his tongue along her skin. She turned her face away, eyes shut tight.

He ran his hand under her leg, grabbed the underside of her thigh, lifting it roughly to position himself between her legs. His hand crept upward until he reached her backside, her skirt around her waist. She struggled and cried out. He pinned her tighter against the wall until she could barely breathe. He raised his head, and she opened her eyes to meet his as he looked down at her.

He smirked, delight dancing in his eyes.

He pressed his mouth to hers, rocking his groin against her. She gagged as the taste of blood on her tongue combined with his stale breath, sour with lingering cigarette smoke.

He reached again between her legs. His fingers slid along the lace edge of her underwear.

She couldn't escape his grasp.

"No," Raveena cried.

She saw the girl rush forward, only to be grabbed by Sanjana, who pulled the girl close and turned her face away.

"You have taught this stupid American a lesson," Tarla said, moving to Shardul's side. "Let her go now. She could call the police. No police here today. Let her go."

As soon as he relaxed his hold on her, Tarla grabbed her by the arm and navigated her toward the door. Sanjana released Raveena and hurried to his side, murmuring in a soothing tone. When he said nothing, Tarla deftly ushered her out into the sunlight on the street, which blazed down on her like a spotlight.

Leslie threw one glance at Raveena on her way out the door. She'd promised help and had only managed to anger the man who controlled the girl's life.

Shardul broke free of Sanjana's mothering clutch and followed her outside, railing at her, fists clenched, shouting that he was not finished with her.

She stood at the curb, watching him approach, dimly aware that Tarla spoke beside her.

Sanjana caught hold of Shardul's arm and tried to pull him back toward the brothel but was no match for his strength.

The man in the street laughed openly at the spectacle.

Prajit appeared out of nowhere. Just as Shardul shook Sanjana off and turned his attention back to Leslie, the taxi barreled down the street, maneuvered around Shardul's parked car, and screeched to a halt before her.

Prajit opened the passenger-side door, calling "In! In! In!" He gestured wildly to her, eyes wide with fear and concern. Tarla shoved her from behind. Prajit grabbed her arm and pulled. Before the door was even closed behind her, Prajit gunned the engine and sped away from Shardul and the laughing spectator.

The door slammed closed. Prajit careened down the street, glancing repeatedly behind them, watching for Shardul. When he left the street and merged into the first traffic circle leading them back to the hotel and safety, he finally began to relax.

She hunched over, gasping for breath. She shook uncontrollably, tears coursing down her cheeks, shamed by the humiliation of being struck and nearly raped. The memory replayed over and over in her mind. If Tarla had not intervened and ushered her out of the brothel, who knew what Shardul would've done to her?

Guilt weighed heavily at the thought of what she might have brought upon the two women and the little girl. She went hoping to help Raveena, and instead found herself in a situation where the little girl tried to help her.

Prajit tentatively glanced sideways at her, probably attempting to unobtrusively size up her condition.

Leslie focused on deep, calming breaths and dabbed the tears that streaked her face. Her cheek was sore and tender. Her lip pulsed. As her heartbeat slowed to a nearly normal speed, she hazarded a look in the rearview mirror. She winced.

Three bright red welts swelled up on her cheek. A small, blue bruise blossomed from the edge of her right eye, bloodshot at the corner. Her lower lip was puffy but thankfully not as swollen as it felt. The metallic taste of blood remained sharp in her mouth, but fortunately only a few smears were visible on her face. Running her tongue over her inner cheek and lip, she found a small, raw cut. Likely, the force of the second slap had caused her tooth to puncture her lip. It ached but could have been much worse.

"Lady, okay?" Prajit hesitantly ventured.

She looked at him. His face told her how alarming her appearance really was.

She nodded anyway, far from okay. "Thank you," she whispered. "Thank you for rescuing me."

Prajit wobbled his head and held up a hand to stop any further gratitude. Thinking back to that frightening moment when she was slapped reminded her that Shardul might now be subjecting Tarla and Sanjana and Raveena to the same treatment. Leslie began to cry again.

"Okay, lady." Prajit attempted to comfort her. "Very bad man. Back to hotel now."

Back to hotel. The words intended to console her stirred new distress. Back to Tom. Before, she'd hoped that, if he lost track of time — as he often did when swimming and lounging poolside — he wouldn't know she'd left the hotel. If he noticed, she could admit to leaving, perhaps on a shopping trip or some innocuous errand.

None of that would fly now. The marks on her face changed everything. She was coming back battered, and there would be no harmless glossing over the incident. He would know how she had walked right into a brothel and placed herself in harm's way. Telling Tom all the lurid details would be humiliating, and he would undoubtedly make it even worse by pointing out how stupid she had been.

Sinking back into the seat of the taxi, she wiped her face of tears yet again, trying to steel herself for his reaction. It was for Raveena. The thought of the little girl under the control of that horrible man stirred up her indignation. She didn't know how, but she would get Raveena out of there. Somehow. Regardless of how many times Shardul tried to run her off. She would gladly take the blows to protect a child.

CHAPTER 13

*L*eslie could tell Prajit relaxed as he pulled through the circular drive and came to a stop in front of the hotel. The doorman rushed out immediately, mopping his forehead with a white handkerchief.

"Thank God," he muttered as he opened her door and held out a hand to assist her. He called to the assorted hotel workers assembled in the entryway. "She has come! She is here!" When she grasped his hand and stood, he caught sight of her injured face. "Oh, my God. Madam, what has happened?"

Tom rushed out of the hotel lobby. Any hopes of quietly returning to the hotel drifted away from her, a balloon snatched by a wild wind. Of course Tom had noticed her absence.

Here we go, she thought. Her stomach clenched again, dreading the next few minutes.

Tom reached her side and grabbed her arm. She winced involuntarily. He pulled her into a protective hug, cradling her head to him. "What were you thinking?" he said, clutching her tightly.

She pressed her face into his chest, relief flooding through her. His warm embrace felt so good, comforting, after everything that had happened this morning. She had not realized how desperately she craved gentle, loving care.

"I couldn't find you anywhere. The doorman said you left hours ago, but he wouldn't tell me where you went." He relaxed his hold on her, took her by the shoulders, and leaned her back to look in her eyes, seeking answers. His eyes took in the bruising and the smudges of blood. The relief of finding her changed immediately to confusion, which morphed into fear for her safety. Then anger rushed in, lashing out, whipping him into a fury. "What happened to your face? Where were you? You look like you've been hit. Did someone hit you? Who did this to you?"

"Please calm down," she urged quietly, aware the doorman and Prajit stood nearby, looking afraid that some of this rage might eventually direct itself toward them.

"Calm down? You leave without a word and come back like this and I should calm down?"

"I went to find Raveena," she told him, hoping he would at least lower his voice. This was going about as badly as she had anticipated. Why couldn't she have been pleasantly surprised just this once?

"The girl? You went searching for — My God, Leslie, you graduated summa cum laude. You're smarter than that!"

"I was trying to help her," she said quietly. "And I won't stop trying."

"Please, sir, let us adjourn inside and let cooler heads prevail," encouraged the doorman.

"My wife has been beaten! How am I supposed to calm down?" Tom answered. "Who did this to you?"

"Shardul," she admitted.

"The man from the zoo? From dinner last night? Jesus, you teach elementary school but can't remember your own lectures about stranger danger? How did you even find him?"

She glanced at Prajit.

Tom noticed and whirled on the driver. "You knew where

they were? And you drove her there? You told me last night that he was dangerous."

Prajit dropped his guilt-ridden eyes. He had failed to protect memsaab, try as he might.

"It wasn't his fault. They tried to tell me not to go. It was my fault for insisting."

"Let us go inside and get some ice for her injuries," the doorman suggested. "We have a doctor available, sir, if your wife requires medical attention."

"So you found Raveena, and this guy Shardul hit you? I will kill the bastard."

"Yes, let's get some ice," she urged. "That sounds good. My face hurts."

"Fine. We can get you some ice and make sure you don't need a doctor. But then I'm finding that son of a bitch."

The doorman led the way back into the hotel and toward the bar located just off the lobby.

"Please, Tom, don't. You have no idea what he's like," she pleaded, following along where she was led. Completely drained, she slumped against her husband. She didn't want to argue. His berating was more than she could handle. Her entire body ached. The sore muscles cried out for her to lie down.

"He's a man who hits women. And more importantly, hit my wife. I intend to show him how I feel about this."

"It's more complicated than that. Please don't upset him. He probably already beat two women who live in the brothel just because they talked with me this morning. He might hurt Raveena, too."

"Live in the...you were in a brothel? Jesus."

The bartender handed a bag of ice cubes to Tom, who rested it against her cheek. The cold stung her raw, bruised face. She winced but held it firmly in place, hoping to minimize the swelling as much as possible.

Watching her, Tom's face softened. He thanked the

doorman for his help. "I'm going to take her up to the room for a while and sort this out," he told the frowning hotel employee.

Lying down sounded good. Dizziness blurred her vision, and her stomach felt as if it were trying to digest razors.

He kept a tight grip on her, helping her into the elevator, holding the door open to their room, then easing her onto the bed.

"Is that better?" he asked, after she curled into a ball on her side.

"Not really. Now my stomach hurts too."

"You should tell me what happened. You found the girl? In a brothel?"

She shared the story with him, describing GB Road and the brothel, the two women who hid her and shared their stories and Raveena's with her, and Shardul's attack when he discovered her there. She left some details out. She couldn't tell her husband how he had touched her—how he'd almost raped her.

"So even these two women told you that you will never be able to get their owner to give up Raveena? And Shardul hit you to scare you off. But you still think you can do something to help her?"

"I'm going to get her out of there somehow. I won't leave her to suffer the same plight as those other women. Can you?"

"She's not our concern, Leslie."

"Now you sound like Shardul." Another sharp cramp hit her in the gut. She closed her eyes. The room spun.

"That was harsh," Tom responded. "And totally uncalled for. I am really worried about you."

"I'm really worried about Raveena." She tried to rise up on one elbow. "Think back to dinner last night. Think about that sweet, quiet, hungry little girl. Can you just sit there unconcerned that any day now she's going to be raped for money? Someone will profit from her violation. It makes me sick."

All at once, she was sick. Her mouth watered and her

stomach heaved. She wobbled to the bathroom, legs like jelly. Closing the door behind her, she bent over the toilet and retched repeatedly.

There was little in her stomach. She'd skipped breakfast, opting for black coffee only. So what was that sweet, spicy taste the bile left in her throat? Even when nothing more was expelled, her stomach attempted to purge itself. She dry heaved for several minutes before slumping to the floor.

Her pulse throbbed in her temples, leaving her feeling as if she'd just run a marathon. When she could move again, she rinsed her mouth, brushed her teeth, and made her way carefully back to the bed.

"You okay?" Tom asked.

"Better now."

"Have you eaten today?"

"No, just the coffee this morning. And then I was at the brothel so I didn't have lunch..." She trailed off, remembering. "Sanjana brought us tea."

"Well, that explains the Delhi belly." He shook his head. "You know better than that. I feel like you've lost all sense lately."

"It would have been rude to refuse," she countered. Though she felt physically better after vomiting, his words stung.

"We're going to the police," Tom decided.

"It won't do any good. The police are part of the problem. They won't help any of the women or Raveena."

"Not for them. I want to file a report of assault and battery. That man had a lot of nerve hitting you like that. I want to see him pay. If you won't let me track him down and kick his ass myself, let me recruit the police to do it." Tom stroked her head, pushing her hair away from her face. His fingers caressed the bruises on her arm.

"I think going to the police will be a waste of time. I don't think anyone will care."

"That's what the police are for, Leslie, to protect the public. This Shardul is a menace. And if he gets arrested for hitting you, he won't be able to hurt anyone else, either. Do you feel up to moving?"

She sat up slowly. Her stomach ached, and she remained weak and woozy, but she no longer felt like she was about to vomit.

"I think so," she decided. "But it will be a waste of time. I would bet money on the outcome. You didn't hear the stories these women told. No one cuts them a break. And no one ever brings these men to justice."

"I will not let them ignore your bruises," Tom told her, his jaw tight and his brow furrowed. "We're going to see some justice today."

CHAPTER 14

*L*eslie smiled warmly when she saw Prajit outside with his taxi, ready to chauffeur them to the local police station. She was starting to think of him as "her" driver. And he seemed to feel the same. He was also eager to make amends for the morning fiasco. He even attempted to refuse payment, but Tom insisted and requested he wait for them. He relented, grabbed Tom's hands in his own, and bowed deeply.

"I wait, sir," he assured them.

Prajit looked so distraught. She feared he blamed himself for her injuries, though she demanded he drive her, coerced him with promises of staying in the locked car, and refused to listen to him. He'd come to her rescue, but he apparently didn't see it that way.

Rattling and honking, traffic in the streets raced by, spewing black exhaust fumes into the air.

She followed Tom into the rundown, sparsely-furnished police station. Officers in tan uniforms, complete with matching brimmed caps, manned the simple desks. Stacks of papers cluttered every desk, some of them a foot tall. Computer screens sat perched atop the desks, but not one of them glowed. In fact, some of the computers were nearly buried under mounds of paperwork. Fans sat motionless. She noticed a bare light bulb in the ceiling above—it was dark. The electricity was out. The windows currently provided the only illumination.

Uniformed men crossed the room, passing in and out of doors leading presumably into private offices. Several sat at their desks hunched over paperwork, writing. Other officers spoke into cell phones, nodding. She wasn't sure what they should do first. She saw a handwritten sign instructing anyone wishing assistance to take a number. Tom ripped the next number from the packet of tickets, and they sat and waited on two metal folding chairs.

She'd never been to a police station in the United States, much less anywhere else. She wasn't pleased to be the cause of this visit and felt oddly disturbed at being here. What would her parents think if they found out she'd prompted a trip to the police? The stomach issues from earlier were not helping. Her empty stomach clenched as she thought of describing the morning's events again. Her mother's voice reminded her, '*We reap what we sow.*'

A fly droned lazily about her, landing again and again on her arm, undaunted by her continual shooing. No one acknowledged their presence.

"I don't feel well," she said. "Can we just go back so I can lie down?"

"We can wait awhile," Tom insisted. "This is important."

The minutes ticked by on her watch. Even Tom began to squirm and huff, looking pointedly at his watch before an officer finally approached the couple.

Dark eyes behind wire-framed glasses took them in with apparent curiosity. He wore the same tan uniform and dark belt as the other officers, but he'd removed his cap. His black hair was trimmed neatly and combed carefully to the side, not a hair out of place.

"Hello." He greeted them with a smile, shaking Tom's hand. His thin, black mustache, clipped and smooth, curled upward. "You speak English?"

Tom jumped to his feet. "Yes, English."

"I am Officer Kumar Verma," the officer said, introducing himself. "Please, this way." He led them to a private office just off the main office area. "Please, sit," he encouraged them. Leaning back out into the lobby, he called, "Chai!"

He went behind his simple wooden desk and took his seat, smiling again at the foreign couple. Moments later, a woman in an unadorned, beige sari entered the tiny office carrying a tray with three cups of tea. A wave of nausea discouraged Leslie from partaking of any more of the beverage.

"It is properly prepared, you can take," the officer assured them. Tom accepted a glass, but she placed a hand on her stomach apologetically. "Ah, not feeling well today, madam?"

"She was ill earlier," Tom replied.

Officer Verma took a cup of tea himself and dismissed the woman, wobbling his head and waving her back out the door.

"How can we help you today?" he asked Tom.

"I want to report an assault and battery. As you can see, my wife has been attacked."

"Oh, my, yes," the officer replied. "How did this happen?" He reached for a stack of paper forms. "So sorry. Electricity is out again. Computers are down. Can you please fill out this form?"

"It happened this morning," Tom began, accepting the paper and pen.

"And where did this occur?" the officer asked.

"I was on GB Road. I don't know the address of the building."

"GB Road, madam?" the officer asked, leaning back in his chair, frowning. "Why were you there?"

"I was looking for a little girl. It's a long story," she told the policeman.

He looked confused. "GB Road is not the sort of place we recommend for our tourists, especially not a woman all alone."

"We realize that," Tom responded. "But she went anyway, looking for this girl."

She began at the beginning, starting with the impromptu visit to the zoo the day before, taking Raveena to dinner, Shardul's behavior toward the orphaned girl, and how she had been so worried about Raveena that she'd convinced the taxi driver to take her to the brothel. As when she recounted the events to Tom, she did not disclose that she was also sexually assaulted. The last thing she needed to hear was that she got what she deserved for waltzing into a brothel. When she finished, she sat quietly, drained.

"I must say, madam, that you are most fortunate nothing further happened. The streets of New Delhi are not safe for women alone. Dreadful things could have happened to you." He took the paper form back from Tom, who had filled in their information as requested.

"Yes, I can imagine." She stared into her lap, wondering if he suspected the part of the story she left out.

"If you read the papers, madam, surely you have seen the stories about women raped on city buses, beaten, and left for dead."

"Look, we understand all this," Tom interrupted. "I'm not happy she left the hotel, but the real issue here is that she was struck. I want someone to do something about this."

The policeman rose from his seat. "I will speak with my supervisor. Please excuse me."

"Why does he need to speak with a supervisor?" Tom wondered. "He can't file a complaint himself? That seems odd."

"I don't know." She leaned forward, resting her head in her hands. "We're wasting our time. I'm tired of reliving this morning. And I'm getting a bad headache."

She rubbed her temples. Tom gently rubbed her back until the policeman returned.

"This is most unfortunate," the officer began, "but I don't believe we can do much here. I am so sorry you have been injured, but you should not have been in a bad part of town." He shook his head sadly.

"Now, wait a minute," Tom spoke up. "Don't blame her for it."

"Sir, in all countries there are places that are not safe. This is a sad truth. But we cannot just go accusing people. Please keep your wife safely with you at all times for the remainder of your stay." He seemed to be dismissing them.

"We're not just accusing someone. We know who this man is, we gave you his name, she knows where to find him. What's the problem here?"

"Sir, we have no proof of who harmed your wife. For all we know, you struck her yourself and are attempting to blame it on someone else."

Tom jumped to his feet, cheeks flushed, eyebrows drawn into a scowl.

"Please, Tom. Don't." She soothed him back into his seat and glared at the policeman. "Why are you dragging your feet? Let me guess—your supervisor is on Bikram's payroll?"

He shifted in his seat.

"Has Raveena been here before? Have you seen that little girl? When you took her from the brothel and forced Sanjana to buy her back with a bribe?"

"Madam, please. I have never done such a thing."

"Please, I just want to help her."

"My hands are tied here. Believe me."

"Why do you even wear that uniform?" she demanded.

"Madam, some days I ask myself that very question. I had such high hopes, such grand dreams. I grew up on the streets myself. I thought I was going to change so many things. That was a long time ago."

"Then help me," she pleaded. "I don't care about filing a report. I just want to get Raveena out of there."

"Why do you even care? This is just one small child. This is not something important."

"Just one small child? The world is full of small children no one cares about. If we all look the other way, nothing ever changes. The question is, why don't you care?"

"Madam, please let this idea go. This is not your problem. You would be well advised to leave India's problems to India."

"I won't let it go. I want to help her. Surely as a policeman you can step in and do something. Answer my question. Why won't you help?"

"Look around you here, madam. Look at our offices. We have so little funding. Look at my desk, my chair. I have repaired the leg on my chair three times. There is no money for buying anything. We are paid in like fashion. It is better than no pay, and I am most grateful I can feed my family, but it is barely enough to get by. I do not take bribes. I never have. But I can understand why some men are tempted to take. Someone like Bikram will double a policeman's salary each month if we look the other way."

"But at what expense?" Leslie said. "Women and children kept against their wills. They're beaten, hungry, raped. And you look the other way?"

"Please." The officer wilted. Shoulders slumped, he dropped his head. "You think I do not know these things? I wish I could help. If I do anything that jeopardizes the status quo, I will be fired. I will have no job. I have to take care of my family. And if Bikram finds out, he may send his men after me. After my family. My hands are tied. If you know what is best, you will not go back. The little girl will be okay."

"Do you have a daughter?" she asked.

"Yes, madam. I have a daughter. And I must protect her."

"Can you imagine how you would feel if Bikram had your daughter?"

"I do not wish to imagine this."

"Now you know how I feel. I don't want to imagine what he's going to do to Raveena."

"She is not your daughter, madam. Leave India to India."

His words stung more than she ever would have expected.

"You told me the police wouldn't help," Tom said to her, glaring pointedly at the officer. "I can't believe you let these men get away with such atrocities. I guess the report we started will go in the trashcan as soon as we leave?"

"Madam, have you been to the Taj Mahal?" Officer Verma removed his glasses and wiped them on his shirt.

She nodded, wondering what prompted the question.

"Is it not the most beautiful structure you have ever seen?"

"Yes, it is."

"Then you have seen the very best of India. The most beautiful monument, an ancient wonder, a tribute to a love so deep, and grief so terrible. The workmanship is staggering. And we take care of it and treasure it today. This is the very best of India—love, loyalty, devotion, hard work. And there in front of the Taj is the reflecting pool, catching the image of this wonderful creation, shimmering there before you, as though she is admiring herself in a mirror."

She nodded. She had been transfixed when she and Tom stood at the end of the reflecting pool. The structure itself was awe-inspiring, its double image below added to the magic of the moment.

Officer Verma replaced his glasses.

"But behind the Taj, in her shadow, is the Yamuna River, polluted and filthy. Raw sewage, pesticides, refuse, and dead animals all enter the river where it flows through Delhi and Agra, making it one of the most polluted rivers in the entire world. This is the worst of India. No one goes around to the back, in the shadows, where it is ugly and dirty. The light strikes the face of the Taj and sends up her lovely image for all to enjoy. Tourists come from all over the world to enjoy the sight of her. But she is to be enjoyed from the front, in the light. Madam, do not enter the shadow of the Taj. Stay where tourists are intended, by the reflecting pool, enjoying all the good things India has to offer."

"I appreciate your advice, but I can't leave Raveena in the shadows either."

The light bulb above them lit, and the fan whirred to life, scattering piles of papers as it turned.

"Ah, the electricity is back! I will get your report filed as soon as possible."

"Let's go," Tom said. "No one is going to do anything for us here. Thank you for your time." He shook Officer Verma's hand before guiding her out of the office. He stalked silently through the police station back to their waiting taxi.

When the doors closed, Prajit turned and asked, "Back to hotel, sir?"

Tom didn't answer. She didn't know what to say to make him feel better, likewise frustrated and at loose ends. Her lip still felt puffy, but the stinging in her cheek had subsided. What bothered her most now was the empty, almost aching pit in the center of her stomach, which had nothing to do with hunger or illness.

She hadn't expected the police to do anything for them, given the stories Sanjana and Tarla told her. And yet, she had hoped and was disappointed that help had been so completely denied. This was a dead end.

Prajit still awaited instructions.

"Okay, I guess take us back to the hotel," Tom said. They drove in silence initially, then Tom spoke. "Well, you were absolutely right. The police did nothing. This was a total waste of time."

"I would have much preferred to be wrong," she answered. She stared out the window, but nothing passing by registered. Her emotions were too confused.

'*She is not your daughter.*' The words ran through her mind again and again. She remembered Tom asking what she would do if she could gain Raveena's freedom. Her main concern was getting the girl out of the brothel and seeing she was safe and fed.

She wondered what would happen to a little girl who had lived all her life in a brothel. What future awaited her? Who would care for her? There must be an orphanage somewhere. Was it as poorly funded as the police station? Would she be able to hand Raveena over to strangers? What if they didn't take good care of her? Could she fly home and never see the girl again?

"Can you take us to the American embassy?" Tom asked.

"Sir?" Prajit asked.

"American embassy."

"American embassy? We go now?"

"Yes, please. We go now. Okay?"

"Yes, sir! Okay!" Prajit wove through traffic, changing lanes for their new destination.

"The embassy?" She was drawn out of her thoughts. "Why do we want to go there?"

"Somebody is going to take notice of how you were treated," Tom said.

CHAPTER 15

*L*eslie discovered that Embassy Row was not, in fact, a row at all but rather a rounded block of convoluted streets threading through a conglomerate of foreign embassies. The broad streets were sheltered by small trees and flanked by clipped, grassy sections. The American Embassy sprawled over many blocks.

Prajit found the entrance they wanted within the huge complex. Armed marines stood before the entrance to the single-story, white building. One of them waved to Prajit as he guided the taxi near the entrance. Prajit rolled down his window.

"No taxis allowed inside. You need to park over there." The guard directed the driver across the street, where numerous taxis and private vehicles waited. Prajit nodded and proceeded to the parking area, indicating as always that he would wait for them.

A good-sized crowd of individuals queued about the front gates as they approached on foot. A large sign above the doors read *EMBASSY OF THE UNITED STATES OF AMERICA*. They stared at the fence, the gates, the armed men, and the crowd of people, unsure how to proceed.

"What do you think?" Tom finally asked, after watching the busy movement in and out of the building. A truck blew past on the street behind them, gaudily painted red with a blue-and-green peacock on the side, decorative chains hanging from the front clanging noisily.

"Maybe we should just ask someone what to do," she suggested.

"Excuse me, madam." A heavily accented voice interrupted them. A middle-aged Indian man approached them slowly and carefully, holding his hands forward in front of him, palms down. "You are Americans, sir?"

"Yes," Tom answered.

"Very good," the man replied, reaching into a pocket and extracting his passport and a pen. "You will please sign my passport?"

"Sign your passport?"

"Yes, sir. Sign here." He opened the passport to a blank page intended for a visa and held it out. When Tom did not accept the document, the man tried again with her. "Please? Madam?"

"We don't understand. Why do you want us to sign it?"

"You are American. You sponsor me. You sign that I am good citizen," the man replied, smiling. "I very good man. Work hard. I go to America, work hard. Need visa. Two times apply for visa, but embassy say no. You sign."

"But our signatures won't help you get a visa for America."

"Yes, yes!" the man insisted. "You sign. American sign for me. Good, hard worker. Madam, please." He thrust the pen at her.

"It won't help," she repeated. "No one in the embassy knows us. Our signatures won't mean anything to them. We don't even know where we're supposed to go to get help ourselves."

"Madam, yes." The man turned to the embassy and pointed. "American citizens, that entrance. Indian citizens, there. My gate." He smiled widely. "You see? I good man. Help you."

Tom took a piece of paper from his pocket, ripped a corner off of it, and accepted the man's pen. He scribbled his signature on the scrap of paper.

"There you go," he said as he handed it back to the gentleman. "You can put that in your passport, okay? Thank you for helping us."

"Yes, sir! Thank you very much, sir!" The man grabbed Tom's hand between both of his own and bowed low over his clasped hands again and again.

She squirmed, knowing the signature would accomplish nothing. She wished she could have helped him understand. And encouraged him to save his money rather than squander it on visa applications that would be denied.

They proceeded to the American citizen entrance. The other gate was thickly queued with people—now including their new friend with his newly acquired but useless signature. But this entrance was empty. The marine guarding the entrance asked for ID, inspected their passports, and waved them through.

The grounds of the embassy were manicured and lovely. Small sections of grass grew around the sidewalks. Trees grew throughout the compound, surrounded by mulched gardens nurturing purple and white petunias, which nodded gently at the visitors.

Passing beneath a large American flag, they continued into the main building. The lobby was strikingly white: white tiled floors, white ceiling, and white partitioned sections with glass teller windows. The brown of the paneled wood walls and the black shelves at the teller windows were all that disrupted the bland, antiseptic room.

Since they had no appointment, they took a number and sat down. Another armed marine stood behind a partition, overlooking the lobby.

The haggard woman who called their number offered a perfunctory smile before requesting passports. She took them, verified they were current and held appropriate visas, then asked, "How can I help you?"

"My wife was struck today by a man she encountered in the street," Tom began.

She squirmed when the woman's eyes shifted to the marks on her face.

"I see. I'm sorry you were a victim of violent crime. That is extremely frightening and traumatic." The woman sounded like she was reading from a script. "Have you filed a police report?" the woman asked.

"Yes, we went to the police station. We attempted to file a police report."

"Do you have a copy of the report?" she asked.

"No, and frankly I don't trust that it was filed, either."

"Would you like to see a consular agent to discuss your concerns?" Still that flat voice.

"Yes!" Tom latched eagerly onto the first sign of progress he'd encountered in his quest for justice. "Thank you."

"Please proceed to the door to your left, at the far end of the lobby," the woman directed. "You will be buzzed in."

The door buzzed and clicked open. Tom pushed it gently and ushered Leslie through. A young man wearing khaki slacks and a navy blue polo strode forward to meet them. The knit shirt stretched taut against his muscular chest and thick biceps. He moved quickly, fluidly, with a light gait. She thought he looked like the type that would have played football in high school, maybe even in college. Dark hair cropped close to his head, his green eyes blazed as he offered his hand to each of them in turn.

"Hi," he said, greeting them. "My name is Ben Gunner, but please just call me Gunner. I understand you've had a little incident today. Would you step into my office?"

Her anxiety diminished, his calm assurance soothing.

The office was just large enough to hold a desk and two chairs. "Please, won't you sit? Can I get you anything to drink? Some water? Sodas?"

"I'd love a diet soda," Tom said.

"I'll grab one for each of you." Gunner sounded as though he'd been waiting all day for the opportunity to serve soda. He hurried out the office door and returned quickly, passing the cold cans to them before proceeding to his own chair behind the desk.

"Okay." He settled in, leaning forward and resting his elbows on the desk. He folded his hands, looking eager to assist. "Why don't you tell me what happened today?"

Throughout the retelling, Gunner scratched notes on a yellow legal pad, nodded, and mmm-hmmm'ed encouragingly. She found herself offering him quite a bit of information regarding the circumstances that led her to GB Road that morning. He smiled when she described Raveena, was impressed that she had wanted to feed her, and gasped concern when she described Shardul smacking her across the face. She even admitted he backed her against the wall and shook her violently, bruising her arms in the process.

"I think he might have..." She glanced sideways at Tom. "...tried to touch me if Tarla hadn't pulled me away." She felt her husband bristle beside her and regretted the admission. She felt dirty even without sharing the graphic details. And now guilty for withholding the truth.

Gunner dropped his eyes and shook his head. "I cannot even imagine how frightening that was. Thank goodness you had people there to help you. Sometimes these stories don't end so well. I know it doesn't feel like it right now, but believe me, you really were quite fortunate."

"So what can we do?" Tom asked.

"Let's talk about that. Do I understand correctly that you went to a police station? And filled out an FIR?"

"What's an FIR?" Tom asked. "We don't know what we filled out. Or tried to fill out."

"FIR—First Information Report. If you went to the police and reported a crime, that would be what you filed."

"Okay, well, we tried to report it. I don't know if it was filed or if it went into the garbage. Can you do anything from here?"

"You did the right thing," Gunner said. "Going to the police was exactly what you needed to do. They have jurisdiction for crimes, with very few exceptions. And if you reported it and filled out the paperwork, I'm sure it will be filed."

"So now what? Can you check on the report? Or contact the police to make sure the man is arrested? Or—"

"I understand you are upset about what happened to your wife, but we really are limited in a situation like this one. This falls clearly under the jurisdiction of the Indian police. And I'll be honest with you—if the embassy gets involved, we will only slow down the process. If you need a doctor or a lawyer, we can definitely provide you with lists of good, reputable resources for that."

"But the police aren't doing anything," Tom insisted. "We know who the guy is and where to find him. Why won't they go get him?"

"What would you want to see happen? Are you prepared to go to trial to testify against him for assaulting you? Sometimes bad things happen, and sometimes we don't see justice."

"So we can't do anything?"

"You did exactly what you could and should do—file that FIR," Gunner reassured him again. "Good job there. I would advise you to avoid traveling alone, Ms. Matthews. That is general advice we give to all women. Try to go out when your husband can accompany you, if at all possible."

She nodded. She already knew it was dangerous. "What about the women in the brothel? No one will do anything for them."

"I admire you for caring, I really do." Gunner leaned back in his chair. "I read a lot of articles in the newspapers that break my heart, too. Horrible. Unfortunately, their situation is truly an Indian matter. We have no business interfering. Especially when the prostitutes are free to leave and choose to remain. If they ever want to leave, want to try starting over, I think there are NGOs here that offer women's shelters and help groups."

After hearing how so many of the girls wound up in the brothel, she bristled at the term prostitute. They were stolen and exploited.

"What about Raveena, the little girl?" she pressed. "Surely the police have to help her. She's going to be sold for underage sex."

"I will tell you that I know for a fact that underage sex is illegal. No question. But no law enforcement agency can move on the possibility of a future crime. She is not being prostituted yet, so the police cannot do anything." He cut her off before she could object. "I know, it breaks your heart. And I am not trying to defend the men holding the girl and taking her into the streets to beg. It does happen, sadly. I agree, she should be in a loving home with parents caring for her."

"Yes. Exactly. She needs to be cared for."

"But if this man claims to be her guardian, there's not much anyone can do, unfortunately. Not everyone is issued a birth certificate here, as we do in America. So disproving his claim of guardianship would be nearly impossible. And I'm sorry to say, funds to support homeless individuals, orphans, and impoverished families are not very robust. With so little to support those in need, they will not be anxious to press this issue." He must have seen disappointment in her face. "I understand. I really do. We just can't save them all."

"What about adoption? Can people adopt Indian children?"

Tom's head turned sharply in her direction, but he said nothing.

"Of course. And there is an orphanage with available children here in New Delhi, if you wish to do so."

"I was just asking in general. What's the process to adopt? Do you know?"

"I know a little bit. Maybe not every intricate detail of the process. But I do know you would need to adopt through CARA—that stands for Central Adoption Resource Authority. There is an office here in New Delhi, if you want to go by. Actually, I think I can find a list of what you need to do. One moment." He turned his attention to the computer screen on his desk, clicking links, searching for the desired information. "Here we go. Yes, you would need an NOC form; a signed letter from the guardian or from CARA, confirming orphan status; passport and visa, of course, prior to leaving the country. Some states do require inspection of the potential adoptive parents' home, background checks. There are age and marriage requirements, but you two fall within those parameters. I will warn you, this can be a lengthy process. So if you are considering adopting, be sure you have enough time left on your visa to begin pursuing that. Are you here for a while yet?"

"We leave next week," Tom said, rather forcefully.

"Oh, okay. I see. Well, that would not be nearly enough time."

"Can we extend our visas and stay longer?" she asked.

"Unfortunately, no." Gunner leaned back, thinking, fingers laced behind his head. "There is another way, though. You can begin the process with CARA now, and you can return to India to pick up the child once all the appropriate steps have been completed." He sat up and smiled, nodding at her, hands out as though offering the solution to her.

"We're not thinking about adopting a child," Tom said.

"Is there anything else I can help you with today then?"

"No, I guess not," Tom answered.

Gunner stood, extending his hand. "Thank you for coming by. Nice to meet you." He shook both their hands before guiding them back to the lobby.

Tom said nothing as they exited the embassy, crossed the street, and climbed back into their taxi, leaving the armed marines and sovereign American soil behind them. Tom told Prajit they wanted to go back to the hotel.

"Why were you asking about adoption back there?"

She stared out the window silently.

She thought she just wanted to rescue Raveena from her situation, help her to a better place. But the policeman's words still stung almost as badly as Shardul's slap. *'She is not your daughter.'* She knew that, and yet she could not explain her protective, almost territorial need to protect Raveena. Leslie wanted so badly to march back into the police station and respond, "Yes, she is mine! Now go get her out of that horrible brothel and away from those disgusting men!"

Her chest ached. She wanted to tell Prajit to turn the taxi around and go back to GB Road. What exactly would happen if she pulled up in front of the building, marched Raveena out, and drove away with her?

She shook her head. Raveena might not even be there. And she had no documentation for her. If Shardul or Bikram came looking for the girl, Leslie would have nothing legal on her side. Knowing something to be right and proving it legally were two completely different matters. That was communicated clearly today.

Raveena was worth too much to Bikram. The police could not intervene. Gunner had told her that disproving guardianship would be nearly impossible. Every idea she had was shot down.

No, you cannot have her. No, she is not yours. Mind your own business. We cannot save them all.

She dropped her head to hide the tears welling in her eyes. She could not stop thinking about Raveena.

"Hey," Tom prodded her. "What are you thinking about? Are you okay?"

"Would you ever consider adopting?" she asked him quietly.

He looked at her as though she had asked if he would consider setting himself on fire. "Are you talking about Raveena? Is that what this is about?" His voice was harsh.

Prajit glanced worriedly behind them. He had seen her get herself into enough trouble today. Tom noticed the look and lowered his voice. "Let's talk about this at the hotel. Okay?"

She nodded again. *How am I going to convince him?* Could she make him understand how important this was to her? She sat up straighter and wiped the tears from her eyes. She would not leave Raveena behind. She might not be able to save them all, but she would save this one little girl.

CHAPTER 16

*L*eslie inhaled the refreshing odor of disinfectant in their hotel room. The day she'd had gave her a new appreciation for it. Crisp towels hung in the bathroom. The surfaces gleamed. The bed had been made, the silky sheets drawn tight, the thick comforter neatly draped over the edges of the bed, and the feather pillows fluffed and arranged. *Stay where you are meant to be. Do not venture into the shadows.*

She thought of Raveena, stuck in that filth-encrusted, dismal brothel, and the room lost its luster. She sank into the cushioned chair and slumped forward onto the table.

Tom stared out the window, propping his chin in one hand as he often did when mulling over a problem or coping with writer's block while working on a grant.

She watched him pacing aimlessly out of the corner of her eye. Finally, she stared up at him. He didn't seem to notice. Or he intentionally avoided her gaze. He appeared to be about to say something, then he dropped his head again, forehead pressed into his hand, squeezing his temples between his fingers and thumb.

When he broke the silence, his words were slow and deliberate, as though he worked hard to maintain his calm demeanor. "Are you really thinking about adopting that girl? Have you actually given this any serious thought?"

"I haven't been able to stop thinking about her," she replied.

"What exactly are you planning?" He looked her in the eye for the first time since they returned to the room. "Tell me that, please, because I'm having trouble understanding. Because it doesn't make the slightest bit of sense."

"I'm not sure," she admitted. "I don't know how to get her out of there. I'm still thinking."

"No, no, no. I'm not discussing your plan to liberate her, which, by the way, kicked off with a great start this morning." He gestured to her face.

She closed her eyes. This was going worse than anticipated. She thought he would at least give her the courtesy of listening.

"I mean, then what? We have this little girl we know nothing about, and…we're going to fly her home with us? Take her to our house? Have her sleep…where?" He shook his head and shrugged.

She bristled. "Generally, when you adopt a child, you take them to your house to live with you. Pretty much the only method of adoption I've heard of."

"Don't be a smartass with me. I'm just trying to understand what the hell is going on here."

"No, you're trying to make me sound like an idiot."

"By asking you to explain yourself?"

"By talking down to me like I don't have a brain."

"Well, frankly, I am starting to wonder." *Ouch.* "Two days ago all you wanted was to go home, get out of here. Today you're trying to devise a way to drag a child home. All of a sudden, out of the blue, you're talking about adopting."

"I know it's sudden. I know. And I can't explain why I feel so strongly about it. But I do. And I'm wondering why you don't show a little more concern. And compassion. You saw that little girl too. You saw her eat like she's been hungry her entire life. If we can fix this, we should."

"What about your job?"

"What about it?"

"How are you going to keep working if we have a kid?"

She laughed. She couldn't help it. "Millions of women do manage that trick somehow. I think I can cope. We live so near the elementary school, she'll attend it for a year, I think, depending on what level she can start at. She'll be right there with me. Several of the teachers have kids at the school."

"Oh, my God." Again, slow and deliberate. "You have actually thought about that?"

"Weren't you just accusing me of not thinking it through? Now you're concerned because I have?"

"This girl is the only thing you are thinking about. What about me?"

"What about you?"

"Have you thought about the extra stress this adds? Isn't it bad enough I'm trying to finish a postdoc and move into a faculty position? Which isn't guaranteed, I might remind you."

"How does bringing her home add to your stress?"

"The responsibility of a child is enormous. I still don't have a permanent position. The whole reason we came here was to help advance my career prospects. Not to add a child to the family. I can't deal with this right now."

"I said I'll handle it. I'll take care of her. Nothing has to change for you."

"Yes, it does. Taking care of another person is huge. I don't know what's going to happen when Dr. Shankar's grant money runs out. He's paying my salary for another year, but there's no guarantee it will be renewed. What happens if I don't get promoted to a faculty position? I'm worried enough about being able to take care of you. Now you want to bring home a child? Who will have a lot of needs, I might point out."

"Something will work out. We'll be fine."

"I don't know that. Look, I'm asking you to support me, okay?"

"Asking me to support—What have I been doing for the past ten years? I've been supporting you all during your graduate studies and now your postdoc."

"I had a stipend. Now I'm on salary."

"Your stipend was nothing. We couldn't live off it. My teaching has always paid the bills."

"When I'm a faculty member, even a junior faculty member, my salary will double. And within a few years I could make twice what you do."

"And you think that makes you twice as important? So you can forget about the years I supported you? If we go by that philosophy, I should get to make all the decisions right now, since I make twice what you do."

"Look." He strode to the table, sat across from her, and jabbed a finger against the wooden surface to emphasize each word. "This is not what we agreed to."

"Agreed to when?"

"We talked about this before we ever got married. We decided we didn't want children. That we couldn't go through that." He sat down in the chair and folded his arms across his chest.

"Yes, we did. And now I've changed my mind. And this isn't an infant we're talking about. She's twelve years old."

"But it changes everything. What if she doesn't adjust well? She's been living in an Indian slum all her life. You think you can just snatch her up and plop her down in another country? That would be taking her from everything she's ever known. It would be a complete and overwhelming culture shock."

"She speaks English. And I'll work with her. I want to work with her, help her adjust. You think she should stay in the slum forever just because that's where she is now? I want to give her a chance for a better life."

"At our expense. We're not exactly wealthy and you know it."

"We get by. It's one child. What are you afraid you'll have to do without? You know we can manage."

"No, I don't."

"Oh, please. It's only your stubbornness that keeps us like this. We could be much better off."

"Don't start this."

"No, you brought up our lack of wealth. Let's explore that topic. You're exactly right—we've spent a lot of years barely scraping by because you refused to accept your trust fund."

"It's not that simple. Don't oversimplify—"

"It is that simple. Your father established a trust fund for you. You refuse to accept it."

"Nothing is that easy with them, especially with him. You have no idea. None."

"How many times have your parents tried to connect? I know your dad has tried to apologize—"

"You don't know anything about it. Okay? You have no idea what he's like. He's a total asshole. We accept that money from him, he regains control over me. That's what he wants. I've told you this before."

"He seemed very nice, the few times I've actually been around him."

"Of course he did. He wants people to think he's a great guy. I grew up with the narcissistic, abusive, alcoholic, wife-beating, sorry excuse for a human being. I know what he's really like—the person who comes out when no one is looking. I don't want him in my life, I don't want him anywhere near you, and I don't want his money."

"I have never questioned that. Not once. All those times they offered to help. They offered to put a huge down payment on a house for our wedding gift. You refused, and we lived in an apartment until we saved enough ourselves. He offered to pay for your graduate studies. You refused, and we've scraped by on my teaching salary so you could keep going, so you could do what you love. They tried to send us on a cruise for our ten-year anniversary. You refused. I've always deferred to you. Always." Always the dutiful wife, as she was raised to be. She didn't marry the man her mom wanted, but that was a different problem.

"Everything from him comes with strings attached. I have explained this to you time and again. Can you please trust me on this? I've had to protect you from him."

"Yes, that's what you tell me. He seemed like a sweet man, but—"

"But he's not. He's conniving and manipulative. Stop this, Leslie. Just stop it."

"I'm just saying I've never once complained, even though that money is just sitting there."

"You're complaining right now," Tom growled. "I'm sitting here telling you I don't want this, and you're arguing and arguing."

"I didn't even want to come to India. Remember? This was your idea. I told you before you applied for the travel grant that I didn't want to come."

"I don't understand that. Why would anyone turn down a chance to travel?"

"I wanted to keep teaching."

"You've only missed a couple months. We'll be back soon."

"But my class started the year without me. They'll have to adjust from the substitute when I get back. And I miss being there. My job is important to me. You wouldn't listen to any of my concerns. At all. And I do not recall that we discussed taking a trip to India before we got married. Things change. I mean, what would you have done if I'd gotten pregnant despite all precautions?"

"That would have been an unintentional accident. This is you deciding what you want and trying to make me agree to it."

"Kind of like you've decided you don't want your trust fund and made me agree to it? And the way you decided you wanted to come to India and made me agree to come with you?"

"This has been a great experience."

"Are you kidding me? Do you listen to a thing I say? Ever?" She took a deep breath. Tried to calm down. "I have enjoyed some parts. I know this has been an enriching experience. And I will probably appreciate it even more once we're home. But I've been bored most of this trip. You left me sitting in our room with nothing to pass the time many long days, Tom. You were out studying crops, taking pesticide samples, driving all over creation. I couldn't even leave the guest compound. Women can't go out alone. I sat in the room, listening to the clock ticking. It never once bothered you. And you accuse me of being selfish?"

"You could have gone out. I suggested you walk down to the shopping center. I didn't tell you to stay cooped up in the room."

"And you never believed me when I told you what happened. I was surrounded by a group of guys all pressing up next to me, walling me in, groping me. And I was nearly shoved into a rickshaw. Where do you suppose they were going to take me? I yelled and yelled for help. No one came to help me. What would you have done if I'd just disappeared? I cannot imagine an attempted kidnapping had any decent intentions behind it."

"Oh, here we go with the kidnapping again. You're exaggerating, Leslie. Just admit it."

"You think I'm exaggerating because you didn't see it with your own eyes. You never believed me when I complained about the way I was treated by the all-male staff in Pantnagar either. If you don't witness it, you don't believe me."

"I believe you got hit today."

"You can see the marks on my face. But I don't think you

believe how horrible that brothel is or you would want to help me get Raveena out of there. You only see what's in front of you. Just like you only see your research, not your wife stuck in the room back at the guest compound."

"Kind of like you won't believe what a controlling, abusive shit my dad was to my mom and me because you've never seen it yourself?"

Foul language, forbidden by her parents, still held the power to burn her ears. "How would you like being left behind while I go to work?"

"While you teach elementary school? Come on, you can't compare the two. This research will help me complete my postdoc project, and Dr. Shankar said he's talking to the department chair about moving me into a junior faculty position. This will advance my career. Plus the work itself has great implications. Decreasing pesticide use is important for the environment. Working with Dr. Hameed, I think we can accomplish some really important changes. And I ought to be able to get my own grant funded instead of relying on Dr. Shankar for everything. This is big. This is our future."

"That's your future. Maybe. Why do you consider everything you do so much more important than what I do?"

"What are you talking about?"

"You just belittled my teaching. And this isn't the first time. How many times have I been up late preparing a lesson or grading projects, and you head off to bed, yawning and complaining about your eight o'clock experiment in the morning? My school day starts at eight too. But you chuckle patronizingly at the shoebox book reports or the science project posters and then go to bed to make sure you get a good night's sleep."

"They're shoeboxes. I mean, come on."

"We all start with shoeboxes, Tom. I stay up later than you and get up earlier than you most of the time, but there I am working my tail off while you head for bed. And on those rare occasions when you have to get up earlier than I do, you flip on all the lights and bang around the house, so you can be sure to wake me up. It's like you have to make sure I see you're up first for once. Make a big to-do about your oh-so-important work."

"I work hard." He sat forward across the table. "Are you calling me lazy? Finally decided your mom was right, huh? What was it she called me? A 'rakish, self-centered, scholar'?"

"Well, that was before she found out you're agnostic. Then you became a 'rakish, self-centered, heathen scholar.' After she found out you're the heir to a small fortune but refuse to accept it, she just called you a fool."

"I didn't want—"

"We could be doing some good with that money. If we could just figure out how to get Raveena out of the brothel—"

"Don't change the—"

"Why will no one close down those brothels? Women and children are kept as slaves. Kept by men. Men like you who think they're so superior they can take advantage of women."

"Men like me?"

"Men who abduct them, torture them, starve them, rape them, and hold them against their wills. Men collect money from other disgusting men and stuff their pockets with it. Men who get rich off abusing them, letting other men use them for their perverted purposes. And why not? They're just women and children. No one cares about them." She rose to her feet, knees shaking. "I may not be able to save them all, no matter how badly I want to. But I won't write off Raveena. I won't leave her in the slum."

"Can you not hear how crazy you sound?"

She braced herself against the table, trying to stop the trembling. "I'm wondering if we ever knew each other. Maybe my mom was right. Maybe we are totally wrong for each other."

"This is what I'm talking about. When have you ever

thought your mother was right about anything? You're not acting like yourself."

"Maybe I've changed. Maybe we both have."

"Where is this coming from?"

"What exactly do you do those late nights you're working more and more frequently? Maybe we need to think about what we want out of life. Because I don't feel like I have a husband lately."

"I'm working hard to help us get ahead. I can't believe you don't appreciate that."

"The secretary has called the house several times looking for you. Said you told her you were going home early. But you don't come home early, you come home late."

He stared at her.

"Where were you, Tom?"

He jumped out of his seat and stormed into the bathroom, slamming the door behind him.

She sat back down, breathing heavily, stunned she'd actually put into words the thoughts she'd been brooding over lately. More stunned he hadn't answered her. He didn't even try to invent an excuse.

The bathroom door flew back open, and he stalked out in his swimsuit, a towel thrown over his shoulder.

"I'm going swimming," he declared. Walking out the door, he paused to yell over his shoulder, "Don't leave the hotel."

She stared at the door, his command ringing in her ears.

So much for convincing him to adopt. She couldn't even convince him to help Raveena. And his silence seemed to all but confirm an affair.

She paced. Her worst fear wasn't even the affair. She feared she'd driven him to it. That stupid purity promise. Her parents left her completely unprepared for any life outside a convent. If she hadn't been so sheltered and protected, maybe that frat party wouldn't have been such a shock.

Maybe that boy wouldn't have been able to manipulate her

so easily. Then she wouldn't have found herself pregnant and alone. She wouldn't have lied to Tom. They wouldn't have married. And she wouldn't be here now, having this gut-wrenching argument.

If he was with another woman, could she ever forgive him? Could she really consider divorce? Images of him with another woman tormented her. If he was having an affair, if the sex meant more to him than anything else she'd done for him, then what other option did she have? But if the marriage was doomed, did she have any business trying to adopt a child?

The thoughts tumbled through her until she shook her head to clear it.

The walls pressed in on her. *I have to get out of here. I have to get out of here before I suffocate.*

CHAPTER 17

The elevator doors pinged to announce her arrival at the lobby, but she stood restless, unsure what to do. She couldn't face Tom right now. But she didn't want to leave the hotel alone again.

A familiar voice called out to her. "When will you come see me? Let me put some bracelets on those poor lonely wrists." The woman in the jewelry shop smiled and beckoned to her. The look on Leslie's face must have told the woman something was wrong. "Oh, my goodness. You definitely need to come see me today. When a woman looks as unhappy as you do, shopping for jewelry is the only cure. Come, madam."

Leslie stepped into the shop with the ever-cheerful woman, who today wore a deep red sari. When she smiled, her eyes crinkled at the corners. The woman seemed to see straight into a person's heart. Her dark hair hung to her shoulders, curling under her jaw, and she wore bright red lipstick and dark eyeliner, somewhat like Raveena at the zoo.

The woman led her past several glass cases to a counter with stools. "Here, madam, sit, please. Let me get some tea."

"Oh, no, thank you. Not now. My stomach is upset today."

"Then you need soda water," the woman crooned, patting

her back. "I will get it. You stay right there." She bustled out of her shop.

The gentle attention was surprisingly soothing. That and the distance from Tom. For nearly six months she'd been isolated from home and friends, cooped up, with Tom as her sole companion.

"Here you go," the woman said, returning. "I had the barman prepare soda with lime."

Leslie's stomach gurgled as she contemplated the fizzy drink. She sipped a bit of it through the straw. It trickled into her timid stomach, cool and soothing. "Thank you. That really helps."

"Rhea knows what makes a woman feel better. Soda for the stomach, jewelry for the soul. Now tell me, what is your name?"

"Leslie."

"And why are you so down today, Leslie?"

Leslie shook her head but said nothing.

"Come now. That is what we women do. We listen to each other. No one understands the way another woman understands. Here. Give me your arm!"

When Leslie hesitantly held her arm out, Rhea grabbed hold with one hand and wrapped her thumb and finger around her wrist.

"What are you doing?"

"Measuring! Very tiny wrist," Rhea replied before turning to her wall of bracelets behind the counter. Row after row of thin, glass bracelets glittered. "No woman should be without some decoration. Let me see." She threw another look at Leslie's skirt and blouse combination before selecting a set of glass bangles. "Give me again."

There was no point to arguing, so Leslie held out her arm. Rhea clasped her hand firmly and worked the collection of bangles over her hand and onto her wrist. They fit so snugly. "I think these are too small," Leslie told Rhea, shaking her arm to demonstrate how little the bangles moved. They did not clatter about noisily.

"No, madam, just right," Rhea told her, holding her own arm out, proudly displaying her deep red bangles painted with gold glitter. "The tighter the bangles, the happier the marriage. You see, mine do not move at all. All married women wear bangles in India."

Considering the fight she and Tom just had, Leslie wondered if she should ask for the biggest, loosest bangles in the shop.

"This trip was supposed to be like a honeymoon."

"Perfect! When an Indian woman weds, her close friend or sister helps her put on the tightest bangles. They use oil to slide them over her hand. The honeymoon lasts until the last bangle breaks."

"It hasn't exactly turned out the way we expected. But these are beautiful. I don't want them to break."

"It is inevitable. They will break. But don't break them on purpose. Only a widow breaks her bangles on purpose, when her husband dies. Broken bangles can be a bad omen or a sign of danger."

"I'll remember that," Leslie said, admiring the glass decorations.

Rhea smiled and patted her hand. "Now, you are a proper Indian woman."

"Thank you. I should have come in a long time ago. I just don't wear much jewelry."

"I can fix that! We have so many beautiful pieces here." The woman brushed her hair back from her face. "Your ears are pierced. We have many earrings."

Before Leslie knew what was happening, Rhea hurried away, flitting from case to case, pausing, mumbling, and bringing her choices back to the counter.

"This one would look so pretty with these clothes. And this

one looks so nice against your hair." She held the earrings up beside Leslie's ears as she spoke.

"My husband and I had a big fight," Leslie confided, staring down at the counter.

"Is that why you are so downhearted?" Rhea set down the earrings and the mirror. "That is not so bad. Husbands and wives argue. It is to be expected."

"We've never had a fight like this."

"Goodness, my husband and I squabble all the time. He will get over it. That is what husbands and wives do. They argue and then they make up. What started it?"

"I was asking him...Well, we don't have children..." She paused. "Do you remember the little girl who was with us last night?"

"Yes, of course. A beautiful girl."

"I saw her at the zoo, begging. She said she was hungry. So I brought her here for dinner."

"So kind of you, madam."

"I found out she has no parents and is being held at a brothel. I want to get her out of there. I don't know how." Leslie told Rhea a short version of her morning's adventures, tired of telling and retelling the entire story.

"If you went to GB Road unaccompanied, you are either truly brave or truly unprepared for life in India," Rhea commented.

"I'm not brave. I had no idea what would happen. Those poor women at the brothel...I ran off and left them there. I'm a coward." Leslie's nausea had passed, thanks to the soda, but her stomach clenched again at the thought of the women left behind to suffer Shardul's wrath. And what would happen to Raveena? Why could she never help?

All she ever did was run away and hide.

"'A coward is incapable of exhibiting love; it is the preroga-tive of the brave.' Mahatma Gandhi's words and so true. Love drove you to the brothel, and only a brave heart can love."

"That's beautiful, but I'm not convinced it applies to me." Leslie remembered watching a little girl being carried away, eyes begging for help, while fear rooted her to the spot. When had she ever been brave?

"I am glad to hear it was not your husband who struck you. When I saw the bruises and you were so shy to talk about the fight, I was afraid your husband had done this to you."

"Oh, I didn't think about that. No, my husband would never lay a hand on me. He's adamant about that. His dad abused his mom...he's never forgiven him. Now I'm glad I told you what happened. He and I were arguing because...I was thinking about adopting Raveena. We thought we didn't want children, and he's not happy I changed my mind. He said I'm being selfish."

"Opening your home to a child who has no home is not selfish, madam," Rhea assured her. "You wish to take her to America?"

"Do you think that would be too hard on Raveena? Tom said I would be taking her from the only home she's ever known, dropping her down in a foreign land."

"The only home she has ever known is not really a home, is it?" Rhea's eyes flashed. "She has been abused and mistreated. A fresh start is just what she needs."

"You don't think such a huge change would be too hard on her?"

"Of course not. Children are very resilient. Look what she has endured up to now."

"That's what I was thinking." Finally, someone agreed with her. "She can speak English. She seems bright. But maybe she should remain in India. I could try to help her get to the orphanage."

"Indian children are adopted to other countries, madam. This happens. The important thing is that they are loved and cared for. Indian orphanages are full. If an Indian family wishes to adopt a child, there are plenty to choose from. Why leave another child waiting for a family if you are ready to give her one? And what would stop someone like the men who have her right now from taking her from the orphanage if you leave her?"

"I know. I don't want to leave her. I want to know she is being loved and cared for. But I keep hearing that it's impossible. I can't take her without proper documentation, of course, and we're leaving in just about a week. I don't know why I'm wasting so much time thinking about it. I can't get her away from the brothel, and even if I could, I don't have enough time left to complete the adoption process. And my husband doesn't want to do it." She almost admitted she feared an affair, but couldn't bring herself to share the raw news. It hurt too much.

"When love is strong, anything is possible, madam. You just need to find the way." Rhea patted her hand. "I think I may be able to help you. This is an issue close to my husband's heart. His sister was taken from their village when she was just a girl, and the family never heard from her again. We work with a group here in New Delhi that offers assistance to women in dire situations. Let me write the name down." The woman hurried away to find paper and pen.

Leslie sat in stunned quiet. Rhea's husband's sister was taken from their village? What were the odds? Here she was, halfway around the world, and she stumbled onto someone whose husband suffered the same horror she witnessed? God works in mysterious ways.

"Here is the address, madam," Rhea said, returning with a slip of paper that she handed to Leslie. "It is just a small local group, doing the best they can with limited means. It is called POW—Protect Our Women. My husband helps and donates when he can."

"You said his sister was taken? Did he see her snatched?"

"No, it was not like that, but he has never recovered. He hopes to prevent others from disappearing. And he still clings to the hope of one day finding her."

Leslie understood that hope only too well. She closed her eyes, images of pleading eyes and kicking feet playing across her mind. The memory she shared with no one. The secret she carried with her every day of her life. "A young girl was kidnapped from my neighborhood when I was little."

"And you knew her?"

She nodded, squirming. Her heart thudded as she thought of her mother's words on the subject: "That which the Good Lord giveth, He also taketh away." Normally instilled to warn of the perils of pride and vanity, her mother fell upon it as an explanation for the kidnapping of a child.

"Was the case resolved?"

"No."

"Then your husband must understand why you feel so strongly about this."

"He suspects, I'm sure. But he doesn't understand. No one understands what it was like. I don't like to talk about it. Not even with Tom."

"But why not?"

"The police, the reporters, everyone wanted me to tell them about it. It was in the papers. People recognized me everywhere as the girl who watched the abduction and felt sorry for me. I just wanted to forget, to put it all behind me and be normal again. My parents became very protective of me. They said we must pray for the girl, that we must trust God, that everything happens for a reason. But where was God when that little girl was stolen?" She choked on the words, fighting the tears welling in her eyes.

At the age of twelve, her mother shamed her for such thoughts. "We must not question the Good Lord's plan." Even then, even as a child, Leslie couldn't accept her mother's rationale. She didn't believe kidnapping an innocent girl was part of a higher plan. Eventually, she came to fear the God her mother described, one who would allow a little girl to suffer such a terrible fate.

When she began dating Tom, his agnostic beliefs rubbed off on her. She still believed in a higher power, but refused her mother's organized religion, her holier-than-thou attitude, and her belief that they were all puppets in a grand scheme.

Rhea watched her closely. "The pain you carry affects you still today, as my husband's affects him. Let your husband help."

"I can't understand why my mom could just accept it and tell me to trust God in all things."

"We all cope with life in our own ways. As Gandhi said, 'But for my faith in God, I would have been a raving maniac.' Your mother needed to believe God was with the missing girl always, no matter what happened to her. My husband needs to believe that someday he will reunite with his sister."

"Do you believe that?"

"It does not matter if I believe it. The idea helps him continue in his life and drives him to help others. And I understand because I know how much he hurts." Rhea patted her hand. "Stop burying the pain from the past. Share the burden with your husband and lighten your own load."

Good advice, but only if her husband was willing to share. Instead, Leslie suspected he was sharing with another woman.

She thanked her hostess but rose from her chair too quickly and grabbed the counter to steady herself, still woozy from her upset stomach. Clutching the paper with the address for POW, she returned to her room and fell wearily onto the bed, only then remembering she had not paid Rhea for the bangles.

CHAPTER 18

*L*ying on the bed, curled into a ball, Leslie remembered the story of Sunita weeping into Sanjana's lap, begging her, "Please, let me keep my baby." Somehow that baby became her hope, the symbol of normalcy in the midst of her chaos. And the three women schemed to keep the pregnancy a secret.

Leslie imagined life in the brothel for a pregnant woman: no healthcare, never enough to eat, no clean water, filthy living conditions. What did she do for maternity clothes?

And then a new thought occurred to her: Did Sunita work during the pregnancy? She shuddered, knowing the answer was "yes" and picturing fetishists seeking her out. She probably also entertained men who were turned on by full, lactating breasts postpartum.

Sleeping with a man while carrying another man's baby… The thought repulsed Leslie. But she knew it was unfair to judge. She wasn't so unlike Sunita, with one exception: Sunita wanted Raveena passionately. Leslie, on the other hand, knelt beside her dorm bed, sobbing puddles onto her comforter, pleading, *Please God, take it back, I don't want it*, over and over like a deranged litany. The pregnancy continued. She decided

God wasn't listening. Or didn't care about her. Or, worst possibility of all, that he was punishing her.

When she realized she'd missed a period, she purchased a pregnancy test from a local convenience store, red-faced with shame. The very next morning, following the package instructions, she used her first urine of the day and sat on the toilet sobbing uncontrollably as the little pink line appeared in the window. She wondered what it was like to stare down hopefully, praying for the little streak of happiness that meant diapers and cribs, bibs and rattles, shared joys and laughter. All she knew was cold nausea and tears, fear and regret. *We reap what we sow.*

She harbored the terrible secret, keeping the shameful knowledge from everyone, carrying it alone. She had no idea what to do with it. Going to her parents was out of the question. She wouldn't even talk to them on the phone, so afraid they would somehow know she was keeping something from them. She was afraid to seek an abortion—scared of the procedure, and even more scared of destroying a life the Good Lord saw fit to create. So she simply ignored it, focusing on her studies, determined to succeed.

Meanwhile, Tom appeared at her library table and kept returning. In retrospect, perhaps she shouldn't have rushed. But his presence had been comforting. He offered solace. He was patient with her. They continued to study. Their coffee dates turned into lunches, then dinner, then movies.

In a matter of weeks, she fell for him completely. She tried to keep her feelings to herself, unsure how he felt about her. Not a day went by that they didn't see each other. "Study buddy," he called her, which always made her smile. She told herself they were just friends, though, nothing more. He gave no indication they were anything else.

As they spent time together, she noticed the looks he drew from other girls, how they always seemed so chipper around him, eager to assist in any way. She also saw the glances in her direction and felt sure they all wondered what in the world he was doing with her. Not that she blamed them. To the contrary, she agreed with them but couldn't work up the nerve to ask him. She was afraid to ask lest he suddenly realize she had a point and start spending his time with one of the many girls in tight jeans and make-up who drooled over him wherever they went.

She couldn't lose him. She struggled through several weeks of morning sickness, hiding the nausea from him as best she could. He was her one comfort during that hideous time. She shared her strict upbringing with him, and though he shared little about his own parents, she felt his relationship with them wasn't good. He seemed to understand. By that time, she no longer believed in her mother's idea of angels, but if she had, she might have believed Tom was heaven-sent.

But she was pregnant, and what guy would want a girl pregnant with another guy's baby? The more she enjoyed his company and cared for him, the worse she felt about the pregnancy. What would she say when she started to show? Could she ever bring herself to tell him about the fraternity party? This must be part of the punishment God was exacting on her. She could see a wonderful future with this guy, but her mistake would ruin it all. No guy could possibly want a girl so dirty.

One day he invited her to go swimming with him at the university fitness center. By then, he'd shared with her that he was from California and grew up in Santa Barbara, spending free time on the beach.

"I can't swim," she confided.

"No problem. I'm a lifeguard. You won't drown. Not on my watch." He flashed that smile that made her stomach flutter, blue eyes blazing. "Lap swim at four, maybe dinner after?"

She just stood there and grinned, marveling at how happy he made her, wondering how she would manage without him.

"I'll take that gorgeous smile as a yes. It's a date!"

Gorgeous smile? She walked away in a daze and only after

arriving back at her dorm room did she remember she didn't even own a swimsuit. Something kept her from thinking straight lately. Whether it was the pregnancy or her feelings for Tom, she wasn't sure.

Her roommate Karen came to her rescue. She had an extra suit and eagerly extracted it from the closet after coercing from her the reason for her sudden desire to swim—and the silly grin on her face. The suit fit well enough, though she noted with alarm the side seams strained against her torso and her breasts amply filled out the top.

"Does this make me look fat?" she blurted, alarmed she was showing already, prompting a critical examination from Karen.

"Hmmm...no, it doesn't. You do look like you've gained a couple pounds since school started." Karen hurriedly added, "But that happens to everybody. And it looks like it all went to your boobs, lucky! You look so good in that, you can keep it. One-piece suits are supposed to be out next summer, and I have a fantastic two-piece. I like to show my stomach."

HE WAS SWIMMING laps when Leslie pushed through the locker room door and into the pool area, leaving behind naked women changing and showering. They apparently didn't share her discomfort with baring her body. She sent up a silent prayer, thanking God that she had worn her newly acquired suit beneath clothing and didn't have to change in front of others.

"There you are!" Tom lit up at the sight of her. He made his way to the side of the pool by the locker rooms. "I was beginning to wonder if you changed your mind and stood me up."

She shook her head, arms hugging her torso, and wondered if that might have been a good idea. She was uncomfortable in the suit, afraid her thickening torso was obvious despite

Karen's reassurances. The chlorine in the air burned her nose and eyes. She wasn't even sure how to get into the lane—the ladder was several lanes over. She stood awkwardly by the pool, feeling plain and out of place.

"Here, I'll help you in," Tom encouraged.

She sat on the edge of the pool, dipping her feet into the surprisingly warm water.

He reached for her, grabbing her under the arms and lowering her into the pool. She held onto his upper arms for support, watching his biceps flex. His bare chest was directly in front of her, just inches away. His warm hands lingered on her body. They faced each other, and she was suddenly aware how very close they were and how very little they wore. His rippled abs made her heart skip a beat and his eyes made her pulse race. She didn't move, not sure where to look. She giggled.

"What's funny?"

"I don't know."

His arms wrapped around her.

"So you can't swim at all?"

He was so close and he made no move to distance himself. Scarcely able to breathe, she shook her head.

"I better keep you close then."

She didn't object. They stayed in the shallow water chatting until he offered a swimming lesson. He demonstrated some basic strokes, which she mimicked easily enough. Her problem, though, was putting her head underwater. The claustrophobic pressure against her face combined with the lack of sensory input from her eyes and ears terrified her. He encouraged her to try it a few times but didn't push.

She dogpaddled alongside him a few laps, watching him easily glide through the water. Trying to be brave, she lowered her face below the surface. She held her breath but wound up with water in her nose. Startled, she gasped, filling her throat with water, too. She tried to stand up as she choked and inhaled another mouthful, but the water was too deep and she couldn't touch the bottom. She panicked, thrashing and choking.

An arm curled around her middle. All at once she was sideways and gliding effortlessly toward the shallow end of the pool. Tom stood her up, and she continued to gasp and cough. He cradled her face in his hands, wiping the water away from her eyes with his thumbs. He asked her gently if she was okay.

She was too embarrassed to meet his eyes. Her throat burned and her lungs felt heavy. She stared at the water, coughing, until she was able to breathe.

"You okay?" he asked again. She nodded. "Geez, didn't believe I was a lifeguard, did you? Had to test my skills?"

She glanced up at him, surprised by the smile on his face. His blue eyes danced without a hint of disappointment. If he'd teased her or made fun of her, she couldn't have stood it. But he didn't. His hands still held her face, his thumbs now simply caressing.

"You were completely honest, told me you couldn't swim a bit. I'm sorry. This was a terrible first date, wasn't it?" He was laughing now, but at himself, not her.

"Date?"

"Well, if you're okay with that." It was his turn to look unsure. "We've been hanging around, and I thought, you know, maybe we could try going out. I like your company. You're smart, unpretentious, don't play games. It's refreshing."

No one had ever applied such words to her. She didn't know what to say to him. When she didn't answer, his brow furrowed, and she realized he thought she was about to turn him down. How could she? This beautiful, amazing boy wanted to go out with her? Still no words came. So she simply threw herself into his arms, hugging him tightly.

"That's a yes, right?" he laughed, wrapping his arms tightly about her.

He situated her on his back after that and dove forward

into the water, allowing her to skim the surface while he swam below, back and forth across the pool. She clung to his shoulders, skin to skin, like a child learning to swim. It was exhilarating, flying over the water, holding tight to her boyfriend.

Boyfriend. What would her parents say? She wasn't talking to them, but that couldn't last forever. She would eventually have to speak to them. They would disapprove of the idea of a boy in general. Would they like him, though?

Then she realized it didn't matter. This wouldn't last. Surely in another month or two her bulging stomach would ruin everything. Almost two months pregnant, she was lucky she didn't show yet.

For the millionth time, she wished she'd never gone to that stupid party. She wished she'd left instead of allowing that boy to convince her to stay. So many things could have gone differently.

Could she tell Tom how stupid she'd been? How would he feel about her? She knew he wasn't religious. Would he shrug it off and suggest an abortion? She wished the baby was his, instead of a total stranger's. An idea dawned on her, rising up out of the dark, angry shame of the pregnancy.

Later, after dinner, when he invited her to his room, she accepted. The girls' dorm had a curfew, but the boys' did not. Shaking, she accompanied him inside. They sat on the bed and watched television, though she had no memory of what was on. She couldn't focus on anything with his body so close.

He put an arm around her. She snuggled closer, resting her head on his shoulder. Heart thumping, she wondered where this was headed and if she would stop it at any point. He turned her face toward him and brushed her lips with his own. It was her first kiss.

He kissed her again, longer this time, and she was startled by a warm sensation flooding through her body. She wanted him to keep kissing her. Shifting to face him, she leaned into him, touching his face with her hands. Something told her she shouldn't be doing this. This was wrong. He didn't know she was pregnant and it was wrong to keep that from him. But she didn't stop, she couldn't. He laid her down on the bed, and before she knew what was happening, he was on top of her, covering her with kisses. He ran his tongue over her neck and looked very pleased when she gasped.

"You like that?"

She nodded, pulling him back to her. The throbbing between her legs grew even more forceful when he shifted them apart and settled down against her. She gasped again as she felt him throbbing in return. He was ready for sex, she could feel it, and she suspected he was willing to go all the way with her tonight. Was she going to agree?

She held very still.

He pulled away and stared down at her. "Have you done this before?"

She remained silent as she weighed the truth against the lie. She didn't remember having sex before, so it was kind of like her first time. Her conscience screamed at her. Thou shalt not lie. But what would he think of her if he knew about the rape? He was a wonderful man. Surely he would understand. Surely he wouldn't think less of her.

But what about the baby? There was no way he could overlook that. Unless…

She shook her head.

"This is your first time?"

She nodded, hoping if the fear thumping through her veins showed on her face, he would interpret it as a virgin's flush.

"Are you really sure you want to do this tonight?"

Was she? How much longer did she have before her bulging belly gave her away? If they didn't tonight, when would the opportunity present itself again? She grabbed him, kissed him hard.

She was certainly awkward enough to pass for a virgin that night. In retrospect, he didn't seem overly experienced himself.

He was gentle and careful but hurt her regardless. She clenched her jaw and held her breath until he cried out and gasped. After he relaxed on her, he kissed her cheek and asked if she was okay and if she'd enjoyed it. She lied and nodded, forcing a smile, as the word Jezebel screamed in her mind.

After that night, they were inseparable. He referred to her as "his girl" instead of "study buddy" and kept an arm around her always.

Three weeks later, she told him she was late for her period.

CHAPTER 19

*T*he hotel room door clicked open. Tom entered.

She sat up, startled, guilt lingering from the memory of their first time together. Would he discuss his late nights? Did she want him to? What if he really was just working? What if he wasn't?

He changed out of his damp suit before joining her on the bed.

"Look," he started, "I'm sorry things got heated. You know how crazy I get about this." He ran his fingertips gently over her bruised cheek. "I can't stand to see you hurting, thinking about that man hitting you. It brings back so many memories. And no one will do anything about it. It's like no one cares."

"That's exactly how I feel about Raveena. It's the same thing." She sat forward, taking his hand in her own, clutching it tightly.

"No, it's not the same. You're my wife. It's my job to keep you safe. That's what a man should do."

"But that little girl needs someone to keep her safe."

He sighed. "I know why this has you so worked up. But there's nothing we can do. It's not our concern."

He knew about the abduction, yes. But he didn't know

she'd been raped in college. Would it make any difference if he did? How could he say a little girl about to be raped wasn't their concern?

"Please let me help her. I can't just leave her."

"I'm trying to be realistic here. Everyone told you this is impossible. What are we supposed to do?" His voice rose again. "I understand—"

"You don't understand. Any day now—any day!—they could decide to sell her. Shardul will come get her, but instead of taking her to beg, he'll take her to some man who will take off her clothes and force himself on her. And you have no idea what it's like to be held down and forced to have sex against your will. None."

Tom snatched his hand away from her, pressing it over his eyes. "And you do? Is that how you feel about being with me? You're forced against your will?"

"What? No. That's not what I'm saying at all. You're twisting my meaning."

"Am I?"

"I'm talking about Raveena. I wish you—"

"I don't want to argue anymore."

"No, you want to just look the other way and pretend everything is fine."

"Stop. Please. We can't fix all the world's problems. Let's get ready for dinner. How's your stomach? Can you eat?"

"I can't think about eating. I'm too worried about Raveena. Shardul hurts those women like your dad hurt your mom."

"Would you stop it? I don't want to think about it."

"I can't push Raveena aside like that. I can't pretend I never met her and don't know what her future holds. How can you? Surely you haven't forgotten what it feels like to be so helpless."

"I haven't forgotten. Just try not to...I don't know...dwell on it." His eyes glazed over. "He was such a prick when I was growing up. He screamed at my mom. Especially when he was drunk off his sorry ass. When I was twelve, thirteen, I started wedging myself between him and my mom, trying to protect her from him, you know?" He dropped his head again.

She took his hand.

"She would stand there wringing her hands, crying, telling me to go to my room and close the door. That she would handle it."

He rarely shared stories from his childhood with her, and when he did, they were only little bits. She knew it was painful for him. With a difficult secret of her own, she understood and never pried, allowing him to share only what he wanted. Today, though, she wanted him to remember. She wanted him to feel something, anything, that would prompt him to help Raveena.

She'd met his parents, of course, and right away noticed his mother was quite a few years younger than his father. Twenty years younger, Tom later told her. His mom still called him "Tommy," which he now detested, a reminder of the youth he wanted to forget.

His father drank heavily, she knew that, and was prone to violent outbursts, venting primarily at his younger, mousy wife. When he couldn't take it anymore, Tom had told her, he rode his bike from their Ojai estate, across the Pacific Coast Highway, and spent hours at the beach.

"She couldn't handle him. Drunk bastard. Thought all that money made him important. Didn't ever stop to think he owed it all to his dad. It was his dad that started the company. He just inherited it. He didn't make anything, he just took over. And treated my mom and me like shit."

"He made you. It's difficult when a child has to take on the responsibilities of an adult. That happens when they don't have someone taking care of them. Just like Raveena."

He turned those blue eyes on her, the shadows of the past clouding their usual brilliance.

"I'm talking about us. Not that girl. You know, it's kind of his fault I met you. Did I tell you?"

This was a new bit, something he'd never shared. She shook her head.

"I graduated top of my class, of course, you knew that. Dad took us out to eat, announced he was paying for any Ivy League school I wanted. Mom said she didn't want me that far away and asked me to think about UCSB or at the worst Stanford. Dad told her he would see which school offered the best business degree, since that's what would help me most. Gear me up to take the reins of the company. I sat there listening to these two people who were so unhappy with their own lives, trying to dictate mine. I mean, they ignored me my whole life. I spent hours every day on the beach just to escape the noise of them screaming at each other. They didn't even notice. So I told him I didn't want his money, or an Ivy League, or his company, and that I'd go to college where I wanted to go. He said we'd discuss it when we got home, which meant he screamed at me and threw me against the wall."

Her husband, already struggling with the emotion of the memories he preferred to forget, gritted his teeth.

"I...I raised my fist to him that day. He kept coming at me. I grabbed his tie and jerked him forward...and realized I was about to land a punch on his jaw. We both stared at my fist. He was stunned. I don't think anyone ever stood up to him. Big bully. Money makes people crazy."

Tom squeezed her hand. She'd never seen this side of her husband, vulnerable and hurting. She thought she saw tears in his eyes.

"I didn't hit him. I could have. He looked so old that day. Did that ever happen to you? One day you look at your parent, someone who was always so much bigger, smarter, and stronger than you, someone you've been completely dependent on all your life, and you're looking at an old person instead. I didn't hit him. I refused to be like him."

She thought of her own father and shivered. He still scared her, even though he had mellowed with age. In her mind, he would always be the six-foot-three pulpit pounder who had terrified her in her youth.

"So I walked away, put myself through college. So what if it wasn't Ivy League. I met you there. And we're doing just fine on our own. At least I thought we were."

"Imagine how that little girl feels, completely at the mercy of the entire world."

"And we're back to the girl again."

"I can't stop thinking about her."

"I thought we were happy. Now suddenly you need a child?"

"Are we happy? Is that why I never see you anymore? Why you disappear and no one knows where you are? Are you going to tell me what's going on?"

"There's nothing to tell. Don't change the subject. Nothing changes the fact that we don't have any recourse here. Even if I agreed to this, what could we do?"

"Rhea—the woman in the jewelry shop—gave me the address of a place that helps women. I thought maybe we could see if they would help."

"And then what? You're not thinking this through. That girl is not our problem."

"But—"

"No. Stop it. I'm done discussing this. I'm just going to order room service."

"Please, just—"

"I said I'm done talking about it. You need to let this go." He turned his back to her and picked up the phone.

CHAPTER 20

The oppressive heat swallowed her, the glaring sun blinding, glinting off the side of the vehicle. Beside the car, a man held a little girl, hand clamped over her mouth and nose. She struggled to breathe, legs flailing, eyes wild with fear —

Leslie bolted upright, drenched in cold sweat, shivering and gasping. She reached out, groping the sheets until she found the warm mass that was Tom, blissfully undisturbed. Pushing the blankets aside, she moved quickly and silently to the bathroom, clicking the door shut, flipping on the light.

She rinsed her face and blotted it dry. The nightmare was the worst she'd had in years. So vivid, she felt as though she'd relived those horrible moments all over again. Taking deep, calming breaths, she glanced in the mirror, where she saw not her current likeness, but her twelve-year-old self, quaking in fear at what had happened at the lemonade stand when she went in the house for popsicles. She had been slothful and succumbed to temptation, bored by the lack of customers, tired of the brutal heat.

God alone knew what transpired that day and what became of little Trisha with her curly pigtails and freckled cheeks. And chocolate brown eyes exactly like Raveena's.

Leslie struggled with nausea as she always did when she dwelt on that sweltering afternoon, now more than twenty years in her past. At first, she harbored hope that someday the little girl might be found and returned home. But Trisha's disappearance remained unsolved. No sightings, no clues, her body never discovered. She just disappeared.

"Leslie?" The door opened and Tom's face appeared, blinking in the light. She jumped at the sound of his voice. "You okay?" he asked, rubbing the sleep from his eyes.

"No," she whimpered.

"Are you sick again?"

"Not exactly."

"Was it the nightmare? Come back to bed, huh?"

She stood there a moment, staring into his blue eyes, awash with guilt for never sharing her darkest secrets with her husband. Rhea was right. She felt the words tugging at her tongue.

"There's something I never told you," she began. Several somethings if she was completely honest, but one step at a time.

"About what?" His eyes crinkled as his brow furrowed.

"It was my fault," she blurted, falling into his arms, leaning heavily against his chest.

"What was your fault?"

"I was supposed to keep an eye on her."

"Keep an eye on...What are you talking about?"

"My sister. The day she was kidnapped. I've never told anyone. I don't like talking about it, and you've never asked a lot of questions which I appreciated."

"It had to be difficult. Seeing your sister kidnapped."

"It was a nightmare. But worst of all...it was my fault."

"No way. There's no way you could have prevented that."

"But I could have. I was watching her. And I left her alone."

"Leslie—"

"We had a lemonade stand. It was so hot, no breeze. No one else was outside. I wanted to quit, go inside where it was cool, watch cartoons." She sniffed, wiped her nose on her sleeve. "There was some toy we wanted, a doll, I think, we were trying to earn money for. I don't even remember. Some stupid toy. Our mom wouldn't buy it, told us we had to earn things in life. 'God helps those that help themselves.' Her usual worthless drivel. She went to the church for prayer group or something and told me to watch her."

She leaned back and stared up at her husband, looking for forgiveness.

"Okay. Still not seeing any blame here."

"It was hot. I went inside to get popsicles." She buried her face in her hands. "I told her to come inside with me. She wouldn't. She just wouldn't come inside. I wanted a break...to cool off..." Her body shook with the violent wave of grief that crashed over her as the memory flooded back. "When I came back outside, there was a car at the curb. I couldn't believe someone had actually stopped. And I missed it. I didn't see Trisha so I hurried down to the stand. Then I saw the man standing by the door of the car. He held her, one hand clamped over her mouth so she couldn't scream. She clawed at his hand. I saw her eyes—huge with fear—and the man saw me. I had no idea what was happening. I was terrified. It must have happened in a second or two. He shoved her in the car and drove away."

He pulled her into an embrace as a fresh round of tears ran down her cheeks.

"I stood there, stunned, while the car drove away. I couldn't believe it. No one was home. I didn't know what to do. I was so scared. And then I thought the man would come back for me, so I ran inside and locked the door."

Tom squeezed her tighter. "Oh, my God."

"When my mom came home, I told her what happened. She called nine-one-one, but I didn't see the license plate. My mom kept asking, 'Why didn't you call nine-one-one? Why didn't you do something?' I could barely even offer a description of the car, much less the driver. I was worthless. I panicked and froze. If I'd done something right away, maybe they could have caught the guy leaving our neighborhood. It's all my fault. I should have stayed with her. Or made her come inside. Or called. Or done something."

Now that she was talking, telling her secret, the words wouldn't stop. All the pent-up grief and guilt poured out. She leaned against him, wracked with sobs.

"I can't imagine how awful that was. I didn't know all the details. I mean, I understand not wanting to keep reliving it. But I didn't know."

"I didn't want you to know what a coward I am," she managed to choke out. "I don't want anyone to know. It's bad enough my parents blame me."

"A coward? You were twelve. It wasn't your fault. Your mother never should have implied that it was. She left you two alone. I can't even imagine how traumatic that was. And you've been holding this inside all these years?"

"I'm sorry I never told you. I should have."

"So your parents never sought counseling? For all of you?"

"No. My mom said we had to accept God's plan for Trisha, not question it."

"Of course she did."

"My dad just sort of faded away. His sermons were much quieter after that. I think he did question it, but didn't want to admit it."

"Something like that is enough to make a person lose faith completely. Trauma like that destroys families. And marriages."

"Not my mom. At least, not that I could ever tell. She said Trisha was so good, she was ready for heaven. Her earthly journey was complete and her soul was pure. So God called her home."

"What about you? I thought you'd put that nonsense behind you."

She considered. The images of her sister in the strange man's arms, his hand clamped over her mouth, haunted her day and night. She couldn't describe the dread of that terrible day to anyone, the bizarre, almost electric fear that coursed through her, followed by a numb loss as policemen tramped through their house, asking her questions she couldn't answer. *Please, God, please,* she'd prayed all day, *please bring Trisha back. Don't let that man keep her. Please, let someone know something and turn him in. Please give my sister back.*

Her prayers did not bring Trisha home. Later prayers did not heal the empty look in her distant father's eyes. The insistence that Trisha was called to heaven because she was so pure comforted her mother. But couldn't you just as easily argue that Leslie was left behind because she wasn't ready? God tested her, and she was found lacking. She couldn't save her sister, so she was left to cope with her loss. Sometimes she even wondered if her parents wished she was the one taken instead of Trisha.

Her mother's praise for her little saint fell on deaf ears as her father withdrew. Eventually, they all stopped talking about her. But Leslie knew they blamed her. The last person to see her sister, she stood by helplessly while a man stole the little girl away. No matter how many good works she tried to offer in repentance, she couldn't make up for the loss, couldn't fix it. Couldn't take away that empty gaze in her father's eyes. She wished fervently that she could be more like Tom and just push all those bad thoughts away. She buried them, perhaps, but couldn't stop them from clawing to the surface.

Tom nudged her. "Hey. You don't believe that, do you? Bad things happen to good people. That's just the world we live in. It isn't fair, but crap happens."

"I wish I could go back and do something different — anything — do something to save my sister." Fresh tears spilled down her cheeks. All her life she'd wished for a way to go back and have a second chance.

Was God finally offering it to her? After all the years of silence, after she spent the last fourteen years refusing to pray, was He finally reaching out to her? Was He offering her the means to mend the rift?

"This explains why you're hell-bent on saving this little girl."

"She asked me to help her. Watching Shardul drag her away—I can't—I don't want to fail again. Maybe this is my second chance?"

"Okay. I get it. Now I understand. So what's this place the jewelry lady told you about?"

"Protect Our Women. She gave me the address. Can we go? Can we see if they'll help us?"

She couldn't judge what he was thinking. But he was thinking. That was something.

"Okay. Tomorrow we'll go see if they can help."

She threw her arms around him. "Thank you. Thank you so much. For understanding and supporting me."

"Don't get too excited. We're just going to talk to them."

"I think we could give her a happy home, I really do."

He unwrapped her arms from his neck. "Leslie, I'm not agreeing to adopt this girl. I'm only agreeing to see if there's a way we can help her escape the brothel. Maybe we can take her away from Shardul. Okay? That ought to piss him off."

It wasn't what she wanted to hear. But it was something. If she could at least save the girl from a lifetime of degradation and nightly disgrace at the hands of strange men, then she would accept that. Maybe that was her mission. Maybe that was the purpose she'd been seeking all these years after the tragedy.

CHAPTER 21

*L*eslie might have questioned their driver if not for the handwritten sign in the window identifying the small, crumbling, concrete building wedged between similarly dilapidated structures. *Protect Our Women*, it read, confirming the location.

"Well…okay," Tom said with a shrug.

"It isn't what I expected either."

"I wasn't exactly expecting bells and whistles or a flying banner, but a little more than this."

"If they can help us with Raveena, it doesn't matter."

The front door to the building was propped open by a rock. As they stepped inside, she couldn't help but think that this place made the police station look luxurious by comparison. There was only one room, she realized as her eyes adjusted from sunlight to the dark, enclosed space. There were no other offices, just a table and a few small desks. One bare bulb in the ceiling illuminated the room. There were no fans, much less something as decadent as air conditioning to cool the rivulets of sweat trickling down her temples. There were, however, telephones, which jangled noisily. And flies buzzing about the room.

Several women wearing saris and *shalwar kameez*, along with a man in slacks and a dress shirt, were preoccupied with the work before them. They glanced at the foreigners hovering in the doorway but did not stop working.

"Maybe we should have called first," Tom said, when no one moved to welcome them.

"I'm not sure they make appointments."

One woman finally hung up the phone on her desk and approached them. She wore a fitted, modern *shalwar kameez*, her thick, dark hair braided down her back. Almond-shaped eyes, accented with black eyeliner, took in the visitors.

"Yes?" she asked, her voice full and resonant. There was nothing timid about this woman. Leslie detected a strong, steely assurance beneath the woman's slight frame. "Are you lost?"

"No, ma'am. We came to see if your group could help us," Leslie said, feeling very out of place and out of her league, like a child asking for ice cream before dinner.

The woman offered her hand. "My name is Gazala. What sort of help do you need?"

"We were told you rescue women and children who have been trafficked and forced into prostitution?"

"Yes, madam, that is one of our purposes." Gazala still looked confused. "I'm sorry, may I ask who exactly told you about POW?"

"Her name is Rhea. She said her husband donates and volunteers. And that they help at the orphanage."

"Ah. Rhea and Maninder." The woman nodded. "I was on my way out. If you will accompany me, we can discuss while we drive."

Tom shrugged and nodded. "Sure."

Gazala gladly accepted their offer to use Prajit's taxi. "The drivers, of course, generally prefer the shopping districts to the slums. But I need to be close to the people I'm trying to help. I hope someday to be able to afford a full time driver. And a car."

Gazala climbed into the front seat and spoke to Prajit in their native tongue. "What is it you want from us? How can we help?" she asked while Prajit guided the taxi back into the street.

"I don't really know where to start. There's a young girl being held in a brothel. Her mother has died, she has no remaining family, and my husband and I would like to help her. But the brothel owner claims she belongs to him and that she owes him money. Something about money her mother owed him before she died."

Clasping her hands together, Gazala nodded. "I do not know how you have become embroiled in this, but the story sounds all too familiar. Was the young girl bred by the brothel owner?"

"No, the women I talked with said he didn't know about the pregnancy until later. And that he was unhappy about the extra mouth to feed."

"Until he realized how much profit could be made from this new slave who cost him nothing to acquire." Gazala gesticulated as she spoke, her passion and frustration overflowing into her hands. "There is no purchase price for infants born to sex slaves. Breeding is sadly becoming more common among the brothel owners. The baby boys will be used for hard labor. The baby girls are future sex slaves. How old is the girl you are trying to rescue?"

"They think she's twelve."

"She has reached the ripe age, then, when virginity is sold to the highest bidder. We see this time and again. Rhea must be thinking of the case from last week. A woman who had escaped a brothel came in begging us to help rescue her daughter. She also had a son inside the brothel. The son was begging for the girl's release, doing what he could to convince the owner not to sell her, to let them go. It was a delicate situation. The woman went back to the brothel trying to rescue them, but the owner had the children beaten every time he caught sight of her. The police were hesitant, but we pushed them hard to raid the brothel to search for minor children. Sadly, we could not coordinate the effort quickly enough."

"What happened?" she asked.

"Her virginity was sold to a man who became quite angry when she cried and fought him. The owner and the gharwali beat her terribly, telling her she will cooperate next time. To make sure she would never fight again, they crushed chili peppers and forced the burning paste into her vagina. The little girl has never even had a menstrual cycle. She is currently in hospital. So horrible."

"That's..." Leslie couldn't complete the sentence. She'd fought images like this more years than not. Even as a sheltered twelve-year-old, her imagination created horrific scenes after the abduction of her sister. As she matured and watched the news, graphic stories added fuel to the fire, conjuring increasingly worse images of torture, no matter how hard she tried to push them away.

"This is unfortunately not the first time I have heard of this method of subjugation," Gazala said.

"Why would anyone do such a thing? And to a child?" Tom interrupted. "That's inhuman."

"This is slavery we are talking about, very simple. People call them prostitutes and sex workers, but this is a misnomer. This makes them sound like paid workers. Even among the women who have 'paid their debt,' living conditions are terrible, the brothel owners continue to overcharge for rent and food, and their pay seems good to them only because they have worked for nothing for so long."

"What happened to the girl?" Leslie whispered, afraid to hear more but needing to know. "You said she's in the hospital now?"

"Upon hearing his sister screaming in pain and begging for mercy, the boy rushed in, caught the owner unaware, and in a mad fit of rage beat him with his own metal pipe. He carried her out of the brothel before anyone could stop him. Luckily, a passing policeman saw them and stopped to intervene. Thankfully, the children have been reunited with their mother. We are in the process of trying to find a home for them and a job for the woman. We hope the young girl recovers from her injuries."

"I can't believe someone would treat children this way," Tom said. "Can't you…I don't know, just walk in and take everybody out with you?"

"I only wish it was as easy as that, sir," Gazala laughed.

"But if they are held against their will—I don't understand how this happens. How can anyone be allowed to do this?"

"Who is going to stop them? You saw my entire staff back at the office. If you have a solution, I am all ears."

"I don't know. What if all the women just left the brothels?"

"And go where?"

"Back to their families? Or to other jobs?"

"I attended university in America, sir, so I know you have never been faced with problems such as we are trying to battle here. This is a different culture—a different world from what you are accustomed to. And frankly, most Indians do not look favorably upon Westerners interfering in our lives. You do not understand the scope of the issues."

"I'm trying to," he replied. "My wife was hit when she went to a brothel trying to help this little girl."

"Yes, I believe it. My staff and I face constant threats. We have been attacked, sent death threats. Our front window has been broken out twice. If these men discover our home addresses, our families' safety will be at stake. You and your wife can go home to America. Our lives are here. We must proceed with caution."

Gazala pointed at a building, directing Prajit to drop them off.

"But I don't understand why any woman stays someplace

when she's being abused," Tom remarked. "If it's that bad, they should just leave."

"If only it was as simple as walking out the door. These women would give anything to escape this nightmare. They are subject to filthy living conditions, starvation, harsh treatment, and long working hours, sometimes servicing as many as twenty men per day. Would you like to have sex against your will with twenty men or more every day?"

Tom squirmed in his seat.

Prajit pulled the car to the curb.

"They are trapped," Gazala continued. "These girls do not deserve this—no one does. Sex workers have a low life expectancy due to malnutrition and disease. Men paying for sex believe they have paid to do as they wish. They refuse to use condoms because they want as much pleasure as possible for the handful of rupees they pay for time with a woman. And the women have no means of forcing their clients to use protection. Some women try to cajole men into using them by suggesting they will withhold sex until the men agree. But then they risk losing the client to another woman who will not insist he use one—and thus losing her potential pay and angering her owner. A client may beat her and rape her if she continues to insist he use one. After all, he has paid for this. He believes he is justified. And the women have absolutely no recourse."

"Someone should close the brothels and set the women free."

"Which is what we wish to do. But if through some miracle we do someday achieve this, then we face the next problem. Where do they go?"

"Back to their families."

"I worked to return a young woman to her village once we liberated her from the brothel. Her family rejected her. They considered her a burden, since she had been 'ruined' and was no longer a virgin. No man would marry her. The community shunned her, convinced she carried HIV and believing that the disease can be spread by casual contact."

"They could find real jobs and support themselves. Women don't need to rely on men."

"Not in the United States. It is a different story here in India. Where would they live penniless, uneducated, and alone? They would be left begging in the streets — at best. We have no food stamps and unemployment benefits here. And if they were ever caught by the brothel owner or his goons, the retribution for running away would be horrific — broken arms are a common form of punishment. There is no easy solution. We are trying to collect enough funding to build a boarding house to provide shelter and protection for rescued women and children. But it is a slow process."

"Why don't the families protect their girls? I don't have any kids, but I still can't imagine allowing someone to take a daughter away, if I did have one."

Leslie stared at him, biting her tongue to keep from reminding him how quickly he dismissed her when she described how she was almost kidnapped. He hadn't given any thought to protecting her that day. He didn't even believe any danger existed.

"The sons are the parents' retirement plan. Families put all their resources into their sons, hoping they will become successful in whatever business they pursue. If they can secure good jobs, they will not only have a better income, but will also command a higher dowry when they are ready to marry. The dowry goes to the parents, so they feel that they are paid back for their investment. Later in life, when the parents retire, they will move in with their son's family, and the son will take care of them in their old age. Again, a good return on their investment. A daughter is often seen as nothing but a burden to destitute families. They do not send their girls to school. Many rural areas do not believe that women should work outside the home, so why should they be educated? This, sadly, is the reality we face in our work. Most days, it feels like pushing an elephant up a hill while others push back against us."

Gazala opened her door and gestured them out. "If you wish to accompany me inside, you will see for yourselves."

The building they approached looked like the others surrounding it—crumbling and sad. A small sign alerted her to what she could expect: *ULTRASOUND CLINIC.*

Gazala pointed to a sign in the window, forbidding the abortion of girl babies. "This sign is here only to protect the clinic. The Pre-Conception and Pre-Natal Diagnostics Techniques Act was meant to curb 'medically terminated pregnancies.' Female abortion and infanticide are still practiced, sadly. Families come to clinics like these to determine the sex of the baby, hoping, of course, for boys."

Leslie's eyes drifted to the demure faces and swollen bellies of the women in the lobby. Older women accompanied most of the expectant mothers.

"Most of these young ladies are here with their mothers-in-law. Family pressure to abort females can be grueling. And most young, often newly married women will not stand up to their elders."

The door to the back office area opened, spilling a stricken young woman into the lobby, supported by an older woman whose strained face contorted in a grimace. A toddler clad in pink trailed behind the devastated women.

Gazala stepped forward, shoulders squared, voice loud enough to carry through the lobby. "I can see you did not receive the news you hoped for. Please, do not despair. Remember sex selection is not allowed nor is it healthy for our country."

The older woman shook her head. "A second girl? No sons? She's worthless."

The young mother moaned.

"But she can't help it," Leslie said. "She has no control over the pregnancy."

Gazala passed a card to the young woman. "You need to protect yourself and your unborn baby. Call us if you need any help."

The older woman snatched the card away. "Our son cannot afford the cost of another girl. Another mouth to feed. Another dowry to pay." She shook the younger woman. "Her parents promised sons. Instead, she has ruined us." The woman pushed past them and out the door, dragging the younger woman, toddler in tow.

"A perfect example," Gazala said, gesturing after the women. "I am certain I know the outcome in this scenario. This is why our population has become unbalanced. India currently has roughly nine hundred women for every one thousand men. In some states, the number of women continues to decline."

Leslie watched as Gazala moved through the lobby, offering support, encouragement, and cards to anyone who would accept them. Would she make a difference? If this strong, outspoken woman couldn't change things, how could Leslie possibly hope to help anyone? How could she save Raveena — before it was too late?

CHAPTER 22

They left the ultrasound clinic. Still stunned by the venom in the older woman's voice, Leslie worried for the young mother. And her two daughters, one of whom would probably not live to birth. The other of whom seemed destined to a life of neglect and resentment at best.

Raveena didn't stand a chance. Even if Leslie and Tom took her from the brothel and to the safety of an orphanage, what life awaited her? Who would adopt a twelve-year-old girl in a culture that desired only sons?

"I two daughter," Prajit said.

She met his eyes in the rearview mirror.

The driver spoke to Gazala, gesturing for the Indian woman to translate.

Gazala nodded. "He says he welcomed his two daughters with love and thanks as the blessings babies should be welcomed as. And he spoiled them as much as he could afford while they were growing up. He arranged good marriages for them to gentle husbands who would be good to them. Some people know to be thankful for what life hands them."

Prajit caught her eye again, his crow's feet crinkled in an encouraging smile.

Gazala continued. "He can see by your face what we witnessed in the clinic. He wants you to know not everyone in India kills their daughters, sells women for money, or strikes foreign guests caught unaware."

"No, of course not," Leslie said.

"He says, 'You just stumbled in with a bad lot.'" Gazala's face softened as she translated. "He's right you know. It's easy to become cynical. The problems seem staggering, but the majority of people are good."

"I know," Leslie said, placing a hand on Prajit's shoulder. "Because luckily, I also met you."

"Okay, lady." He brushed away her thanks, wobbling his head.

"So we can't solve the entire problem today," Tom said. "What about Raveena? Can you help us get her out of the brothel at least?"

"We were hoping maybe you could intervene," Leslie added. "Or tell us what we can do."

"I'm not sure how much help we can offer. POW is a non-governmental organization. We must work with police. Have you talked with the authorities?"

"Yes, we went to the police to report Leslie's assault. They wouldn't do a damned thing. And she asked about Raveena there, too. Same story."

"If they have already indicated they will not help the child, we have no way to force them. In the case we were discussing earlier, we were approached by the children's mother, and even then we were unsuccessful. You have no direct tie to this child." Leslie began to speak, but Gazala cut her off. "Yes, I know you wish only for the child's best interests. I understand your intentions are good. But on what grounds could we even seek to remove her? We cannot use the future plans of prostitution—it has not happened yet."

"Okay, yes, I understand that. I get it," Tom said. "But

what could these characters do if we just go take Raveena from them?"

"Report the kidnapping of a minor. That is an allegation the police will respond to."

"How would they find us?" Tom asked, crossing his arms.

"You are registered as visitors in this country," Gazala replied. "It would not take them long to track you down. And I presume you wish to take the child back to America with you?"

Leslie looked at Tom. He said nothing.

"You lack the necessary documents to take her with you. When you failed to produce them, the authorities would take her from you at the airport and expel you from the country."

"We know about the documents," Tom answered. "But we don't want to adopt. We just want to get her to a safe place. Like an orphanage."

"In that case, it would not take the brothel owner long to find her, declare guardianship, and demand that she be returned to him."

"He isn't really her guardian," Leslie insisted. "Raveena told me so. And the two women I spoke with confirmed that."

"But what proof? Without proof, there is no means of denying him the child."

Leslie's breath caught in her throat, choked by the imagined screams of Raveena, locked in a room, approached by a strange man, helpless to escape or protect herself. No one would answer her cries for help.

Brothel baby or not, no twelve-year-old was capable of coping with such a trauma. She would wind up like the others —hollow, scarred, beaten down, and convinced it was her fate in this life. Leslie clenched her fists, frustrated by the doors closing every way she turned.

Gazala reached into the back seat and squeezed her hand. "I know. The problems seem insurmountable. I deal with it every day. We root out corruption in one location and it scurries to another. We raid a brothel, gather the workers, jail the owners—and the following day bribes have exchanged hands, the owner lures his girls back, and they open for business as usual without missing a night. Even proof of harboring a minor is no longer a guaranteed means to close a brothel."

Gazala's eyes narrowed. "But we won't stop fighting the evil. All it takes is a few more to join us and a few more and a few more. People who refuse to look the other way. When we all join together, determined to put a stop to it, we will rise up like a tsunami and wash this evil away."

But what would it take to make people pay attention? To stop looking the other way? To stand up and make a difference?

Leslie saw an elderly man begging on a corner. "The poverty here drives people to do horrible things. Parents sell their children or believe stories about great paying jobs for their children."

"I told you money makes people evil," Tom said.

"It isn't money causing problems. It's the lack of money."

"The lure of making money is what drives this system—the trafficking, the slavery. It's all about the money."

"Not for Raveena. Or any of the women in the brothel. They weren't trying to make any money. It's the men profiting off of them who are evil. They keep them ground down and dirt poor."

"And make money off them. That's the point I'm making. Money makes people evil."

Leslie looked out the window and recognized where she was. She clutched Tom's forearm. "This is the street where Raveena lives."

"This is where you came yesterday?"

She nodded, craning her neck to see down the street.

"Which brothel?" Gazala asked. "I make regular visits to GB Road. I am familiar with most of the gharwalis here."

"It's farther down."

Prajit spoke to her.

Gazala frowned. "I believe I am familiar with the brothel."

GB Road was busier later in the day. The roads that were nearly deserted in the morning now teemed with activity and traffic. People shuffled from shop to shop. Vendors pushed carts of goods for sale.

Ragged children threaded their way through the gathering crowd. Some appeared to play, some begged, some offered shoe shines, and some dug through trash.

Men squatted on curbs, staring blankly ahead. She saw one man lean over and blow his nose into the street, pinching residual mucous with his thumb and forefinger and flinging it onto the pavement.

Prajit pulled up to the curb in front of the brothel.

"I know this brothel," Gazala said, voice hesitant for the first time all day. "The owner is known for his enormous wealth. And his cruelty. His name is Bikram. He is feared by many."

"That would explain the reaction at the police station," Leslie said.

"Yes. The police are known recipients of his bribes. He orders hits on anyone who tries to stand up to him. And I strongly suspect he is responsible for our broken front window. Both times."

"He's worse than other brothel owners?" Tom asked.

"Yes. They are all unsavory, to be sure, but he is a monster. He owns several brothels. One of them he acquired after the suspicious death of the previous owner—which was never solved and only barely investigated. He also brings a lot of the drugs plaguing New Delhi into the city. He drives the most expensive cars, wears designer clothing, surrounds himself with bodyguards at all times, lives in an enormous estate, walled and guarded."

"And with all that wealth, he's still determined to sell

Raveena to the highest bidder?" Leslie's stomach turned, bile rising into her throat.

"How do you think he acquired all that wealth? Selling drugs and women to the highest bidder. It's what he does. Demand for younger and younger girls is rising. He provides what his repulsive clients demand."

Leslie gritted her teeth. "So you've been here? Have you ever seen Raveena?"

"I did not know her name, but I believe I have seen the girl a few times. These women are difficult to talk to. Bikram is so feared, it is difficult to reach out to them. But I try."

"I want to go inside," Tom said, hands fisted.

"That may not be wise. Especially if one of his men is here."

"There's one in particular I'd like to get my hands on."

"Bear in mind, Bikram supplies much of the opium on our streets. His employees probably have access to it and may not be rational if they partake of it."

Leslie's eyes searched the faces in the street then glanced up to the windows of the building, but she saw nothing of concern. Even the lounging man no longer reclined by the front door. "Can we see Raveena? You've been inside, right?"

"I have not been inside this brothel, and I do not know the gharwali. They may not open the door to me. We should go."

"I don't think Shardul is here. I don't see his car. Can I at least say goodbye to her? If she's here?"

Gazala hesitated, appearing torn. "If he is truly gone, this may be a good chance to finally meet the gharwali. If they will let you in to see Raveena."

They crossed the street, knocked, and waited. The building remained still and quiet, the girls resting during the day to prepare for their work at night.

Leslie wondered if perhaps someone had identified them from a window upstairs, and they were being intentionally ignored. But a moment later, she heard the bolt disengage. The door opened a crack.

Sanjana appeared. The lack of surprise in her eyes convinced her that they had been seen from above. She stared at her, then Tom, then eyed Gazala. Shaking her head, she tried to close the door.

Tom leaned against it. "Wait."

Leslie heard a voice behind Sanjana. "Tarla?" she called. "It's Leslie."

Sanjana opened the door a bit more, and Leslie saw to her dismay that the woman's face was bruised, much like her own. Shardul must have taken out his anger on her.

"I'm so sorry," Leslie whispered.

The older woman merely shook her head.

"She does not blame you," Tarla said, and Sanjana opened the door a bit wider. "We are not angry with you. But we cannot let you in again. If Shardul learns you were here, he will be furious. There will be no stopping his anger."

"Is he gone?" Leslie asked, heart galloping at the thought of the brutal man appearing behind the women.

"He is gone."

"Did he hit you too?" Tom asked, his voice shaking with fury.

"Please, sir, this is not unusual. We can take it," Tarla assured him.

"It shouldn't be usual. He has no right to hurt you," Tom insisted. "I want to talk to him. We'll wait."

"No!" Tarla said. "Please, you must go. If you make him angry, we will all suffer at his hands. All of us. Including Raveena."

Gazala held out her hand, holding another business card. "My name is Gazala. I work for Protect Our Women. I want to give you my contact information, in case you or any of your girls ever need help or want to leave the brothel."

Sanjana shook her head. "I cannot take it. If Shardul saw it and told Bikram..." She shook her head, shivering slightly at whatever she imagined would happen.

"Perhaps you can hide it?"

"I cannot take the chance." Sanjana turned back to Leslie. "If you truly care about Raveena, you must leave right now. We will take care of her."

"But you can't stop these men from hurting her." Leslie pressed forward, knowing this might be her last chance to say anything. "Do you want to see Raveena treated like this her entire life?"

The women blanched.

"Of course we do not want this," Tarla replied. "But this is our fate. And it is Raveena's fate too. There is nothing you can do to change it. Bikram will never let you take her from him. His 'Cherry Girl' is too valuable."

It wasn't going to happen. Leslie had to accept it and move on. She'd failed Raveena just as she'd failed Trisha.

"Can we at least say goodbye to her? Is she here?"

Sanjana and Tarla looked at one another. Leslie could see they struggled with something. They spoke quietly in Hindi, shaking their heads and staring into the street furtively.

Finally, Sanjana rolled her eyes and appeared to give her consent.

Tarla turned and called up the stairs, "Raveena!" Then she said, "You really must just say goodbye and leave. Please, if you care about her and us, do not linger."

"Auntie!" Raveena stood at the top of the stairs, beaming down at her. Her deep brown eyes shone all the way down the stairs and across the tiny front room. Raveena leaped into her waiting arms. "Auntie."

At the sight of Raveena's face, anger bubbled within Leslie. New bruises on her cheek and a fat lip told her the girl had been beaten. Again. Leslie gritted her teeth and fought back tears, knowing more of the same and even worse awaited Raveena soon.

Images of birthday parties and shopping, movies and homework, parks and picnics, tears and hugs played in her mind. She forced herself to let go of the impossible future. The potential years together were lost to them all. Just like her sister.

She clutched Raveena for the last time. She had no words to tell her how much she loved her, how hard she had tried to fight for her, how much she wanted to take care of her. She also realized speaking such words would help nothing and make leaving even more difficult for them both. How crushing it would be to tell her she wanted to take her away from this and then leave her behind, helpless to the coming horrors.

"Raveena," she began, stroking her hair, trying to ignore the marks of violence on her face. "I will miss you. We both will miss you," she added, gesturing to Tom.

"You are going home to America, Auntie?"

"Yes, we are. We wanted to tell you goodbye."

Raveena hugged her tightly. "Goodbye, Auntie," she whispered, her voice quivering. She turned her attention shyly to Tom. Then she threw her arms around his waist, hugging him tightly. "Good-bye, Uncle."

Tom looked stunned. He placed a tentative hand on her back. He took her arms in his hands, staring down at them. His fingers brushed over marks on Raveena's arms she hadn't noticed before. Cigarette burns.

Tom's expression hardened. He turned to Sanjana. "How much does he want for her?" he asked.

"Sir?"

"How much does the bastard want for her?"

"I am sorry. I do not understand."

"I want to know how much money this Bikram claims the girl's mother owed him. How much he expects to make from her to pay off this supposed debt."

Leslie's mind raced as it occurred to her what he might be thinking. Was Tom offering to pay this debt? After all his talk of being helpless and his insistence that she let the idea go, was he presenting her with the solution?

Sanjana and Tarla conversed in rapid Hindi.

"How much to buy her?" Tarla clarified. "You will pay and take her away?"

"That's right," Tom nodded. "I will pay off her debt, and Bikram will let her go. If everything revolves around money here, then so be it. Those sons of bitches think they can do whatever they want. Beat up on women and sell them to the highest bidder. Not this time."

Leslie put an arm around Raveena. "Bikram needs to sign that he is not her guardian. We need a document stating that he relinquishes any claims of guardianship and verifying that she is an orphan."

Tom nodded. "Make sure he understands that. We are paying off her debt completely, and he will relinquish all claims to her. We want it in writing. Do you have an idea how much he will want? How much does he claim her mother owed him?"

"No one is sure how much they owe," Tarla told him. "There is no telling how much he will demand in payment when he hears this. But we can guess how much he expects for her that first week. She will be young, most prized. He will ask the highest amount for her. Around seventy thousand rupees."

"How much is that in dollars?" Leslie asked. "Exchange is about fifty rupees to the dollar. So I think about..." She clutched Raveena but could not think. Excitement clouded her thoughts. She could barely breathe.

"Fourteen hundred dollars," Tom supplied.

She could see the revulsion in his face. Fourteen hundred dollars to rape a little girl for a week. He looked down at Raveena and shook his head.

"But he will want more than that," Tarla told them. "Men pay a higher price for young girls even after they are no longer virgins. We think he will ask for maybe hundred-fifty thousand rupees to take her away."

"So maybe three thousand dollars?" Tom calculated aloud.

Tarla shrugged. "We are guessing," she said.

Leslie's hands shook. Was she really standing here hoping a man would sell an orphan to them? For three thousand dollars? It seemed so little, and yet—where would they scrape together that kind of money?

"Tell Bikram we will give him three thousand dollars if he will sign a document relinquishing all claims of guardianship," Tom told Tarla. "It will have to be fast. We only have a few days left. Will you tell him? Or should we wait and tell Shardul ourselves?"

Tarla and Sanjana spoke quickly.

"We will tell," Sanjana answered. Sanjana bowed and patted her hand. "Good woman. Good man." Then she grabbed Raveena by the shoulder and led her away. "Come now."

Leslie watched Raveena go, wondering if she would ever be able to hold that little girl without someone taking her away.

CHAPTER 23

Though euphoric as they returned to the taxi, Leslie knew getting the money would be challenging. She wanted to discuss Tom's plans for getting it. But Gazala turned and spoke before she could ask him.

"I must tell you in my official capacity that purchasing a slave is highly discouraged."

"We're not buying a slave," Tom said. "We're buying her freedom."

"I understand. But this is not considered an acceptable means of liberating anyone. In fact, it only adds to the problem in the end, since the purchase supports the idea of trading money for a human life."

"We don't have any other options," Leslie said. "What else can we do? Except leave her there."

"As I said, I felt I must give you the official view of this. Unofficially, I cannot help but cheer you on. Nothing would make me happier than to see Raveena escape Bikram's brothel." The woman smiled for the first time since they'd met her. "And now that I've met the gharwali, perhaps eventually they will talk to me and come to trust me."

They returned to POW and dropped off Gazala. The

woman wished them luck one last time before they said good-bye.

"You were brilliant back there," she told Tom.

He offered a tight smile. "Thanks."

"Really. I should have thought of that myself. But I didn't. Thank you."

He nodded. "Thank me after they agree to the deal. We have no idea what will happen. Bikram may not have any interest in our scheme."

That was true. And even if he did, they had to come up with three thousand dollars. How would they get their hands on money like that in India? She had no idea how to transfer funds before their departure in a few days.

Her mind drifted to her parents. Their church was comfortable financially, but they weren't wealthy people. Would they give her the money? They didn't pay a cent for her wedding, but that was because they didn't approve. Surely they couldn't object to helping a little girl.

She tried to imagine the conversation. She pictured her father, reminded of Trisha, receding further into his emotional vacancy. Her mother...her mother would hear brothel and sex slave and her face would pinch into righteous disapproval. She would refuse to listen to any more. Then the two of them would dissolve into an argument about God's children and helping each other and What Would Jesus Do until her mother seethed at her in silence. No, they wouldn't help.

The look of hope in Raveena's eyes troubled Leslie. She'd put that hope there. She'd goaded Tom and pleaded with him until he found the solution. And now what? How could they make this happen? She wanted to ask him but couldn't bring herself to say the words. The look on his face told her he didn't know, either.

Prajit followed the curving drive to the front door of the hotel. She watched her husband pull several bills from his pocket and instruct their driver to keep the change before heading for the door. She scurried after him.

She stopped short at the sight that met her in the lobby. Shardul leaned against the countertop on his elbows, speaking softly to the front desk attendant.

He turned, looked about the lobby, and met her gaze. Recognition sparked in his eyes. Slowly, he drew himself up off the counter, like a cobra uncoiling, preparing to strike. He smirked at her, his eyes traveling to her bruised cheek as though admiring his handiwork. He held an unlit cigarette in his hand, which twitched violently. Ignoring the baffled desk attendant staring after him in confusion, he slowly approached the couple. He squared off directly in front of Tom, still smirking at her, hand twitching.

Leslie was paralyzed, a cornered rabbit, transfixed by his gaze. This was how Raveena felt at the zoo, she was sure.

His face gave away nothing save amusement. She remembered his hands between her legs, his mouth hard against hers. Sweat broke out under her arms.

Tom finally broke the silence. "Do you have a message for us?"

Shardul's heretofore unwavering gaze released her and shifted to Tom. She felt no relief. The two men stared, each silently sizing up the other.

"Yes." Shardul finally acknowledged the question.

"Well," Tom prompted. "Is he going to let us have Raveena or not?"

"Why do you want her?" Shardul asked, his hard, dark eyes drifting back to her, drinking her in from head to foot. "Your wife cannot give you a child?"

"That's none of your business," Tom told him.

"Why do you wish to buy a filthy Indian girl? Are you so weak you cannot give your wife a baby?" He rocked his pelvis forward.

"Look," Tom answered through gritted teeth, "I am not going to explain myself to you. Do we have a deal or not?"

"Ten thousand dollars," Shardul said, hand twitching, face impassive.

"Ten thousand?" Tom recoiled, taken aback, she imagined, by the inflated purchase price.

"Ten thousand US dollars," Shardul stipulated.

"That's not—we said three thousand dollars."

"You want the girl? Ten thousand."

Ten thousand dollars? The words landed on her with all the weight of the world. That amount of money was astronomical to them. Unattainable.

"And in exchange, he will sign paperwork giving us guardianship of Raveena?"

Shardul's head wobbled almost imperceptibly. "Tomorrow. One o'clock."

"I can't get my hands on that kind of money by tomorrow."

"Tomorrow," Shardul smirked again. "You come to GB Road. Bring the money. I will have Raveena."

He brushed past her as he sauntered toward the door, leering into her frightened eyes, clearly enjoying the knowledge that he scared her. She watched him ooze out the door. Before he left, he turned, smiled, and waved to her.

CHAPTER 24

*L*eslie and Tom were the only people in the bar. It was early for the dinner crowd. But Tom wanted a beer. And hadn't eaten all day. He nursed his Kingfisher quietly.

"Who does that asshole think he is? I should have kicked his ass! That man…" Apoplectic, he clenched his hands futilely.

She barely heard him, annoyed at her inability to react to Shardul's taunts and insults. She didn't do anything, couldn't say anything while in Shardul's presence. He had screamed at her and hit her, and she cowered in his presence. She understood how these men exercised such complete dominance over the women they bought and used. No wonder none of them "just left," as Tom had put it. If she was so easily controlled by one slap and some groping, how would she feel if she had been drugged, raped repeatedly, starved, held against her will? She shuddered, pushing away her plate of spiced biryani rice that the bartender had ordered for her. Her food grew cold while she racked her brain for a way to get her hands on ten thousand dollars.

"I'm a complete coward," she muttered.

"No, you're not."

"All these years later, and nothing has changed. I just stood there," she answered. "I didn't say anything. Couldn't do anything. Except hide behind you. I kept thinking about him hitting me and touching me, and how scared I was that I would never get away from him." How must Trisha have felt when she was scooped up and carried away from her home? *While I stood by and watched.*

"Son of a bitch." He tossed back the remainder of his beer and turned his attention to the curry in front of him.

"So what are you thinking?" she asked hesitantly.

"I don't know."

"Ten thousand dollars. How are we going to get money like that?"

"I don't know."

"How were you going to get three thousand?"

"I don't know."

"Oh." That was disappointing. She thought he at least had an idea. Something clever up his sleeve.

"I thought I could come up with something. I'm sorry." He forked another bite of curry chicken and rice, refusing to look at her.

"So what are you thinking?"

"Nothing, Leslie. I've got nothing. Can you understand that?" Another bite.

Her heartbeat accelerated. Surely he wasn't giving up so easily? Not after she was so relieved, so excited, so proud of him. "So we're just going to show up tomorrow without the money? See if he'll give us more time?"

"No. We're going to pack and go home."

She spoke the unthinkable. "And just leave her?"

"I don't see anything else we can do at this point."

"But...you must have had an idea. You promised three thousand dollars for her."

"I guess I thought we could call the bank or something. See

about a loan. We can't get ten thousand bucks. Not by tomorrow, for sure. I don't know if they'd loan us that kind of money at all. And over the phone? I wasn't thinking clearly. The marks on the girl—"

"She heard us. She knows we said we would pay her debt and take her away from the brothel."

Fear of failure escalated like panic in her chest as she imagined Raveena waiting for them, waiting for a rescue that never came. Like Trisha. How long did her little sister live after the abduction? Where was she held? For years she struggled with the images her imagination conjured—dark rooms, basements, slimy walls, her sister gagged and blindfolded. She imagined Trisha listening intently for sounds of someone coming to save her. Praying for a rescue.

Which never came.

"I'm sorry, Leslie. We tried."

"No, we didn't. We haven't tried anything."

"It's ten thousand dollars. We don't have it."

"Three thousand dollars was okay, but not ten? How can you make that distinction? How can you put a price on her like that?"

"I didn't!" he snapped, bringing his fist down on the bar. He looked at her, eyes blazing, voice quivering. "I didn't put a price on her. They did. This is not my fault."

"We could get it." She was desperate, almost pleading.

"Please tell me you're not suggesting what I think you're suggesting."

"I don't understand how you can sit there shoveling down curry, knowing that girl is hungry and abused and in real danger of being sold and—"

"Would you stop?" He dropped his fork, pushed away the nearly empty plate.

"What if someone could have saved Trisha, but gave up because they thought it was too much trouble?"

"This isn't the same thing."

"We can get the money. We should."

"It's not that simple. I hate it when you oversimplify things."

"She needs us. We have access to the funds if we want it. All it takes is a phone call. Or an email."

"No."

"It's just sitting there —"

"Stop it!" His whole body shook with fury.

She climbed off the barstool. "I can't believe you can look the other way. You're going to go home and pretend this never happened? Ignore it, like you do everything else you don't like?" She stopped before adding, *the way you've been ignoring me lately.*

"There's nothing we can do. Some things in the world just suck. And there's no magic wand we can wave to fix all the problems. I can't make the assholes keeping that girl give her to us, okay? So stop blaming me."

She pushed away from the counter and stalked away, sandals clacking against the tiled floor. How could he do this? She crossed the lobby to the elevators, punching the up button repeatedly. There had to be a way. No, scratch that. There was a way. Why wouldn't he consider it?

They could help Raveena. He just wouldn't agree to their demands. Sure, ten thousand dollars was a lot. But it was a bargain for the life of a child. How many people paid several times that amount for fertility treatments? How many people drove cars that cost several times that?

She wished he could feel the depth of pain she harbored for her sister. It never left her. Maybe in the morning after he calmed down, she could try again to explain.

Please, God, please. I'm trying to make it right.

In their room, she paced, changing direction only when confronted with an obstacle. Was she willing to defer to him on this? All those times his parents reached out to help them, she allowed him to make the decision. Never complained, never said a word. Always supported him in everything. Now that she asked for something, he refused.

She opened his laptop and pressed the power button, praying he would break his strict one-drink-only rule. Or at least stay in the bar long enough for her to do this.

The computer whirred to life, waking from sleep mode. Clicking the mouse, she discovered what she hoped to find — his Gmail account was open.

Heart pounding, ears straining for the sound of footsteps in the hall, she quickly scrolled through his contacts, then composed an email. Guilt churned her stomach, but still she typed. Finally, she navigated the mouse to the send button. Her conscience screamed at her to stop and think about this. God helps those who help themselves, she answered. She clicked. It was done. She put the computer back in sleep mode and lowered the lid.

The elevator pinged. Footsteps approached. She turned on the television and threw herself into a chair, praying she didn't look as guilty as she felt. This was important. Surely he would understand. Eventually, at least. She hoped.

CHAPTER 25

*L*eslie barely looked at Tom when he stepped through the door, still as hangdog as she left him, and rested a hand on her shoulder. "I'm sorry. I really am. I don't know, I guess we can still try to call the bank. It's early in the morning back home right now with the time difference, so they're not even open yet."

"But you don't think they'll send the money?"

"No, I don't."

She said nothing, just stared at the television, oblivious to what droned from it. Her heart hammered. He wouldn't be happy when he found out what she'd done, but she hoped he would forgive her, even if he couldn't understand. If her idea worked, if she could rescue Raveena, it would be worth it.

He flipped off the television and stood in front of her, arms inviting. "Come here."

She offered her hands and allowed him to pull her out of the chair. He caressed her cheek. "This looks a little better." Soft as a whisper, his lips brushed her bruises. "How's your arm?"

"It doesn't hurt anymore." She stared into his eyes, which

practically glowed with desire. Unexpected, considering his silence during dinner.

Without warning, he lifted her blouse over her head, dropped it on the floor, and kissed the purple splotches on her bare skin. She shivered at the sudden nakedness.

He moved his lips back to her face, hovering over her mouth. "And the swelling is almost gone here." He kissed her puffy lip gently. The sharp tang of beer clung to him. She never liked the sour scent, but tonight it carried her back to the fraternity house and the memory of fingers fumbling with her jeans. She tried to push the thoughts away, but the door wouldn't close.

His kisses lingered, lengthened. He opened his mouth, tongue seeking hers. His hands snaked around her, pulling her close, then moved over her breasts. His tongue traced a line down her neck, raising goose bumps on her flesh. The smell of beer, his warm breath on her neck, and searching hands on her skin intoxicated her.

Warmth throbbed between her legs even as she shivered. She drew her husband closer, pulling his arms about her, pressing her mouth to his, trying to drown out the memories of other bodies entwined with hers.

"You like that?" he murmured.

Excited, possibly more aroused than she'd been in a long time, she wanted someone inside her, feeding her desire. Tom curled his arms around her, sought out her bra clasp. In one flip, it sprang apart. He lowered the straps from her shoulders, tossed it to the floor, pressing his chest against her.

Images of the brothel clouded her mind—filthy rooms, naked bodies, bruised girls, wasted lives. She shook her head and tried to think only of her husband. This was not the frat boy or Shardul. This was Tom. Her husband. Nothing illicit or naughty about sex with her husband. Nothing to feel ashamed about.

Her thoughts galloped out of control, placing her on the

rancid floor of the brothel, one imagined man after another lowering himself on her, touching her, running his tongue and hands over her. She gasped, horrified that her brain could conjure these nightmare images and even worse that they excited her, sent her pulse racing, made her pull her husband toward the bed.

The shame swelled, justified. This was wrong. She shouldn't be turned on by perverse thoughts. *Focus on Tom.*

He laid her on the bed, hovering above her. Pressing his hard groin against her, he grabbed her butt and squeezed. Like Shardul yesterday morning. Her stomach lurched at the thought.

Panic, bubbling at a low simmer, boiled over. She pushed him off, broke away from him. While he stared, bewildered, she grabbed her shirt from the floor and held it over her bare front.

"What's wrong?" he panted.

"Nothing. I'm just not in the mood." Hands shaking, she replaced the bra and wiggled back into her shirt, refusing eye contact. The thought occurred to her that she should try to please him, keep him happy in light of the email she'd sent. Perhaps he would accept her actions better if she satisfied him tonight. But she couldn't bring herself to do it. Not feeling like this.

"It felt like you were in the mood."

"I'm not." Still unsure where to look, she returned to the chair, picked up the television remote, and flipped on the TV, searching for distraction. "Want to watch a movie?"

He snatched the remote from her, punching the power button, silencing the droning noise. "Why are you suddenly shutting me out?"

She shrugged and shook her head. She smoothed her hair but nothing could smooth her rumpled emotions.

"I get it," he continued. "This is about the little girl, isn't it? You're mad about the money, so you let me get all hot and bothered and ready to go and now you're putting on the brakes. I'm trying to be close to you and you keep putting that girl between us. This is shit."

She blanched at the curse word. "That's not—"

"Great. Nice. You put more value on that girl than our marriage."

Unconvinced he cared much about the marriage, she didn't know how to answer. He misunderstood. Would he understand if she finally told him about the rape in college?

But that revelation would lead to another discussion she really didn't want to have. She fingered the bangles on her wrist.

He sat heavily on the edge of the bed, head in his hands. "You know what I was thinking about while I was swimming yesterday, after we argued? I was thinking about our first date. You came swimming with me, remember?"

"Of course." She would never forget, any more than she would forget the first time she saw Raveena.

"You couldn't swim, didn't even want to swim, but you came anyway. Just because you wanted to be with me. You climbed on my back and laughed and laughed while I swam. I wish you would come swimming again and let me carry you through the water like that. You enjoyed being around me then."

"I swim sometimes. I'm just tired of it. I like other things better."

"I'm sorry you've hated our time in India. I thought...I don't know, I guess I thought it would be like that first date—a fresh start. We never had a honeymoon. Your parents hate me, wouldn't pay a dime for the wedding. And I won't take money from my parents. I know you don't agree with that decision, but I wish you'd at least trust me."

She finally met his eyes, now a stormy cataclysm of the emotions churning through him, likely a mirror image of her own.

"I really thought we'd enjoy ourselves here. Six months overseas—that beats the one-week honeymoons most people get. At least that's what I thought. Apparently all I do is make you miserable."

"That's not true." She joined him on the bed, leaned against him, ran a hand up and down his arm.

"Forget it. Not now." He pulled away.

"I wasn't trying to start anything. I just wanted to be close to you."

"I believe it. You never start anything. You make me beg for it."

The words stunned her. Before she could shape her startled thoughts into a coherent reply, he continued.

"I know you don't enjoy sex. You really think I can't tell? All these years, I kept thinking I could do something different, better, I don't know. I mean, I know I was your first, but I always thought you'd start to enjoy it at some point. You've never once initiated sex. This can't all be because of your purity pledge. If you liked me and were attracted to me, you'd want it too."

She blinked at him, jumbled images tumbling through her mind, sifting through memories for something to prove him wrong. Nothing surfaced. She liked being with him. She loved him. But sex made her feel dirty. She'd internalized all the admonitions, all those years of being told she must remain chaste and pure and not let anyone ruin her. Now sex remained taboo in her mind, no matter how much she wanted to change that. How could she explain that to someone who had nothing similar in his past and couldn't understand? He could only infer she was unsatisfied with him. And probably wouldn't believe her.

Tom pulled away from her. "I'm right, aren't I?"

"Please, Tom…"

"So you're disappointed in my work, don't enjoy being around me, don't enjoy sex with me, and, oh yeah, are more interested in a little Indian girl than me. Why are we together?"

"That's not—"

"Don't worry. I'll never touch you again. You can take another purity pledge as far as I'm concerned." He stood up, but the room offered no refuge.

She followed, plucking at his sleeve, frustrated with his misinterpretation of everything. "It's not like that. I do like being with you. I can't...it's hard to...I wish you could understand."

"Oh, I understand just fine. You're upset about that Indian girl and you don't want to be with me anymore. So I don't get any. Well, guess what? Guys have needs."

His words hurt like a slap across the face. "Guys have needs? So do women. We need to feel appreciated and loved in return. We need a little quality time out of your day. Do you have any idea how insulting it is to be ignored all day and then have you crawl in bed and start pawing me, demanding sex? And then you're mad that I don't enjoy it?"

"And now we're getting down to the real problem. You are mad and punishing me by withholding sex. I knew it."

"No, that's not it at all. You still misunderstand. I'm just saying I'm not the only one who has some room for improvement. Maybe you can try coming home earlier occasionally. We can spend some time together."

"I have to work, Leslie. I can't change that."

"Except sometimes you're not at work when you claim to be. And you won't tell me where you go."

He glared at her. "Don't henpeck me. I'm a grown man."

"With a secret he doesn't want me to know about. This is really starting to worry me. Is it another woman? Are you having an affair?"

"What if I am? What do you care? You don't want me. You just said so."

"I said no such thing." She could barely get the words out.

She couldn't breathe. He couldn't have hurt her any worse if he'd punched her in the gut. "I can't believe, after everything we've been through, everything I've done for you, you'd throw it all away over sex."

"I'm not throwing anything away. And I never said I'm having an affair. I just don't see why you should care if you don't want me."

"You never denied an affair. And won't say what you're doing. So something isn't right."

"And what do you mean, everything you've done for me? What have you ever done for me?"

"I supported you. Always. You wouldn't be where you are today if it wasn't for me."

"Oh, please. Sure, getting married right out of college helped so much."

"That was your idea. You proposed.'

"Because you were pregnant," he snarled. "And I always keep my promises."

"But you didn't change your mind after—All these years, I thought you really loved me. I thought we were building something together. But all you're interested in is sex."

"Quit being melodramatic."

"I can't be around you right now." She slid her shoes on and pushed past him to the door.

He grabbed her arm. "Where are you going?"

She shook free. "What do you care?"

She slammed the door behind her.

CHAPTER 26

*L*eslie went straight to Rhea in the jewelry shop. Where else could she go? The closest thing she had to a friend right now, the Indian woman's buoyant personality drew her.

"Have you come for jewelry, chai, or both?" Rhea asked with that dazzling smile.

Leslie didn't hesitate as she slumped into a chair. "Both."

While Rhea bustled away for the milk-and-spice tea, Leslie leaned her head back and took deep breaths, twisting the snug bangles around her wrist.

She needed to think clearly. No good would come of assumptions, heated words, and rash decisions. But if he was having an affair, could she forgive him? Could any resolution other than divorce possibly result from this? Was she willing to go through with that?

Divorce. Wouldn't her mother gloat? The words "I told you so" might not ever pass her mother's lips, but Leslie knew the glow of being right would burn in the woman's eyes.

Ten years. Wasted.

Did Tom realize ten years had passed? Their tenth anniversary had gone by unnoticed. Not by her. She'd planned a romantic evening for them. She hurried home that afternoon after seeing all the children safely delivered to their parents. She stopped on the way to pick up a bottle of red wine, selecting one she'd seen Tom choose before, and debating whether or not to join him and drink her first full glass of wine.

She'd planned dinner to include all his favorites: baked tilapia, rice pilaf, and garlic green beans, served by candlelight. A cheesecake had chilled in the refrigerator for dessert. A romantic film waited on the entertainment system.

He'd promised to be home by six when she asked that morning as casually as she could manage when to expect him for dinner. She wanted to surprise him. He worked so hard lately, staying later more and more frequently, always with the promise their time was coming. The words sounded less credible the more he said them.

Ten years together was an accomplishment, and she was disappointed Tom hadn't mentioned anything special for this anniversary—at least not that she knew about. He hadn't mentioned reservations or told her not to plan anything for dinner, but he could be keeping a secret like she was. As she pulled the tilapia from the refrigerator, she smiled at the thought of his face if he walked in expecting to sweep her off to dinner only to discover the lights low, candles burning, and wine chilling in the fridge.

His parents had offered to send them on a cruise. After hearing their message on the machine, daydreams of lounging on a sunny deck and white sand beaches cluttered her thoughts, but Tom adamantly declined. Why did he have to be so stubborn? So they didn't need a cruise. Time together was something they had too little of these days. Work stress combined with her monthly struggle to make their income cover the bills frayed her nerves.

Monthly issues. That was more stress she didn't want to think about. The general lab work from her annual checkup with her gynecologist—mostly to renew the birth control prescription she grew to resent—flagged her hormone levels low. Her doctor wanted to run more tests to determine if she was premenopausal. "Your childbearing years may be drawing to a close. Nothing to worry about just yet, especially since you don't want children. But you could be experiencing premature menopause. And we may need to supplement your estrogen to protect your bones."

She seasoned the fish and turned on the oven. As she spread and smoothed the tablecloth and centered the candles, she wondered if she could just stop taking birth control. If her body was infertile, what was the point? And why did she feel so sad? How odd to think she'd been actively prohibiting pregnancy all these years, and now that it wasn't necessary, now that she no longer needed to remember to take that little pill every night, she suddenly wanted the option. All those years the thought of pregnancy brought only memories of sobbing desperation. Now that the choice was gone, she felt a different type of desperation.

Maybe she did want children.

She hadn't told Tom, and she hadn't gone back for the additional blood work. Some part of her wasn't ready to have that choice taken away.

The table was missing something, she decided as she studied her work. Inspiration carried her to the mantle, where she took down the silver-framed wedding photo. A thick layer of dust fuzzed the top edge. A cobweb drooped from the corner. The picture sat on the mantle, familiar and taken for granted. She wiped the photo carefully before settling it on the table to oversee their anniversary dinner.

Tom's eyes stared out of the picture, her own gaze firmly set on her new husband. They looked so young, so excited, so ready. Ten years sounded like a lot but had passed by in a flash. Projects, goals, bills...so many things took their attention. Hard to imagine, but the first group of children she'd taught after finishing her degree would be eighteen years old now. She tried to picture them as young adults—graduating high school, driving cars, working starter jobs, and leaving for college. That was the age she'd been when she first met Tom. It didn't seem possible.

Her mother's tight smile and acerbic graciousness the day she took her vows impressed even her. Without frowning once or saying a single negative word, her mother managed to convey deep disapproval of the wedding in general and Tom in particular. That was the only time both sets of parents were together with their children. Tom's father drank quite a bit of champagne—further galling her mother, who thought the reception should be dry—and grew more boisterous as the night progressed.

Her mother had called earlier that day, wishing her happy anniversary in her bright, chirpy voice. "How *are* things?" she'd asked, pretending to delight in her daughter's report that everything was just fine. "Do you remember that sweet boy from the church? Darren? He's your age." Of course, Leslie remembered him—her mother had thought he was perfect for her and tried to push the two together. How many times had she urged her daughter to talk to him after service? "I ran into him after church Sunday. He's in town visiting. So successful. He always was such a charming boy! Would you believe he's never married?"

Leslie heard the unspoken questions beneath her mother's feigned pleasure. Somehow, she thought her mother would prefer to hear that her husband was the abusive, alcoholic, philanderer she'd long predicted he'd turn out to be. That was what her mother cared about—being right.

Just as she'd cracked the oven door to check the fish, squinting at the surge of heat that rolled up into her face, the phone had rung.

"Hey," Tom's low voice greeted her when she picked it up. She could tell by his tone he was about to say something she wouldn't like. "I'm really sorry. I know I said six, but I'm up to my elbows right now. I'll be late tonight."

"Oh." She waited a moment, expecting a punch line. He said nothing. "How late?"

"Gosh, I don't even know. Maybe eight or nine."

It had to be a joke. Even if he wasn't planning anything for their anniversary, surely he wouldn't work late.

"What about—I—I'm cooking dinner."

"Yeah. Sorry. Just put my plate in the fridge. I'll heat it up when I get home. I gotta go."

She heard the click as he hung up his line and stared in disbelief at the phone in her hand.

He hadn't even remembered their tenth anniversary.

She'd placed the phone in its cradle and walked slowly back to the stove where the green beans had hissed at her, sizzling in the pan. *How* are *things*? Her mother's question had echoed in her mind as she turned off the heat and packed the food in leftover containers, wiping away embarrassed tears that burned her cheeks.

Her stomach churned a rock that night as she'd put everything away, hiding her humiliation that she had been so excited to prepare a surprise for someone who had other matters in mind.

She grappled with that humiliation all over again, magnified by the knowledge he probably hadn't worked late that night. He'd most likely spent their tenth anniversary with another woman.

How are *things*?

Rhea returned with chai and pressed a cup into her hands.

"There we go." The woman brushed a hand across her puffy lip. "Feeling better?"

"Yes. And no." Her bruises were better, but a new wound gaped—this one on her heart.

She sipped her tea and hazarded a glance at Rhea's eyes.

The happiness in them combined with the dark brown color that exactly matched Raveena's sent Leslie over the edge.

Tears flowed from her eyes, dissolving the false, forced smile. Setting her tea to the side, she hid her face in her hands and gulped back the sobs wracking her frame.

"I'm sorry. I'm so sorry," she choked as Rhea placed a hand in her shoulder. "I'm okay. Really. I'm fine."

"I can see you are not okay. But that is okay." Rhea held her chai in front of her. "Drink."

Hands shaking, Leslie accepted the cup and sipped quietly. "I think my husband might be having an affair." She blurted the words without thought.

Rhea's brow furrowed. Whether in sympathy or disgust or confusion, she wasn't sure.

"I can't believe I just said that. I'm so sorry. I'm a complete mess. I should go. I don't know why I told you that."

She stood to leave, but Rhea grabbed her arm. "Sit down, please. You need to talk to someone. That is why it came spilling out. Just drink your tea. And breathe."

Who else could she confide in? Even back home, this wasn't something she would discuss with anyone.

"You have had a long day," Rhea said. "Relax for a moment."

Leslie took a deep breath.

"Now," Rhea said a few sips and deep breaths later. "Do you merely suspect your husband of infidelity? Or are you certain?"

"I'm not certain. And he hasn't admitted it. But several times when he told me he was working late, the department secretary called the house looking for him. She told me he left early, saying he was going home. The last time she called and I said he wasn't home, she just said, 'Never mind' and hung up. I don't think I'm the only one who's suspicious."

She deteriorated into tears again.

"Hmm." Rhea stroked her hair. "It is rather discouraging."

Leslie sniffed, gathering her composure around her like a tattered gown. "For the first time in my life, I'm starting to think maybe I made a mistake. Maybe I should've listened to my mom."

"Because her decisions are always correct?"

"Well, no."

"Because you normally allow her to make the important decisions in your life?'

"Definitely not. Not since I was old enough to move out on my own. But I've been screwing up ever since." A fresh wave of tears broke free, reducing her to a blubbering mess.

"I do not believe that is true." Rhea patted her back. "You are focused on the mistakes now. But that does not mean they are the sum total. You have forgotten the good things."

Rhea lifted her chin and dried her tears with a tissue.

"But it's true. Ever since I left for college—"

Rhea clucked at her. "I do not wish to hear this list of mistakes you think you have made. We are going to talk about the good things you have done."

"But I haven't—"

Rhea clucked again. "I will start. You saw an endangered girl and brought her to eat and spent the day trying to help her."

"But I didn't rescue her. I failed again."

"Gazala does not rescue every woman she attempts to free. Maninder and I do not rescue all the children we try to help. Does that make the attempts mistakes? Or mean we failed?"

Leslie sniffed and drew in a deep, quivering breath.

"Now tell me what you do back home."

"I'm a teacher."

"Then you are doing good things every day. And I am sure you spend your own money on things the children need."

Leslie nodded, wiping a sleeve across her face. "Sometimes."

"We are alike, the two of us. No children of our own, but

helping many children. And supporting our husbands in their work. You came all this way to be with your husband while he works."

"I've always supported him. I pay the bills while he works on his degree. But he doesn't seem to appreciate it at all."

"I am sure he does. You both have seen a lot of stress today. I am glad you came to see me. I think you both needed a break. Things will look better in the morning after a good night's sleep. It is late. Time to close the shop. And you should return to your husband and prepare for bed."

Leslie remembered the email she sent and squirmed. Tomorrow would probably be another stressful day, regardless of how well they slept tonight.

CHAPTER 27

The smell of coffee woke Leslie. The wispy scent crept in and wrapped around the first threads of awareness, grabbing hold and luring her back to consciousness. Breathing deeply, she luxuriated in a satisfying stretch. It was a rare night she was able to sleep without dreams—and, even worse, nightmares. She reached for Tom, but he wasn't in bed.

She sat up. He was at the table in front of his computer, his back to her. A breakfast tray sat beside him, apparently untouched. Her stomach growled as she tried to see what he'd ordered.

Then she saw the computer screen. His email was open.

A chill shivered down her spine.

Immediately she sat taller, trying to read over his shoulder from across the room. Was there a reply to her email yet? She couldn't judge by his posture.

"You're up early," she said, trying to gain his attention.

"Sleep okay?" He sounded normal. She couldn't detect any undercurrent of suspicion.

"I did. Very well."

"I ordered breakfast. Got you some coffee. Then I checked my email."

Her stomach stopped growling and clenched into a fist. All thoughts of food were pushed away. The hotel room felt ten degrees colder. His voice remained calm and even, but something was off. He still didn't turn around to look at her.

She pulled the sheet tightly around her.

"What—was there—"

"Do you think I'm stupid?"

"No."

"Are you trying to punish me?"

"No."

"Then what is this?" He gestured to the computer.

"Is it from your dad?"

"You did this, didn't you?"

"For Raveena. We can't leave her in a brothel."

"Helping her won't bring your sister back."

She sucked in her breath. "No, but it's still the right thing to do," she whispered. "I wish you felt the same way."

"And since I don't, you went behind my back? I can't believe this. You've walked right into his hands. Just wouldn't believe me. He won't just give us the money."

"He didn't send it?"

"Oh, he sent it. Right away—before we could change our minds. This is exactly what he's been waiting for."

She couldn't understand what he was so upset about. "What is? What did he say?"

His voice took on a hard, sarcastic edge as he read. "'Dear Tommy—So good to hear from you. Of course I'll send the money. I don't even care what sort of trouble you've gotten yourself into that costs you ten grand to get out of. Just like your old man! I'm looking forward to seeing you soon. Go ahead and book flights for yourself and lovely Leslie for the holidays. While you're out here, we can discuss your future with the company. If you're not ready to let go of your crazy idea that you want to be a professor, I'll ask around, see what I can get for you closer to home. Until you're ready to transition into a leadership position with me.' And then he has the wire confirmation information." He stared at her, his blue eyes full of disappointment and sorrow.

"I'm sorry. I didn't realize…"

"You didn't trust me. And I don't understand that. When you were pregnant, did I run?"

"Of course not." She wanted to go to him, wrap her arms around him, and try again to explain why it was so important she rescue this little girl. But she didn't move. His voice nailed her to the bed.

"I told you I'd always take care of you. I held you while you cried. Have I ever failed you?"

"No."

He stood, knocking the chair backward. "Hell, maybe that's why you cried so hard at the clinic when you had a miscarriage. Not because you lost the baby, but because you thought I'd run. You'd never get your hands on the money."

The clinic. The campus health services clinic. They didn't know where else to go when she began cramping and bleeding. She remembered his face, watching helplessly as she doubled over, moaning, arms across her abdomen.

In the exam room, she sat in a paper robe on a cold table, her tiny new engagement ring glittering accusingly in the harsh light, waiting for a doctor, sure she was suffering for her sins, further punishment for her faults. The doctor—blessedly female—examined her and declared she had "lost the pregnancy" and mistook her tears of utter relief for grief, assuring them they could "always try again, maybe in a few years after college."

That which the Good Lord giveth, he also taketh away. She bled away the proof of the rape and her lie. And she was glad. Though Tom had proposed, neither of them knew what they would do with a baby, how they would finish college with no support from their parents.

Granted a clean slate, she determined Tom would never

know what she'd done, never know she'd lied to him. Of course, she'd worried he wouldn't want her anymore, once the baby was out of the picture, but he didn't call it off. The money didn't cross her mind. She was just so happy he stayed, that he didn't end the engagement. The thought he truly loved her was almost more than she could bear. If only she'd known what a huge burden the secret would become — the constant knowledge that he trusted her and she'd deceived him. And she'd rejoiced in the death of another human being.

"How could you even think that?" She fought to blink back the tears threatening to spill down her cheeks. She didn't want him to see her cry.

"What am I supposed to do now?" He bent down in front of her. "Everything I've worked for, you just swept away with one email."

"We can send the money back. I'm sorry. Send it back. Or tell him no. It's your money."

"It's not that easy," he yelled, startling her. "You opened a door I closed a long time ago. Handed him the one gift he always wanted — my failure."

"You haven't failed. I'll tell him it was me."

"But you found a problem I couldn't solve and went to him." He grabbed her arms and shook her, squeezing until she felt each of his fingernails digging into her flesh. The bruises Shardul had left screamed in pain.

He'd never laid a hand on her, rarely raised his voice to her. There was something ugly in his eyes, a smoldering fire she'd never seen before.

She stared up at him, her head snapping back and forth, teeth rattling.

"You're hurting me," she whimpered, tears leaking down her cheeks.

He released her as if she burned him and stared at his hands like he didn't know whose they were. She sat down hard on the bed. One of the glass bangles on her wrist broke, clattering to the floor.

"I'm sorry," he whispered. He pressed his palms to his eyes and shook his head. "I told you — money makes people crazy."

Silence. She didn't know what to say.

"I have the bank confirmation number for the wired money." He sounded like a deflated balloon — empty, withered. "We'll go get the girl. I told her I'd get her out of there, and I always keep my promises. You can do whatever you feel is best for her. It's your decision who you want in your life — Raveena or me."

CHAPTER 28

*L*eslie wiped the sweat from her brow. The midday sun beat down on the taxi. Though GB Road bustled with afternoon commerce, silence roared inside the vehicle. Prajit watched her and Tom nervously in the rearview mirror, glancing from one to the other, like a child watching helplessly as mom and dad argued.

She glanced at Tom, wanting forgiveness, longing for peace, not sure how to achieve either. His clenched jaw and knitted brow told her to stay quiet. Would he really throw away ten years together and their future? She thought if she handed him a divorce decree right now, he would gladly sign it.

The day of her miscarriage, when relief flooded through her, she truly believed that nothing in her future could equal the embarrassment and shame she felt draining away. But here she was again, faced with a difficult choice, wanting to make the right decision. How did anyone ever know what right really meant?

And what was she willing to sacrifice for Raveena?

The brothel was quiet. All the curtains were drawn, the windows like the closed eyes of a sleeping monster—a monster that gobbled up women and children and fed them to the god Desire.

Her mother's dire warnings of a fiery inferno—eternal damnation—paled beside the life to which fate damned Raveena and others like her. The life of a sex slave meant stolen freedom, never-ending clients, groping, pawing, starvation, abuse, and helplessness. It wasn't life at all. It was hell.

She prayed for strength and success...and forgiveness. Because in that moment, staring up at Raveena's window praying for a glimpse of the girl, trying and failing to imagine coming home to an empty house or apartment, she knew she would do anything to drag Raveena out of her shadowy existence. This little girl wasn't falling through the cracks into the waiting hands of a monster.

And if Tom couldn't understand that...

A growling car engine caught her attention. It sounded like the car that frightened the women in the brothel the day she ventured inside and unwittingly began this entire ordeal.

"What did his car look like?" Tom asked, finally breaking the silence.

"I don't remember. I didn't get a good look." She'd been too scared, focused only on Prajit's taxi in her flight from the brothel, to pay attention to the other car. "It was a dark color and a sports car, I think." *Please don't stop loving me*, she wanted to add.

"This looks like it matches that description."

Prajit craned his neck, watching the approaching vehicle, eyes wide with anxiety.

The sleek, glossy, black car pulled to the curb on the other side of the street and stopped.

Tom, sullen all morning, whistled his appreciation. "That's an Audi. I don't recognize that model, though."

"R-Eight," Prajit said.

The luxury car with its sweeping lines rode low to the ground on a wide chassis, sides flared out. The headlights scowled perpetually, matching the angry growl of the revving motor. The driver killed the engine, but even silent this vehicle screamed muscle car for a muscle man.

The window lowered. Shardul. He took a drag from his always-present cigarette. Smoke curled indolently from his mouth. Lowering his sunglasses, he locked eyes on her as they stepped out into the street.

His dark eyes bored into her. Her pulse raced. Her hands shook uncontrollably and while she had been sweating just a few minutes ago, her blood now felt like ice. He smirked at her and her stomach dropped. Struggling to gain control, she broke eye contact with him, searching the car for any sign of Raveena.

The R8 sported only two doors and no back seat. The little girl was not beside the driver. So where was she? Had they decided against the deal?

Shardul opened his door and stepped out onto the side-walk, facing them squarely, raking his eyes up and down her as he puffed on his cigarette. He tossed the smoldering remnant into the street and smiled widely.

Prajit mumbled to himself, and though she could not understand a word he said, she was pretty sure she agreed with him. From the corner of her eye, she was certain she saw movement at the windows of the brothel and knew the women inside watched, eager for Raveena's escape, glad to witness the transaction. One of their own was about to evade their captors' grasp. Perhaps it would give them hope.

Escape. Not exactly true. Escape implied breaking free and running away. Raveena was about to be bought. She couldn't hedge around it or gloss over it—she was buying a child. As she stood there in the quiet afternoon, she knew this was the right thing to do. Yet, she felt dirty, like she was part of a drug deal in a dark alley.

"You have the money?" Shardul asked, reminding her even more of a drug deal.

"Where is Raveena?" Tom asked.

Show us the goods. Her mouth went dry. She couldn't talk even if she wanted to.

"Money first," Shardul said in his smooth, self-assured tone. His arrogance was maddening.

Tom laughed. "No way. You were supposed to bring the girl."

"She is here."

"I don't see her." *No goods, no money.*

Shardul stared them down before he stepped backward, black eyes piercing her as he moved. He opened the car door and flipped the driver's seat forward, revealing Raveena crouched in the cramped space behind it.

At the sight of them, the girl brightened and sat up straighter. Tears threatened, stinging Leslie's eyes. She blinked them back and returned Raveena's wide smile.

"She is here," Shardul repeated, gesturing to the child.

And you have her smashed in the nonexistent backseat, she thought.

"Money," he breathed greedily, his eyes searching for cash as hungrily as they had sought a glimpse of Raveena.

Tom peered over both shoulders before reaching into his jacket pocket to extrude the bank envelope that held the thick stack of hundred-dollar bills.

"Open it," Shardul instructed, one hand creeping down to block Raveena, who appeared ready to bolt to her side.

Tom rolled his eyes but lifted the flap and stretched the sides of the envelope to reveal the contents. "Okay?" he asked, gingerly fanning out the bills.

"Bring it." Shardul waved him over. Tom started to make the exchange. "Wait." He raised a hand. He turned his dark eyes on her and sneered. "Send her."

Every nerve in her body tensed. *No more, please.*

Tom glanced at her, his eyes that knew her so well recognizing the cornered-rabbit fear thumping in her chest.

"No way." Tom spoke firmly, shaking his head. "It's all here. I'll bring it to you and let you count it right here in the street."

"No." Shardul's eyes danced as he answered.

"I'm not sending her over to you. Do you want the money or not?" He held it in front of him, a matador trying to interest a bull in his red fabric.

Raveena, so excited before, now looked stricken.

"You want Raveena?" Shardul replied, stepping aside and gesturing to her.

"Auntie!"

"This is ridiculous," Tom said. "Just let me bring it to you."

"She can bring."

"No. Absolutely not."

Shardul shrugged, pushed the seat back into place, and started to get back into the car.

"Auntie!" Raveena cried from the back seat, eyes wild.

The girl's frightened voice reached inside her hammering chest, wrapping around her heart, the gentle tendrils stabilizing the chaos. "No." Leslie's voice returned. "Give me the money." She reached to take it.

"And send you over to the man who attacked you? Not happening."

"We don't have a choice."

"We always have a choice. I don't like the choices you're making, but that doesn't mean I'm going to let someone hurt you."

"Then you must understand why I really don't have a choice. I can't let him hurt Raveena anymore."

"We could stand our ground and tell him no."

"And if he drives away? If he takes Raveena from us again? I don't think I could handle that. Not after we came so close to getting her. I'll take it to him. I don't care."

"And if he hits you or shoves you into the car? I know I can't handle that."

These were the same possible outcomes her imagination currently played out for her. She refused to let it change her mind.

Tom's blue eyes pleaded with her. The emptiness that pervaded them all morning was gone, replaced by concern.

"I believe God sent me here to rescue this girl. My mom always said, 'We are the words and hands of Jesus in the world.' I think I finally understand what that means. I'm here to help her."

"Now you're quoting your mom?" Tom stared up at the sky then shook his head in frustration. "I don't like it," he reiterated.

"I can't leave her again. I can't lose another child. Not when I can do something about it. I watched a man carry my sister away and did nothing. I'll never forgive myself if I let it happen to Raveena."

Finally, Tom nodded his agreement. He turned to Shardul. "Let Raveena out of the car first."

This time Shardul hesitated.

"Let her out or forget it. We'll take the money and leave."

Shardul tipped the seat forward and spoke rapidly at her.

Raveena clambered out of the vehicle, nearly tripping in her haste. The girl's terror was surely mirrored in her own face. Leslie tried to give Raveena a reassuring smile, hoping she appeared more confident than she was.

Tom handed her the envelope. He closed his hands around hers, started to say something, then shook his head. She opened her mouth but couldn't form the words. Maybe what she was feeling couldn't be expressed in something as ordinary as words. Ten thousand dollars. And possibly the end of their marriage. She wasn't fool enough to believe his protective nature indicated forgiveness. If she had to choose between them, how could she?

Time slowed as she approached Shardul, who shifted from

foot to foot. His hands fidgeted. He lit another cigarette and pulled long drag after drag as he watched her.

"Hey!" Tom yelled from where he waited by the taxi.

The sharp sound startled her, nervous energy flooding through her like a jolt of electricity. She stood motionless, afraid to turn and look, scared of what could be happening behind her.

"Don't forget the documents. We asked for paperwork giving us guardianship."

A moment lapsed before the meaning of his words was clear to her — no emergency, just documents.

"The papers," Tom repeated when Shardul did not respond to the request. "Documents?"

The man merely looked confused, shook his head, and shrugged. He was either truly baffled or was the best actor she'd ever seen.

She didn't dare turn her back on Raveena. But handing over the money and taking her without the documents would be foolish. Now what?

Prajit's voice called out from behind her. He spoke to Shardul in words she could not understand but must have conveyed Tom's message. Shardul nodded, leaned into the car, and removed an envelope from the glove compartment. He held it up for the Americans to see.

"Okay?" he asked.

"Okay," Tom answered.

Once again, Prajit had come to their rescue.

Raveena, still focused exclusively on her, tried to step around Shardul. He grabbed her arm roughly and yanked her back.

Leslie longed to tell him off, put him in his place. Why didn't she just collect the shaking child in her arms, soothing her and protecting her from any further mistreatment? Ashamed of her weakness, she stood helplessly as Shardul separated them.

He took a long drag from his cigarette, exhaling a cloud of acrid smoke while he looked her up and down. Her skin crawled, remembering his hands all over her.

"Give me money," he encouraged when she made no move to do so, his voice soft and silky.

She wasn't fooled. Get Raveena first.

She shook her head. He puffed on his cigarette and scowled.

"You want her?" He gestured at Raveena, his dark eyes glowering.

She nodded.

"Let her have Raveena," Tom called from the other side of the street. "Then she'll give you the money."

"Money first," Shardul growled.

"No way," Tom argued. "Don't do it, Leslie. If he won't release her, bring the money back."

Shardul's smooth, clean-shaven upper lip curled into a scarred snarl. The cornered dog showed them some fang, but he still had the advantage. Because he still had Raveena.

He took another deep pull on his cigarette, admired the smoldering remnant as he exhaled the smoke, then flicked it into the street, where it joined the other detritus accumulating there.

He relaxed his tense stance and held up his hands as if to surrender. "Okay. I give you these papers." He gestured to the envelope. "Then you give me money. Then I give you Raveena." He stepped aside, allowing a clear path between the girl and the woman.

There she was, so close, small and disheveled, the same dirty, threadbare outfit hanging from her thin, undernourished frame.

Shardul twitched again, watching for her answer. His hand kept drifting up to his breast pocket. She could see the outline of his cigarette pack there and suspected he really wanted another one. The smile and cordial behavior was a very thin mask and undoubtedly difficult for him to maintain.

"Okay," she finally answered.

"Be careful, Leslie," Tom cautioned.

Shardul glared at him then forced his smile back into place for her benefit.

"Okay." He held the envelope of documents in his right hand. The fingers of his left hand quivered spastically, as if playing a demanding concerto on an invisible piano.

His broad shoulders and lanky frame towered over her before she even registered he was moving. The stale stench of cigarette smoke pervaded his clothing and skin. Her stomach clenched at the musky sweat and heavy cologne she now associated with being slapped and groped.

He bent low to her neck but didn't quite touch her. She thought she heard Tom and Prajit talking, but she was unable to understand what was being said. She was too distracted by Shardul, only aware of his breath, his nearness.

He lingered, seeming to enjoy her fear and Tom's indignant cries.

"You smell good," he whispered heavily in her ear. "Fresh and clean."

She stood there, waiting for this to end. Was this how the women in the brothels felt every night? No more fear, no resentment, no fight—no life—just a void of nothing, waiting for it all to end.

"Hey! Back off!" Tom's voice finally broke through her clouded mind, bringing her back from the void. Relief coursed through her limbs. She longed to escape to the safety of his side, the warmth of his comfort. If he would offer any. Maybe he thought she deserved this. Maybe she did after going behind his back.

Smirking, Shardul stepped away. She could breathe again.

As if he could see she was regaining some sense of self, he

raised a hand to her cheek, stroking the bruises he had inflicted on her. "Does it still hurt?"

"Auntie!"

"Hey!" Tom called again. His voice was louder. He must have started toward them.

Shardul's eyes flicked over her shoulder. "Stay there. Or no Raveena."

Her stomach lurched as she leaned away from his touch. "Please, just do what he says," she called over her shoulder.

Shardul retracted his hand, sneered at her, and handed her the envelope.

She stood for a moment, recovering. Her stomach quivered, her hands shook. Handing over so much of Tom's money was more difficult than she anticipated. She swallowed hard and gathered every bit of strength she had left within her. For Raveena, she could do this.

She held the envelope out to him, but he didn't take it immediately. Leering at her, he stared her down contemptuously and left her standing with her arm suspended.

"What's the problem?" Tom called.

"No problem," Shardul whispered. He moved closer, invading her space but not quite touching her.

She wanted to run from him but was unable to break his gaze. Beads of sweat broke out on her temples. Why didn't he take the money?

His gleaming eyes never left her even as he jerked the money from her hand.

This was why he had insisted she bring it. He wanted to subjugate and humiliate her again. The ten thousand dollars wasn't quite enough — he wanted control too.

As soon as the envelope left her hand, she scooted hastily backward several feet, out of reach.

Shardul peered inside the paper packet. The delight on his face at the sight of the money irritated her.

He spoke to Raveena, who stared up at him expectantly. At his words, the girl lit up.

In a grand gesture, he bowed low, his arm sweeping out to tell Raveena she could go.

She squatted down and held her arms wide to welcome the precious girl. Raveena beamed at her.

The girl only made it three steps. Shardul's arm caught her about the waist and scooped her off the ground.

Raveena struggled and cried out. Shardul clamped his hand over her mouth. The girl stared, eyes pleading for help.

It was happening again.

Leslie froze in place, just as she had twenty years ago. Raveena kicked her legs, writhing in his arms.

Not again, don't let it happen again. Her feet responded, and she raced to snatch Raveena from him.

Shardul was too quick for her. He stuffed the girl into the back of his car like a wadded up blanket.

"You have the money," Tom yelled. "Let her go!" He dashed toward them.

Shardul whirled around as she tried to push past him. All she saw was Raveena's hand, reaching out, so close, just out of reach. He grabbed her, spun her around to face her approaching husband, and pinned her against his own body. Something glinted in his free hand. A knife, she realized.

He pressed it against her neck.

Tom skidded to a halt, hands in the air. He shook his head.

Holding her across the chest, Shardul clutched her body against his own, one hand fondling her breast. He rolled his hips against her and pressed his face into her hair. Stomach lurching, she struggled to free herself.

"Let go of her!" Tom shouted. He started toward them again, face contorted.

Shardul brought the knife to her cheek, the sharp metal biting into her skin. She cried out as the warm blood trickled down her face. She couldn't move, could scarcely breathe.

Tom pulled up short again and took a few steps back, hands in front of him.

The hand on her breast crept slowly down. He caressed her stomach as she held perfectly still, knife back at her throat. She closed her eyes and gritted her teeth.

His hand edged beneath her blouse, the rough fingers sliding over her bare skin. He found her waistband, groping fingers sliding easily down her skirt. She whimpered and thought she might be sick.

"You son of a bitch!" Tom yelled. "You have the money! Let go of my wife and give us the little girl!"

Shardul retracted his hand from her skirt and shoved her forward. She sprawled onto the street, knees and palms scraping against the asphalt. Pieces of shattered bangle scattered into the street.

She jumped to her feet, dimly aware of Tom running and Prajit yelling, but only concerned about Raveena, still just a few feet away.

Tom raced forward, but Shardul slid deftly into the driver's seat of the R8 and popped the ignition. He revved the engine, threw the car into gear, and with one last merciless grin, slammed the door and sped away.

She watched him escape, wind tugging at the hem of her skirt. The last image she saw, indelibly seared into her mind, was Raveena's terrified face in the back window, her little hands pressed against the glass, as she silently cried out one word: "Auntie!"

CHAPTER 29

*L*eslie stared at the disappearing vehicle, all her hope vanishing with it. Her feet refused to respond to the commands blaring through her mind—to run, to move, to do something. If only she possessed a superpower—strength or speed or the ability to clap her hands together and destroy evil—she could tear after him, issuing justice. But she didn't. She had no special powers or abilities. Her life felt like a long series of failures and disappointments. And God never gave her the chance to make up for past mistakes.

Her mother would say God created obstacles to test her. And that she still had a chance at success. But she couldn't bring herself to believe that. And then a new thought took shape. Maybe God wanted her to lose Tom. Maybe God wanted to punish her for her deception. And for turning her back on Him.

Be careful what you wish for.

No second chance—just more of the same. Unable to bear her weight, her legs crumpled beneath her, dropping her painfully to the exposed flesh of her raw knees.

Pounding footsteps brought Tom at her side. "Come on," he panted, hoisting her to her feet.

He dragged her back to the taxi. She struggled to place one foot in front of the other, wondering why God took away her sister, why He wouldn't let her help Raveena, why men used women without a second thought to the rotting sickness it left in their souls.

Prajit sat in the driver's seat of the taxi, the engine already running as he waited for the Americans. He hung out the open window, banging his hand against the side of the old car, urging them to hurry. "Lady! Come!" He beckoned her forward impatiently.

Sanjana and Tarla stood in front of the wide-open brothel door, their faces stricken as they clung to each other for comfort. Some of the other girls hovered at the windows, peeking around tattered curtains. A few had even ventured out onto the balconies. They stared down into the street, silent witnesses. Sanjana slowly shook her head and seemed on the verge of tears. Tarla, on the other hand, looked furious. The angry scowl on her face silently screamed, "Go get her!"

Tom scrambled to open the taxi door, fumbling with the silver latch, first unable to get a good grip then yanking repeatedly before succeeding in opening it. He pushed her in, clambering after her.

"Go, go, go!" he yelled to Prajit the moment he was inside the taxi. Their driver had the car in gear and took off before he managed to close the door.

God works in mysterious ways. Yes, very. She wanted to hear her mother explain this one. How could He allow tragedies like this to happen? This should have been a simple exchange, the money for the girl. *Jesus loves the little children...*

The song skipped through her mind, memories of vacation bible school bubbling up with it. Do the right thing, God will reward you. Stray from the path, God will burn you in hell. So why wasn't Shardul roasting? Why did her sister's kidnapper elude authorities? Where was the justice?

Chasing after the R8 struck her as ludicrous, but she held

her tongue as the taxi puttered along as fast as Prajit could coax it.

Tom remained silent beside her. She couldn't bring herself to look at him, unable to face the accusation she knew would roll off his tongue in tidal waves. Would he be able to forgive her for the loss of so much money?

Her skin crawled remembering where Shardul's hands had touched her. She shuddered, wrapping her arms around herself, warding off the phantom touch. She couldn't think about that now.

In the distance, she caught sight of the tail end of the glossy black R8. She sat forward. Maybe this wasn't over yet. Remembering the choked streets surrounding the train station, she latched onto the hope that they still had a chance of catching him. She pictured herself throwing open the door of the black car and pulling Raveena to safety. How many times had she replayed her sister's abduction? Over and over again, she saw the man stuff her into his car and drive away, nothing stopping him from destroying her family. Over the years, her mental movies morphed as she thought of ways she could have stopped him, dozens of reactions all resulting in the same outcome—she saved her sister. She was praised by her parents, lauded a hero. If only...

If Shardul outran them to the huge traffic circle, his options were endless. The convoluted jumble of streets that spider-webbed across the city would offer him innumerable hiding places. He undoubtedly knew the back alleys and escape routes well.

The R8 took a hard turn to the right. Prajit mumbled to himself, shaking his head. He dragged his sleeve across his forehead, mopping the nervous sweat collecting there.

"We're going to lose them." She broke the strained silence that had settled over the taxi for the second time that day.

"I'm pretty sure that's what he wants," Tom replied.

She glanced at him, startled by his harsh voice, the voice of the angry man who shook her fiercely this morning. His scowling brow knitted above dark eyes.

Prajit stomped the gas pedal to the floor. The overworked engine clattered and groaned. Even full throttle, the engine increased their speed only negligibly.

Peering anxiously through the windshield, she leaned forward, gripping the front seat, as if she could will the car to move faster.

Prajit slowed slightly and glanced only perfunctorily to verify that there were no approaching vehicles before he took the turn much too fast. She was thrown against Tom. His warm skin burned as if fire blazed through him. He didn't catch her or console her. She never feared her husband in all their years together, but today the look in his eyes—fixed forward, following their prey—terrified her. She sensed the raw anger coursing through his veins.

The taxi was in no shape for a chase and complained bitterly, creaking loudly, shuddering, threatening to come apart. DB GUPTA ROAD, the street sign read.

She righted herself and scooted away from Tom.

Prajit attempted to coax more speed out of his reluctant taxi.

The R8 turned sharply to the left—she imagined she heard the tires squealing as it rounded the turn. They lost sight of the car as it sped away. The taxi followed, puttering along after him.

Shardul's slick sports car stuck out amid the trucks, rickshaws, and dented vehicles sharing the road with him this afternoon, making him easy to spot. The traffic congealed in front of the entrance to the train station. Shardul could not advance.

"There!" she exclaimed, pointing excitedly.

Prajit nodded.

"He knows," Tom snapped. He was more volatile than she'd ever seen him.

The R8 was in the farthest lane from the train station, unsuccessfully attempting to avoid the clotted traffic. Though slowed, Shardul still managed to nose through the mess. He would leave them behind long before they caught up.

The car in front of them turned, leaving a gaping hole in traffic into which the car beside them quickly lunged.

Prajit wasted no time. He floored it and turned sharply, cutting off the other car. That driver honked long and loud, gesticulating wildly. Prajit stuck his arm out the window and waved him off, easing the taxi into the space.

The slow progress was maddening. They seemed to pull no closer to Shardul.

Where would he go, if he managed to lose them? Back to the brothel? Surely he would expect them to look for Raveena there. Maybe he considered them so woefully out of their league that he simply didn't care. He had just proven them completely unequipped to grapple with the likes of him. *Stay where you belong.* This was what Officer Verma warned her against. She didn't belong in the shadows.

She pictured Raveena huddled in the back of the R8, bewildered, upset. Snatched away like Trisha. Was Raveena watching them? Could she see them following? Was the girl young enough to still harbor hope? Or was she already resigned to her fate as Tarla claimed to be? She imagined Raveena weeping silently, shaking in fear as she had at the zoo, when she clung to her and pleaded for help. *Help me, Auntie.*

She grabbed the handle and threw her shoulder against the door, tumbling out into the street. She only glanced at Tom, glad to see she'd startled him. The angry man she didn't recognize as her husband scrambled after her.

"Get back in here!" he insisted. "You cannot keep putting yourself into dangerous situations like this." Closing her ears against his complaints, she slammed the door shut.

She threaded her way through the creeping traffic, ignoring indignant yells and catcalls. Hunkered down, she approached the R8. She caught a glimpse of Raveena crouched in the back. She hoped the girl knew she would never give up. She reached out her hand and could almost reach the passenger door.

A hand grabbed her arm roughly and spun her round.

"What are you doing?" Tom demanded. "That guy is a psycho. Come back to the taxi."

The R8 revved noisily, jerking forward and backward like a horse eager to run.

"Help me get Raveena!" She wriggled out of his grasp. "He's stuck in traffic…"

Her hand closed on the handle. She pulled. It was locked. Desperate, she slapped her palm against the window. Another bangle broke. "Give her to me!" she yelled at the man on the other side of the glass. She smacked the glass again and again until her skinned hand burned and her blood smudged the window.

Tom grappled with her. "Leslie, have you lost your mind?"

The wheels of the car jerked sharply. The R8 bucked backwards. Tom grabbed her, pulling her to safety. Shardul backed up as much as he could manage without crunching the car behind him. The driver laid on his horn.

He gunned the engine and hopped the curb onto the sidewalk, scattering shoppers and knocking over a fruit cart. Drivers, bicyclists, and pedestrians shouted at the crazy man driving his sumptuous car down the sidewalk.

Ignoring the protests, he crept along the sidewalk, passing the tangled snarl of traffic. Easing the R8 back into the street, he jumped ahead of an oncoming truck and took off with another squeal of his tires.

Tom's fingers dug into her arm, restraining her as though concerned she might take off after him again.

"What the hell were you thinking?" Tom asked her after they climbed back into the still-creeping taxi.

"I was thinking that if he got away we would probably never see Raveena again."

"You have to stop behaving like this."

"I couldn't sit still and do nothing."

"Now he's even farther ahead of us. You spooked him into driving on the sidewalk." She said nothing. Because she knew he was right. "I didn't want you to take the money to him in the first place. And you walked right into it. Put yourself completely at his mercy. I feel like your brain turns off every time you get near that girl."

"Were we just going to leave? Keep the money and go? Abandon her to that horrible man? He knew we wouldn't do that."

"He knew *you* wouldn't do that! So now he still has her. You didn't accomplish anything other than to hand over ten *fucking* thousand dollars to that son of a bitch."

"You agreed to it." Guilt bubbled up like a toxic ooze. "Buying her was your idea, not mine. What would you have done differently?"

"What would be different? I wouldn't have seen that man with his hands all over you." His voice caught in his throat. "I watched him...touch you...like...like one of those whores." He turned away.

"They are not whores. Don't call them that."

"Men paw them and—"

"And abuse them. It's not their fault. Do not blame those women for the atrocities—"

"Can you imagine how I felt?"

"How you felt? Are you seriously acting like this affected you?"

"He held you at knifepoint, ran his hands...all over your body. I couldn't do anything."

"That's how the women feel—powerless. They can't fight back."

214 | LARA BERNHARDT

"I couldn't stop him. Do you have any idea how I feel every time that man hurts you?"

"The same way I feel every time he takes Raveena from me."

"No, no fight now," Prajit interjected. "Raveena." He gestured ahead, trying to redirect their attention. He had navigated them out of the clogged traffic.

She stared out the window, trying not to cry. Tears filled her eyes. Her attempts to blink them back were unsuccessful. She rubbed her cheeks angrily with the back of her hand to hide the wet trails left there.

She ached at the thought that Raveena would slip through her fingers and back into the clutches of men who would allow her to be raped for their profit. They would delight in her suffering as they gleefully raked in money. No one deserved that.

Prajit picked up speed. She peered frantically into every street, alley, and parking area they passed, desperate to catch a glimpse of that expensive car purchased with money made off enslaved women.

Minutes passed. No sign of them anywhere. *Come on. Where did you go?*

"He could be anywhere," Tom said.

She ignored him. He just wanted her to give up, let him go back to life as usual.

The taxi approached the outer edge of the big traffic circle. Streets fed into it like the spokes of a wheel. Had Shardul made it this far? Worse yet, had he already sped along ahead of them and left the circle far behind? If so, he could be anywhere. Their chances looked grim.

"There! There!" Prajit cried. Somehow while negotiating the chaotic traffic around them, he had managed to catch a glimpse of the R8 in the street ahead.

A scooter zipped past, weaving between lanes of congested

traffic. Auto rickshaws chugged along, maneuvering between the larger vehicles, spewing black exhaust into the air.

Prajit muttered again. The taxi driver squeezed his vehicle into a tight space to get them into the flow of traffic traveling around the wide circle, like blood pumping through a clogged artery. He slammed on the brakes to avoid a lumbering truck that cut in front of him. She lurched forward. Tom reached out a protective hand to catch her, but retracted it almost as soon as he touched her. He crossed his arms over his chest and scowled out the window.

An auto rickshaw riding too close to their bumper beeped at the sudden stop. The driver pulled sideways and cruised past them between lanes of swirling, swerving vehicles, the engine buzzing like an angry bee.

They watched as the R8 left the traffic circle and the suffocating traffic behind, exiting onto Barakhamba. Prajit followed.

Barakhamba, a wide, tree-lined stretch of road with two lanes in each direction, seemed empty compared to the chaos of the traffic circle. Shardul gunned the R8's engine, putting space between them at an alarming rate. She gritted her teeth, silently begging for a miracle. *If not for me, for Raveena.*

The distance between the two cars increased. Still they followed diligently, refusing to give up even as the cause looked more and more hopeless. Shardul swung quickly through another traffic circle, the taxi chuffing along after. He continued around halfway, passing numerous streets, then exited onto Copernicus Marg. She knew this street—they had come down it to see a monument shortly after they first arrived in New Delhi.

They would never catch him now.

"Wait a minute..." Tom shifted, sat up straighter, and looked as if he'd been hit upside the head. "What's wrong with us? We should just go to the police."

"The police? Again? They were so much help before." She shook her head.

"This time they have to help us. We have the documents. You have the envelope with the guardianship papers. If we can't get the money back, we can at least force him to keep his part of the bargain."

The documents. She retrieved the crinkled, smudged envelope from the floorboard near her feet, where it had fallen sometime in their earlier scramble. Perhaps, as Tom thought, the police would be obligated to help them now. Shivering at the memory of Shardul tormenting her during the exchange, she lifted the triangular flap and extracted the piece of paper inside.

He took the paper from her hands and unfolded it.

It was blank.

She blinked, confused, and peered back into the envelope. Nothing more awaited discovery. She'd been duped, she realized. Why hadn't she opened the envelope and looked? Why on Earth had she trusted Shardul to uphold his end of the bargain? He'd distracted her with his lecherous behavior. But then again, she should have seen something like this coming. Another failure on her part.

"I'll be damned," Tom muttered. "He did it. Took us completely." With a growl, he crumpled the paper between his hands, wadding it into a ball. Prajit watched his employer with a concerned expression.

The previous hope of success, buoyed by the belief that God offered her a second chance, sank quickly, drowning in harsh reality. She watched the R8 barrel down Copernicus Marg.

Shardul changed lanes. A large truck obscured their view. The truck turned, but the R8 did not reappear. She stared anxiously, watching for any sign of the black car. Nothing.

A painful realization pricked at her, even as she attempted

to ignore the obvious, trying to believe they still had a chance. *You aren't getting her back — he won.*

God is not on your side.

Copernicus Marg dumped them into another traffic circle, a squashed hexagon surrounding a park and monument. India Gate loomed above them, a monument inspired by the Arch de Triomphe.

The taxi continued around the entire circuit of the hexagonal traffic circle. The R8 was nowhere to be seen. Shardul had finally succeeded in outrunning them, in addition to outsmarting them.

"He must have come this way…" She trailed off, unable to finish the sentence. Even she could hear the flimsiness and recognized how unconvincing the argument was. He was gone.

Another failure. And why should she succeed? She didn't want the baby He gave her. Why should He give her this one?

CHAPTER 30

*T*he what-ifs reared on hind legs, demanding Leslie's attention while Prajit navigated traffic. What if she hadn't gone behind Tom's back and lost his money? What if she hadn't insisted on visiting the zoo? What if she'd stayed home instead of coming to India in the first place? What if she'd never met Raveena?

She tugged each distinct thread that wove together the fabric of her existence, testing the tenacity, trying to imagine removing any one of them—or all of them—if that possibility were available to her. Raveena, Tom, the rape, the miscarriage, her lies—all distinct colors, weaving together her life.

The brightest thread of all was Trisha—her thread wound throughout the entire warp and woof. Though Trisha had disappeared from her life, her remnant remained, producing the loudest what-if of all: *What if it was me instead of her?*

Beside her, Tom picked at his fingernails, teeth clenched. She'd seen a stranger peering at her from his eyes. She wondered if he grappled with what-ifs too. For him, there was probably only one: What if he'd never married her?

Could he snip her thread, unravel her completely from his life, knit it back together, and go on as though she'd never existed in it? As if the two of them never twined together? Watching him, she realized she didn't want to do that. If she clipped his thread, she would unravel and be left with nothing but a jumbled mess and no idea how to weave it back together.

The problem was, now she had a new thread—the vibrant baby pink Raveena introduced. It didn't stretch back as far as Trisha's, but it would continue forever. How could she knit them all together? Or would she be forced to let one go?

When Tom spoke, she jumped. "When the yelling was more than I could take, I used to sneak out the back door and ride my bike aimlessly around town, trying to forget my dad's drunken screams and my mom's pitiful whimpering. The first time I rode all the way to the beach, I broke rule number one —don't ever cross Pacific Highway. I knew I'd get in trouble but I didn't care. I parked my bike, yanked off my shoes, and sat in the sand, the crash of the surf drowning out their blasted bickering. I didn't want to leave. I trembled all the way home, knowing I was about to get in trouble."

He seemed to lose himself in the past. She was afraid to say anything, scared to provoke him. She waited for him to continue on his own. Sometimes silence was deafening.

"Funny thing was, nothing happened. I walked in, shaking in my boots, waiting for the yelling to turn on me. Hell, if my dad was drunk enough, he might've knocked me around a little too. The house was silent, which scared me more than the yelling. At least when they were yelling you knew where they were and what they were mad about. I brushed off every speck of sand, but for nothing. They never noticed I was gone."

She thought about her own youth—actions dictated, activities supervised, friends scrutinized. If she'd ever disappeared for hours on end, she was certain the police would have been at her house upon her return. She'd come to resent her mother's clinging watchfulness. Listening to the pain in Tom's voice, she realized absence was worse than hovering. At least she'd known her mother cared, even if she was suffocating.

Raveena crept into her thoughts. What if she adopted the girl and took her home? What would she do the first time Raveena wanted to go to a movie or to the mall with friends without her? The panic that sent her heart pounding startled her. She imagined men like Shardul lurking in dark recesses, waiting for the opportunity to lure Raveena away, to snatch her from the people who loved her.

So this was how her mother felt all those years.

"After that, I went to the beach whenever I wanted. I started wearing my trunks, sure that my wet suit would give me away. I think at that point I hoped they would figure out what I was doing. Nope. I just tossed the trunks into the washer when I got home, and our housekeeper never said a word. She was probably too afraid of them to say anything, if she even cared. I loved the beach—the warm sand, the rocking waves. I learned how to body surf—it was like flying. I'd stare out at the ocean, all that possibility stretching off into the horizon. I started thinking about my parents' house—sterile, spotless. It wasn't a home. A home has smudges and clutter, scuffs and dust. Homes should be hugs and laughter and vanilla, someone making your favorite foods, and…"

He glanced at her, searching for something in her face. She saw his eyes drop to her cheek. He blanched at the red wound and turned away again. She wasn't sure where this conversation was going. She wasn't sure she wanted to know. He was so serious, sharing more than normal. This sounded like the type of conversation that ended with "We did our best, but it wasn't enough."

"I started imagining the home I would have when I was older," he continued. "I wanted a home near the beach so my kids could run and play and hear the ocean all the time. It would be a home, not a house, with their growth charts penciled on the walls and drawings on the refrigerator. And I wouldn't get upset about the sand, either. I imagined sweeping and sweeping and never getting rid of all the grit underfoot. I would teach them to swim in the sea."

He'd never mentioned any of this before. His dreams of a happy home filled with children mirrored her own. But neither of them ever shared with the other. She was afraid to talk about it, because he'd been so vehemently opposed. He'd been very clear: no children.

"You won't turn into him. I know you won't."

"I used to believe that." He stared out the window.

"We could still have that happy home." She reached for him, grabbed his hand, the drying blood on hers tacky. "You're nothing like him."

He turned to her suddenly, his eyes blazing. "He laughed when I told him about the baby." He peeled his hand from hers, the sticky blood holding fast, refusing to let go without a fight. Clenching his fists, holding tight to something she couldn't see, he stared down at her blood smudged on his hands.

"What baby? Our baby? You never told me you—"

"I called to tell him about you, about the baby on the way. And he laughed. Said he knew I'd be back as soon as I got myself into trouble." His voice shifted as he mimicked his father's. "'How long did you last? Six months?'" Eyes squeezed tight against the memory, he breathed evenly. She suspected he was fighting tears. "Trouble. That's what he called you and his grandchild. Of course, he was thrilled about getting his way, getting me to work with him after all. Damned drunken bastard. I swallowed all the things I wanted to tell him and just thought about that dream I had when I was younger. Maybe we could have that little house on the beach."

Was this his way of telling her he might consider adopting? Her heart beat faster. Was he unbolting the door he'd closed? If he once wanted children, why couldn't he again?

"We still can. I know we can make it work."

"Then you had a miscarriage."

She'd never thought about the impact the lost child made on Tom. She assumed he was simply relieved, as she'd been. They got to stay in college, grow up slowly, pursue his career goals. It never occurred to her that he mourned the loss. Of course, he didn't know the origin of the pregnancy.

"It felt like a message, like the universe telling me that I wasn't meant to have kids. How could I be a good dad when he's the only example I've had?"

"Oh, Tom…" Her voice caught in her throat, a lump cutting off her air. Everything was wrong. She was like Midas who ruined everything he touched. She never meant to hurt anyone, least of all her husband. She had to release him from that pain, even if it meant losing him forever.

She thought she'd experienced every emotion in the rainbow. She knew the hue of them all, refracted through her heart, knew the taste in the back of her throat as they clawed at her chest searching for escape. The terror of Trisha's abduction, the anguish when Trisha never returned, the humiliation of rape, the embarrassment when it left her pregnant, the joy she experienced as a teacher watching children learn and grow, the fear that she disappointed everyone—her parents, her husband, God. She knew how every last one of these flavored her tears.

Today she tasted remorse, bitter and metallic, like the bite of a wishing penny or the blood that seeped from a wound. She closed her eyes and prayed. *Please, God, don't let me fail again.* She opened a musty compartment in her heart and released the moldy secret hidden away there.

"The baby wasn't yours."

CHAPTER 31

Tom didn't speak a word. He sat still, pale, chest heaving, eyes bouncing, seeking something solid upon which to rest. In the ensuing silence, her pulse pounded in her ears. The look on Tom's face told her the damage was irreparable. The disbelief in his eyes left her wondering if there weren't times when the truth was better left hidden.

The truth will set you free. For her, this verse conjured images of caged birds diving through an unhinged door, winging into the sky, soaring. It did not describe how she felt now that she had finally released the truth. Instead of exhilarating freedom or the relief of unloading a heavy burden, the words left destruction in their wake and a nasty taste in her mouth.

Prajit seemed to realize something had shifted between them. Of course, he couldn't possibly fathom the canyon she'd rent between the two of them. She saw concern in his eyes when he parked the taxi in front of the hotel and hurried to open her door. He looked eager to do something to make it better. Nothing would fix this, though. Nothing could undo the past. If only he knew. What would he think of her?

Tom trailed behind her, distracted, like someone walking through a fog.

Rhea called to them across the lobby. "Namaste." The woman held her palms together at her chest.

Leslie swam out of the haze suffocating her, disoriented. "What?"

"Namaste," Rhea repeated. Were her steepled hands an invocation to prayer? How could she explain she was never praying again? That God didn't listen to her, and she only made a mess of things? "How a proper Indian woman greets others."

The woman's smile shone like a beacon until she stepped closer and noticed Leslie's fresh wounds. "Oh, my. What has happened now?"

"Well, we..." Leslie turned to Tom, only to discover him staring back toward the hotel exit. Was he contemplating a run for it? Completely abandoning her? He may be physically present, but mentally he was nowhere near her.

Rhea made a dismissive sound Leslie was sure she couldn't replicate if she tried and ushered her toward the jewelry shop. She forced her smile back into place. "Come in, come in! I will get tea."

Tom finally spoke, his first words since she'd dropped the bomb on him. "We've had a rough day—"

Rhea cut him off with her clucking sound again. "Yes, I can see. We need to help your wife." She ushered them both into her shop, guiding them to seats. "Sit down."

Tom tried to protest, mumbling something about needing some time alone. Rhea was gone. She'd disappeared behind the counter into a back room, presumably for the tea. He stared down at his hands, patting them together, clasping them tightly.

He didn't seem inclined to talk to her. But then, what had she expected? She wanted to explain she never meant to hurt or upset him or make him feel like a fool. The choice she made as a desperate eighteen-year-old completely in love with him seemed right at the time, but she knew how terribly wrong it sounded now. "Tom…"

"You said I was your first," he whispered, staring into his lap.

She was caught off-guard. She expected accusations and name-calling, yelling, fury. Not the quiet, quivering whimper of hollow desolation that echoed disappointment. "I…I know."

"But there was someone else? You were…dating someone else?"

"No, how could you even think that?"

He jerked at her sharp response, turned to face her. "Then…" His eyes searched hers, pleading with her for something to bandage the wound she'd inflicted on him.

"Here we are." Rhea trundled back through the door, carrying a tray that she set on the small table before them. She placed a cup of tea in front of each guest and settled into a chair beside her. She shook hands with Tom. "So nice to meet you. Now tell Rhea what has happened. Madam, you look as if you have lost something precious. Something worth fighting for." Rhea lifted a warm, damp cloth from the tray and draped it around her hand, gently working away the dark crimson smudges.

Precious. Yes, that was the problem. She'd lost too many precious things. Trisha, Raveena, her husband's trust. They took little pieces of her with them, eroding, leaving her hollow. Empty. Leslie looked to Tom as Rhea moved to her other hand. Being wiped off and cared for like a child embarrassed her.

"The…" He cleared his throat. "The organization you mentioned…"

"Protect Our Women?"

"They couldn't help us. With the little girl."

Rhea's eyes scanned them both. She thought she saw understanding dawn in the woman's eyes as she pressed the cloth to her cheek.

"Here. Hold it tight."

Leslie peered into one of the many mirrors balanced on the counters and hung on the walls, intended for women to admire their contemplated purchases and decide what they couldn't live without. Lowering the cloth, she inspected not a draping line of silver links about her neck but a bright red line oozing blood from her cheek. Only a scratch, she realized, just a hint at what Shardul could inflict on her. The blade could have sunk deeper and left a gaping raw gash. Something that would have required medical attention, stitches even.

He still had Raveena. What pain was he inflicting on her?

"Madam, who has hurt you?" Rhea asked.

"We tried to pay Raveena's debt," Leslie admitted, knowing this was not an officially acceptable solution. What would Rhea think of her now? Was she any different from the traffickers? She'd tried to buy a child.

Rhea's eyes travelled over her injuries again, as if seeing them in a different light. "But I see you do not have the girl."

Leslie shook her head, feeling foolish. Why had she thought, for even a moment, that she could help anyone? She'd actually imagined Raveena sitting on the plane beside her, flying to a new life, every day a new discovery, a new adventure. She lowered the cloth, pink-tinged, and wilted in her chair. How many times did she have to fail before she accepted that she would never be allowed to make amends for her mistakes?

Tom spoke when she remained silent. "The guy took the girl and our money and ran. We couldn't catch him. He hurt Leslie. Again."

"Perhaps you should seek help from the police."

"We tried that," Tom said. "They don't help. Said she shouldn't have been there in the first place."

"Surely he will return her to the brothel where you first found her. You can go there to retrieve her."

"She still won't be ours. They didn't give us documents for

guardianship." He lifted his cup of tea but seemed to forget about it halfway to his mouth.

"Besides," Leslie added, "Shardul might hurt the women there if we do anything. It's hopeless. We did everything we could."

"Madam, nothing is ever hopeless. If something is worth fighting for, you must never stop fighting." The woman looked back and forth between the two. She thought perhaps she meant more than Raveena. "Look at my husband—for so many years he searches for his sister. He has not yet found her, but he will never stop looking."

Leslie picked up her teacup, breathing deeply of the cinnamon and clove perfume before sipping the milky sweetness. She closed her eyes. "It tastes just like Sanjana's," she murmured.

A hand gripped her arm tightly. She opened her eyes to find Rhea staring at her with wide eyes, fingers trembling as she clutched her wrist.

"What did you say?" Rhea asked.

"Sanjana, one of the women in the brothel, made tea for me. It tasted just like this."

"It is the spice mixture my husband learned from his mother. This was at the brothel where you found the girl? You could lead me to it?"

"Yes, but he won't give us the girl."

Rhea reached into a pocket and extracted a cell phone, releasing her wrist. "Please, excuse me just a moment." The woman disappeared again into the back room.

In the empty silence, Leslie wanted to ask Tom what he thought that was about, wanted to fall against his familiar chest and succumb to the fatigue and weariness that pulled at her aching limbs like a leviathan dragging her to the drowning deep. She wanted to tell him she was sorry, that she would give anything to be able to go back in time and change the past. It wasn't possible any more than it was possible to know what her future might be.

"So...who was...the father?" Tom stared at his hands as if expecting the reply from them. "The guy you weren't dating."

Words rose up in her throat, words she'd never spoken before to anyone, not even to herself in the dark of night while weeping uncontrollably. She found she didn't know how to say them, couldn't dislodge them from her vocal cords. Guilt sunk its vicious fingers into them and held fast with its heavy weight. She cleared her throat and took a deep breath.

"I was raped." The words tumbled off her tongue, an avalanche, leaving her icy in their wake. She didn't look at him, afraid of the disgust she would see in his eyes. "A guy at a party gave me a drink with something in it." She broke off, unable to divulge anything more. She didn't want to hear her own conscience echoed in Tom's words and prayed he wouldn't ask why she was at a party like that anyway.

She was falling, tumbling into a trap of her own creation, nothing to grab to halt her descent. Maybe she would go back to the brothel, steal Raveena away. What did she have left to lose? She imagined herself in Sunita's place, alone, no hope brightening her future—until Raveena changed that.

Tom must consider her on par with the women in the brothel—and didn't they, in fact, share common abuse at the hands of men? She remembered Sanjana speaking of girls drugged with opium to subdue them. Wasn't that just what happened to her? She'd been drugged and raped. Just the once, and not repeatedly, as the brothel women were, but it was the same. The thought sickened her.

Why should she feel ashamed? She was guilty only of trust. *You shouldn't have been there. You should have known better. You should have left and not followed him to his room.* Blaming herself was like blaming the girls in the brothel for their treatment, when they were helpless and abused. Why wasn't she disgusted with the guy who administered the drug and forced himself on her? All these years, she still blamed herself.

She remembered how effortlessly Sanjana and Tarla shared their experiences. Was it easier to talk to another woman? Or was the casual discussion indicative that rape had become a normal part of their lives? They discussed it as though talking about what they might cook for dinner. *This is our fate.*

"Was that...before us?"

"Before I even met you."

"And you're telling me now?"

Rhea returned, beaming, cheeks pink. "So sorry. I have phoned my husband. Will you please join us for dinner tonight?"

"I..." Leslie wasn't sure what to say. Tom wouldn't look at her. She suspected he might never speak to her again.

"How about six o'clock? At Taj Palace? We will see you there." Rhea patted her hand before turning her attention to another customer entering the shop. She hurried to his side. "Hello, sir. What are you shopping for today?"

Leslie slowly rose from the chair, drained, disappointed, trying not to imagine what would happen to Raveena next. And what she had just done to her marriage.

CHAPTER 32

eslie slumped beside Tom, plodding toward the restaurant to meet Rhea and her husband. She threw glances at him, and, despite all his balled up anger and frustrations, he reminded her of a little boy she'd encountered at the elementary school once, years ago.

She'd met the boy during recess, when she should have been eating lunch in private, away from the children. That day, though, all the duty assistants had called in unavailable due to illness and personal issues. The children could not go unsupervised, so the principal asked that one teacher from each grade volunteer. She agreed to take the four third-grade classes.

While the other kids tore around the playground, this one little boy stood quietly by her side. He wasn't in her class. She didn't know his name. But she recognized his round face and knew he tended to keep to himself. She thought he was shy.

"I'm writing a story," he finally said.

"Are you? About what?"

"About living on Mars."

"I'd like to read that."

"I write it in my room when my dad screams at my mom."

She felt as though a bucket of ice water had been dumped

on her head. She opened her mouth but seemed unable to form words.

"She's going to have a baby," the boy continued. "I wish he wouldn't hurt her."

She didn't know how to respond. When she looked down at him, she imagined Tom, who by then had shared that his father abused his mother.

"My mom and I were going to run away, but now she's going to have another baby."

Why, she wondered, was he telling her? Was it easier to tell someone you didn't know?

"Sometimes he gets mad at me too. I wish I had a space-ship. I would take my mom to Mars."

He stared down at the ground, tracing lines in the dirt with his worn shoe.

That was when she noticed his arm. "What happened here?" she asked, pointing to a bruise.

"I made too much noise while my dad was watching TV. I'm glad it was his favorite show cuz he only hit me once so he could watch the rest. Cigarettes are the worst." He raised his other arm to show her a red, blistered circle in his flesh.

How did no one see this and realize what was happening? Or did they all look away, not sure what to do? She placed a hand on his back, wishing she could scoop him up into a hug and hide him somewhere safe.

"My mom says if he hits me again, we'll run away to grandma's house. But she said that before."

Another child ran up to her. "Teacher, I'm hungry. Is it time for lunch yet?"

Glancing at her watch, she discovered they were five minutes late. She blew the shrill whistle around her neck, wishing it could drown out the words she'd just heard.

At the end of the day, heavy with the weight of what the boy told her, she went to the school counselor, who helped her write an incident report. Anyone who worked with children was required to report abuse allegations. This felt like a betrayal of trust, but the counselor quickly assured her the boy was probably hoping for help.

Leslie wished she could have given him a spaceship instead.

Today, Tom looked like he needed a spaceship. Leslie forced herself to smile at the restaurant maître d.

"Welcome to Taj Palace," he said, greeting her.

His youthful face seemed out of place above the starched, stiff, traditional costume—formal jacket buttoned tightly up the front and headdress perched firmly on his dark hair.

The rapid approach of clacking high heels preceded Rhea, out of breath but smiling.

The maître d greeted her. "Good evening, Auntie."

"Manish, we would like a table for four, please. Something quiet." She pressed a handful of rupees into his hand. "And Uncle will be joining us shortly. Will you kindly show him to our table when he arrives?"

"Of course, Auntie. This way."

"You know him? Is he actually your nephew?" Leslie asked quietly as he walked ahead of them, leading the way. "Or does he call you Auntie like Raveena calls me Auntie?"

"He is one of the orphans we helped," Rhea answered, her clacking heels quieted by carpets covering the restaurant floor.

Tom followed behind the women, his hair damp from the hours he spent in the pool. He'd spoken very little when he came back to the room to dress for dinner. Safe comments about what he should wear and how nice she looked and why in the world did Rhea invite them to dinner with her husband —things you might say to a total stranger.

They helped him avoid the huge issues too large and new to grapple with.

A mural of the Taj Mahal covered one entire wall. Maharajas atop elephants, leading large parties on hunting expeditions, scowled down at her as if they knew she did not belong in their country. Candles flickered on the tables, and the light grew dimmer as they moved further away from the entrance. Sconces hung on the walls, scattered between the tables, a soft glow emanating from each to envelop the tables in welcoming warmth.

Their young host stopped at a large table. "Is this table to your liking, Auntie?"

"It is perfect, Manish. Thank you." Rhea slid into the seat he withdrew. He hustled around the table and pulled Leslie's seat back for her as well.

"Madam, please." He gestured as he spoke, gazing at her with a fervor that approached pleading. As she lowered herself into the seat, he moved it forward with perfect timing. Assured repeatedly of her satisfaction, he finally nodded. "Your waiter will be here shortly, and I will bring Uncle." He turned on his heel and hurried to the front to await the next guests.

"You met that boy at the orphanage?"

"Yes," Rhea replied. "He had a very difficult start to life. He was rescued from a carpet maker. The conditions were deplorable. The boys were starving, abused, filthy." Rhea shuddered.

Their waiter approached, served tea, and left menus, promising to return when their party was complete.

She blew on her hot tea. After an afternoon of silence, company and conversation felt like a crocheted blanket draped around her shoulders. At the school, her hours were filled with schedules and lessons, bells and whistles, giggles and chatter. Even quiet time was filled with whispers, the scratching of pencils or crayons, scissors clattering to the ground. She'd had enough silent, empty days in Pantnagar to last a lifetime. "How did you find him? How were you able to rescue him?" *And why can't I do the same for Raveena?*

"We did not find him ourselves. My husband and I were already volunteering at the orphanage. One day, we heard the manager discussing a rescue attempt—a carpet factory was holding boys as slaves. She said another villager had called the police to tip them off about it. The police were afraid to act on the tip—the owner was a wealthy, powerful man they did not wish to cross."

"Like the brothels. The police don't want to anger the owners."

"Yes, that is it exactly. I am sure bribes exchanged hands. I believe a local NGO applied pressure until the police finally stormed the building. The poor boys were terrified. They had no idea what was happening and tried to run and hide. The police grabbed as many as they could and loaded them into the van. The owner's thugs arrived before they had all of them, and the police sped away with the boys they had grabbed. Many of the boys were rescued, but those who fled into the streets were likely recaptured or returned willingly to the factory later."

"Why did they run?" Tom broke his silence. "Why were they scared? They were being rescued."

"Yes, but the rescue happened so quickly. It had to—the boys are rarely alone. They had been so badly mistreated, they had no reason to trust adults." She paused, staring down into her teacup. Her eyes misted over. She was far away, revisiting a time long past. "My husband and I were at the orphanage when the van arrived with the boys. We had previously agreed to be there to help orient them. It is quite traumatic on children." She shook her head, struggling with the memory. "They were so scared. We brought them inside. We were smiling, trying to help them see we were going to help them and not hurt them. They were emaciated, every one of them, so thin we could see their bones. So timid, so frightened. And covered in filth. Some of them were bruised and burned. One small boy wept. I asked him his name, but he would not speak. He just stared at me, eyes full of terror." She paused again, composing herself.

"Food helped." She smiled at that memory. "Those hungry little boys were allowed, no, encouraged, to eat as much as they liked. We gave them new clothes, let them wash, showed them bedrooms. My husband and I continued volunteering, helping with the care of the boys. Very slowly, over several weeks, they came to trust us. They suffered horribly, but we began to see signs of recovery. They began to play and attend classes with the other children in the orphanage. Once we knew their names, we searched for their parents. A few of the older boys remembered the names of their villages—we were able to return them to their homes quickly. Others did not remember, and we had to search very hard for their families. Some of the boys had been plucked from the streets—they had no parents and remained at the orphanage, hoping for adoption. The little one, the little weeping one who would not tell me his name that first day—that was Manish."

"The young man working here now? But he's so bright and happy. I never would have guessed."

"Many of us hide our scars. No one wants to be defined by the pain they have suffered." Rhea stared pointedly at her.

Leslie flushed. Who would have guessed that she'd watched her sister's abduction? That she'd been raped? That she'd lied to her husband? Didn't she try to forget these things?

"How long ago was this?"

"Ten years now. He told us his name but did not know the name of his village or where he was from. He was so young. We think he had maybe six or seven years then. He said a man took him away and made him to make carpets but that was as much as we learned. It was all he knew."

"How do you track down their families?" Tom asked. "Do the police have records of missing children?"

"No. It is so difficult. These men who steal children prey upon the most remote, impoverished villages. In a village without clean water or schools, you can imagine how difficult it would be to even report such atrocities. They have no computers, much less internet. Sometimes the parents do not even realize they have been lied to, duped out of their child. In those cases, they have no idea their child is being brutalized and starved. So heartbreaking."

"Did you find his parents?"

"No, we never did. We visited him often in the orphanage, assisted as much as we could. We even drove him around a few times in the hopes he would recognize something. Those drives are fond memories for us now. We would take him to lunch, and my husband would always buy him ice cream. We came to care for him so much. We watched his grades, bought his school supplies, made sure he had new clothes. He adjusted very well. And oh, how he ate! One day I came to visit him and realized his face was full and round, his eyes were bright. He was no longer that scared, starving little boy. That day, he smiled when he saw me, hugged me, and called me Auntie for the first time. I fell completely in love with him. No one had adopted him yet, and I realized I wanted to adopt him myself."

It seemed so easy. Why couldn't Leslie help Raveena the same way? Why would no one see, as she did, that her predicament was just as horrible? Why was she written off as a brothel baby?

"My husband of course felt the same. We both wanted Manish to join our family. We had not been able to have children of our own, and we adored Manish. We still do. Such a sweet boy. But he did not wish to be adopted."

"Why not?" Leslie tried to imagine how she would feel if she freed Raveena, offered to adopt her, and the girl rejected her.

"He missed his family so much. We tried to find them, but it was impossible. Still, he thought they would come looking for him. He was afraid they would come and he would not be there because he had been adopted. We told him we would keep checking, that we would never give up. It did no good. His little heart clung to the belief his parents were searching for him and would find him. That hope kept him going. I think it still does. He is such a good boy, so smart. And so patient."

"But he chose to stay in an orphanage? He could have lived with you all these years. You would have been his family."

"The heart cannot be explained. Can you explain to me why you have fallen in love with an Indian girl and want to adopt her? Why that child? Orphanages are full of children needing homes, here and in the United States. But until you met Raveena, you were not moved to adopt a child. Do you think now you could walk into an orphanage and just choose another child?"

"No, you're right. It wouldn't be the same at all."

"And you cannot explain it. I know, I understand. I have felt it myself for Manish. No one can explain the human heart. It is no different than falling in love with your husband. Why this man? Why him and not one of the other hundreds of men you must have encountered in your life? No one knows. It is a great mystery."

It was no great mystery to Leslie even if she hadn't encountered hundreds of men, as Rhea assumed. She glanced at Tom and found him watching her, an odd look on his face. He looked like he was tracing each feature, trying to remember them. Was he making a mental image, something to remember when he left her? He started when he met her eyes and quickly shifted his gaze.

"Manish is a delightful boy. We watched over him all these years, let him know we are always here for him. Still, he clings to the hope of being reunited with his family. Who could fault him for that?"

"Gazala spoke of children being sold. She said the parents thought they were going to work but were tricked. You think that happened to Manish's parents?"

"It is quite possible. We know this happens. Or he could have been plucked from the streets as he believes. It is also possible that his parents sold him outright, knowing what they were doing. Sadly, this also happens when a family is starving

238 | LARA BERNHARDT

and the parents see no other option. Of course, we never said such things to Manish."

"But maybe if he knew the truth—"

"It would only break his heart. And for what? He has grown up happy and healthy. We helped him get his job here. He will be just fine. Why should we break his heart? So that my husband and I can have things our way? It is not worth hurting the boy. And no one knows what truly happened anyway. He could be correct."

"Did you ever think about adopting another child?"

"We did. Years we waited for Manish, hoping he would change his mind and decide he wanted to be part of our family. That did not happen. Now we are older. We have opted not to adopt, to help as many children as possible through the orphanage rather than just one through adoption."

"I still can't believe he wouldn't let you adopt him," Tom said. "That doesn't make sense to me."

"It is his choice. He should do what makes him happy."

"But he's probably waiting for people who will never come looking for him."

Rhea wobbled her head in a figure eight. "That may be true. Some people wait all their lives for someone or something that will never come. And some people search all their lives, yet never find what they are looking for. Who are we to tell them to stop waiting or stop searching? Who is to say that those who let go of their dreams are taking the correct path?"

"Sometimes things just don't work out. They aren't possible," Tom insisted, and though he spoke to Rhea, he looked at Leslie.

He was talking about their marriage. He couldn't forgive her for lying to him.

"Perhaps. That is one view. Some of us believe that when love is strong, anything is possible. As Gandhi said, 'You must be the change you wish to see in the world.' Ah—here comes my husband now."

Manish approached with a man wearing an elegant suit and carrying a briefcase. Even in the dim light, she noticed he was a strikingly handsome man. Tall, he carried himself at his full height, his stride sure but graceful.

"Uncle has come!" Manish announced with a wide smile. "Your waiter will be back soon."

"Thank you, Manish." Rhea's husband shook his hand before the boy left to return to the front of the restaurant. "He looks good. I think he likes his new job."

"This is my husband, Maninder," Rhea said.

He offered his hand to Tom, who clasped it and murmured, "Nice to meet you."

"Very good to meet you and your lovely wife," Maninder replied, turning his attention to her. The light from the wall sconce illuminated his face, framed by dark hair, silver confetti sprinkled throughout. He clasped her offered hand gently between both of his own and smiled warmly. "My wife insists we must meet. I believe we have something in common."

$\mathcal{M}$aninder offered to order for everyone. Leslie didn't know what he ordered and she didn't care. People required more than food to survive. She was pretty sure Rhea wanted them to meet due to the shared loss of sisters. But she didn't feel like talking about it anymore.

Tom ordered a beer. The distance between them swelled with each silent moment. He hadn't invited her swimming with him that afternoon—he just changed clothes and left the room, leaving her alone with her emptiness and guilt. His detachment would spoil dinner. She wished she hadn't agreed to come. She longed for warm arms around her, comforting her, reminding her love existed and good things sometimes happened too. She didn't want to be alone anymore, but that was where she would find herself after the divorce.

Her scraped knees and palms burned, another reminder of her failures. She didn't dare complain—that would only invite comments that she asked for it, brought it on herself. She wrapped her hands around the glass of water in front of her, hoping to soothe the raw wounds.

How would they split things up? They could sell the house, retire the mortgage. She wouldn't want to stay there without him, surrounded by memories of their life together. He could take over repaying his student loans. She thought of all the payments she'd made over the years—the bills, the loans, the house—all investments in a life that would now yield no return. Would he continue to refuse his parents' money when he was responsible for meeting all those monthly expenses?

He elbowed her. Heat rose in her cheeks. Had he somehow read her thoughts?

The waiter was gone and all eyes were on her, deepening her embarrassment. Maninder repeated the question she'd missed.

"Are you recovered from your injuries?"

She ducked her head, hiding the bandage on her cheek, but not before his eyes drifted to it.

"It's just a nick." She'd cleaned herself up while Tom swam, carefully dislodging the grit ground into her palms and knees. She'd even ventured to the front desk for antibiotic ointment and bandages—and learned to request plasters for the scrapes. Once the blood and dirt were wiped away, they didn't look so bad. Not even the knife wound on her face. She covered it with a plaster anyway so she didn't have to see it.

"What brought you to India?" Maninder asked when no further conversation developed.

"My work," Tom answered. "I'm a postdoc. Hoping my research will help me into a faculty position."

"Leslie, Rhea tells me you two have grown quite close. She says you are quite similar."

Leslie smiled at the woman, touched to hear her feelings of friendship were reciprocated. "She's been a very good friend to me."

"And you are trying to help a small girl?" Maninder asked.

"Yes, but it isn't working out. I lost a lot of money trying to get her."

"I know it is frustrating. We've encountered similar situations working with Protect Our Women. Perhaps we can help you in this matter?"

"I wish you could, but we've been to the police, the embassy, Protect Our Women. No one offered any hope. And trying to buy her freedom didn't work either." She grasped her tea, clutching it tightly in her hands, as if holding on could keep her from falling apart. She had to find a way to let go, to put this child out of her mind.

"Rhea tells me you and I have something in common as well. You lost a sister? When you were very young?"

"That's right. Someone abducted her."

"I understand the pain you carry. I also lost a sister. An older sister." She met his eyes, a mixture of sorrow and sympathy swirling in the dark brown irises. A black hole, like the one she carried, that sucked away the light and never let her forget. She felt the tug of time and distance, the dissonance of unresolved issues. Yes, he did understand. "Was your sister ever found?"

She shook her head. Shared pain or not, she really didn't want to discuss it. Surely he could understand that. Then again, she doubted he was responsible for his sister's abduction as she was for hers.

"What was her name?"

"Trisha." Her voice caught in her throat. The little freckled face and sandy pigtails swam up from her memory. What would she look like now? For a few years, she'd been included in "Have you seen this child?" posters and ads, and eventually her photo was subjected to computerized age-progression, coaxing her features to resemble an older version of a child who no longer existed. Could a ghost haunt you from the future? Where would she have gone to school? What career path would she have chosen? If her life hadn't been snuffed out.

"We never forget, do we? I still search for my sister. For all these years, I kept searching. I will not stop until I know where she is. I remember the day she left our village. It was so bright, the scorching sun blistered the earth."

"It was hot the day Trisha was kidnapped too. I went inside to cool off." She didn't want to relive it. Didn't want to think about it anymore. Couldn't bear to let others know how she'd failed. This was why she didn't tell Tom—or anyone else.

"Relief." He nodded in sympathy. "My mother sought relief too. Our village starved, we suffered the worst drought anyone could remember. My father had traveled to a city, looking for work, anything to make some money to buy food for his starving family. A man came to our village, offering money for girls. A lot of money."

Money for girls. Hadn't she heard enough of these repulsive stories?

"He would take the girls away to Agra, he said, where they would sew handicrafts and clothing for tourists. He promised to send money each week, so much money. Our mother accepted the offer so she could feed her children instead of watching them starve."

She lifted her eyes to meet his. Sewing and Agra. This sounded uncannily similar to a story she'd heard in the brothel.

"When our mother realized no money was coming, and we had no way to know where my sister was, she was distraught. There was no way to find her." He hung his head. "It was a terrible time. The entire village starved, desperately trying to survive. Our mother, and the other mothers, hoped to send their daughters to a better life. The money the man promised— they couldn't turn it down in the face of starvation. Our baby sister, Adi, died that year. Our father returned, and when he heard one daughter was gone and the baby had died, he said, 'Now we gain four dowries and no longer pay two.' Our mother just stared at him. I think something snapped that day. She was never the same after. She mourned both daughters as if dead. Baby Adi, and Sanjana, taken away by a strange man."

Sanjana. He repeated Sanjana's story, though his ended

where she was placed in the van and disappeared. Like her, he watched a sister taken away, left to cope with the aftermath, never knowing what happened next.

Leslie looked to Rhea, who appeared ready to burst. *Am I right?* her eyes seemed to ask.

"We four boys felt so helpless. Our mother wept for weeks. She was inconsolable. She kept saying, 'I have sold one daughter, now the other has died.' She thought she was being punished."

"I know that feeling," she said, while Maninder sat silently. Beside her, Tom shifted. She thought he almost reached for her, but instead he signaled for another beer.

"I had only ten years," Maninder continued finally. "Watching our mother like that, I swore I would find Sanjana and bring her home. I imagined beating the man who took her and bringing her back to our mother. I was so young. Now I know how quickly these girls change hands. Finding the man who stole her would be more difficult than finding Sanjana herself. She was likely sold several times."

Leslie knew that thirst for justice, the longing that somehow, against all odds, a sister could return home. No matter how many years passed, she grappled with the guilt that Trisha would be fine if she'd simply stayed outside with the little girl.

Her parents coped in their own ways. One preached goodness and forgiveness while receding from the world that allowed a man to pluck his daughter from the street. The other threw herself into religious fervor.

"Many years passed, but I never forgot her. None of us did. Some days, I found my mother just sitting, staring. She missed her daughter. Well, both daughters."

She thought of her own mother, hands clasped, lips moving silently in prayer, beseeching the Lord to watch over his newest angel until she herself was deemed worthy for the rewards of heaven.

"When I was old enough, I began my search. I never told

my mother. I knew it would be difficult to find her after many years had passed. I made my way to Agra."

She hesitated a split second before blurting out, "They didn't go to Agra."

"Of course they did not. I know now that Agra is not known for its Red Light District. But I was young. I have learned much since then. I met many people while searching for her. It was while in Agra that I found my profession."

"He was apprentice to a jeweler in Agra," Rhea explained. "It was there he learned his craft." Rhea looked meaningfully at her. *Let him tell the story.*

"I am grateful for that," Maninder said. "I started out taking any job I could get. Then I began running errands for a jewelry store. The jeweler liked me so much he decided to teach me the art of making jewelry. Later, I began to bargain for gems for him. It was good experience."

"And he has natural talent. Every piece in our shop, he made himself."

"Everything?" Leslie asked, thinking of the glittering silver and gold chains, the tiny links arm in arm creating a home for the delicate floral bursts of gems. "You are very talented."

"Well…" Maninder tried to wave away the compliment.

"It was also in Agra that we met," Rhea said, curling around his arm and resting her cheek against his shoulder.

"Yes, I found my calling and my wife in Agra. But not my sister. She was not there."

"As soon as we could, we moved to Delhi," Rhea said. "We became involved with any help groups that accepted us as volunteers."

"My jewelry business thrived, but we never had a child, and I never found my sister. So we help at the orphanage and at women's rescue groups."

"A guest here at the hotel first told me about Protect Our Women," Rhea said. "It was just starting and they were in need of funds."

"Rhea shared the information about POW with me. I later met with the woman who started the group."

"Gazala?" Leslie asked.

"No. Gazala has taken over. The woman who started the group was named Aleyamma. She barely lasted the first year. The death threats from the brothel owners became too much for her. Gazala also changed the name to Protect Our Women. She studied in America, you know. She considers herself fighting a war. She's a strong woman."

"That first year was so difficult," Rhea said. "We made a slow but real impact on the brothels. We helped women leave. We helped them find jobs. But even those women who have paid their debt and are supposedly free to leave are captive. The owners do not let them leave easily. They threaten us for helping the women escape their grasp."

"I agreed to help after my very first meeting with Aleyamma," Maninder said. "We were so proud of our work. But the brothel owners are never happy to see one of the workers leave. Replacing them requires the purchase of a new slave. We were menaced by their thugs many times. Aleyamma had the idea that we could try to stop the problem before the girls reached the brothels. So we began to enter the villages and educate the people, warning against these men who promise money for children, especially young girls. We tried to change their opinions—tried to convince them not to value boys over girls."

"Did you have any luck?" she asked.

"Very little. It is difficult to change customs thousands of years old. It is a fundamental problem. So many people still prefer sons to daughters. Daughters are a financial hardship to destitute families. Even those who welcome daughters are less enthusiastic when it comes to the burden of paying a dowry."

"I thought dowries were outlawed."

"Yes, but it is much more difficult to enforce a law than to enact it," Rhea said. "We are battling a deeply entrenched custom."

"In many rural villages, the people have no knowledge of anti-dowry laws. They only know customs that have been passed down for generations."

"Imagine your parents given the two options, Tom. Tradition dictates that a scholar such as yourself with a secure future would command a good dowry. Now say the parents of two women approach to arrange your marriage—one girl's parents point out demanding a dowry is outlawed, the other girl's parents shrug and offer thousands of dollars. What would your parents do?"

"Money is certainly the only thing that matters to some people." He glanced at her then returned to his beer.

"He could have married someone better than me," Rhea told them. "He could have commanded a dowry if he chose. I grew up very poor. My parents had no money to pay a dowry."

Rhea's words rang true for Leslie as well. Tom could have married anyone. The wall rising between them told her he wished he had chosen someone else. He thumped his beer bottle on the table.

"The first time I saw her," Maninder told them, "she was at the market. She held clusters of cut roses. The most beautiful woman I had ever seen."

"The first time I saw Leslie," Tom said, "she sat right next to me in Biology."

"I sold the roses I had cut from rose bushes that did not belong to me," Rhea giggled. "Just a step above begging."

"I bought them all," Maninder said, gazing at her as though seeing her again for the first time. "And asked her to dinner that night."

"She didn't wear a bit of makeup." Tom seemed to be talking to himself. "Her hair just rippled naturally over her shoulders. And she didn't even notice me." He barked a laugh. "She was easily the most attractive girl in the room, without even trying. And so confident. She knew she didn't have to try."

Confident? That was one thing she'd never been. Then again, so was attractive. Trisha was the cute one, her parents always said, telling anyone who would listen what a beautiful woman she'd grow to be. No one ever said Leslie was pretty. Except Trisha. If that's what he'd thought of her, no wonder he was disappointed.

"I was surprised," Rhea admitted, laughing. "But I was also hungry. I thought I would at least have a good meal. I never imagined he would ask me out again."

"And again and again. I knew after our first dinner together that I had found my wife. She is my jewel. My '*choti gulabo*.'"

"She was so damned smart." Tom continued his own story, though Maninder and Rhea didn't seem to notice. "A on every exam. I had to get close to her."

"It means 'little rose,'" Rhea explained for them. "He chose to forgo a dowry, took me as his bride with nothing in my hands. I could never understand why he would settle for me when he could do better. The heart wants what the heart wants. Who can understand it?"

Tom laughed suddenly. "The heart wants what the heart wants," he echoed, tipping his Kingfisher at them before downing the remainder.

Leslie's cheeks burned. She wished her husband would be quiet. Any moment now he would open his mouth and spill her ugly secret: how she lied to him about carrying his child, how he'd proposed quickly as a result. That she'd basically trapped him. Fortunately, Maninder and Rhea were wrapped up in their own memories.

"Who could want more?" Maninder asked. "Look at her— beautiful, hardworking, and smart. I make the jewelry, she operates the shop. A perfect team. And I know I can trust her.

What other employee can I trust this way? She has no incentive to steal from me."

"As long as you treat me right." Rhea winked at her as though they shared a joke.

Maninder threw back his head and laughed. "There you go —you see how she keeps me in line. We are very happy together, despite the difficulties we have faced in life." He clouded over again. "But I miss my sister. I would give anything to know where she is."

Rhea turned to Leslie, nodding, eyes bulging with her surprise for her husband. ...*and now you tell the end*.

One wary eye on her husband, Leslie took a deep breath. "She's in a brothel on GB Road."

CHAPTER 34

*S*he reminded herself she loved him. *For better or for worse, in sickness and in health…*

The elevator pinged. Tom pulled himself off the wall and attempted to shuffle through the opening doors.

"Whoa, not yet," she said, pulling him back by his shirt. She felt like she spoke to a toddler. "This isn't our floor."

She smiled, embarrassed, as they were joined by another couple. They huddled on the opposite side of the box and watched Tom with curiosity.

He stumbled back a few tipsy steps and bumped into her. She had never been tipsy. Other than sips of champagne at special occasions, she didn't drink. Her husband's unwieldy gait might have amused her if she wasn't in such a bad mood.

When they arrived at their floor, she offered to help him walk, but he pulled away.

"I'm not drunk, for crying out loud. I didn't drink that much."

She wasn't sure what to expect from him. How was she supposed to know? She had no idea how much liquor intoxicated a person. Other than the writhing revelry at the frat party, she had no experience with this. And Tom normally limited himself to one drink.

He sat on the bed and wrestled his shoes from his feet. "Can we talk about this?" His shoe popped loose suddenly.

What did he want to talk about? Her lies? The money? Raveena? Sanjana? Divorce? Each topic of conversation pounded against her temples like she was being punched from inside her skull.

"Tom, I'm really tired."

"Me too. But I'm not gonna be able to sleep now. Can you?" He tilted his head, trying to force eye contact.

As drained as the last few days had left her, she thought she could sleep for days. "I need some sleep. We can talk tomorrow." She didn't add, *after you've sobered up.*

"Look, I'm not...I don't wanna fight. I just don't think we should go to bed mad."

"I'm not mad. Really. Let's just get some sleep so we can get up in the morning. We promised Maninder."

"We haven't talked about that. We haven't talked all day. At least, not since..."

This was why she didn't want to talk. She didn't have the strength to wrangle with the pit of snakes writhing in her stomach. "I promised him. I'm going to take him to Sanjana, see if she really is his sister, and see if she's willing to leave. He's been looking for her for years. It's the least I can do. I hope she is his sister. I'd love to see a happy ending." She didn't want to admit how badly she wanted this. She needed to see someone return home safely. And if she angered Shardul in the process, so much the better.

"I don't see why you need to be there. Prajit can take him."

She sighed. He obviously hadn't been listening. "He doesn't want to scare her. He thinks she's more likely to listen to another woman than a strange man who says he could be her brother. Even if he is her brother, she probably won't recognize him. She hasn't seen him in decades. He was only ten when she was stolen."

"I don't have a brother or a sister. I can't imagine what you've been through. But I don't want you to go back to the brothel. I don't want you in danger again."

"Maninder will be there."

"I'll be there too." He spoke entirely too loudly. "You don't think I'd let you go alone, do you?"

She remembered the last time he spoke those exact words, scoffing at her for suspecting kidnapping and dismissing the idea she'd ever been in any real danger. He must have, too, because he dropped his eyes quickly.

"Let's just go to bed. Please." She moved to unbutton his shirt. He grabbed her hands.

"I wasn't a virgin when we met, either." He pulled her so close, she thought he wanted to kiss her. He smelled heavily of beer. She drew away. The scent frightened her, dredging up a symphony of jarring chords. "And I wasn't forced, so it still isn't even." He released her hands, scratched his head.

She wasn't strong enough for this right now. She just wanted to roll him under the blankets, fall asleep, and pretend none of this ever happened. Tomorrow, if the day went as she hoped, she would bring home a lost girl.

"Just tell me what you're feeling. Please." He took her hand again. The tenderness in his eyes caught her off guard, prompting the painful words from her lips.

"I was raped. I lied to you. And you're having an affair because I'm lousy in bed. I feel stupid." Her voice quivered.

"You shouldn't feel stupid. I'm not having an affair." He glanced up. She saw fear in his eyes, cowering behind the beautiful blue pools. "But I do need to tell you something." He dropped his head into his hands, stared at the floor.

"What is it?" She took a step back, bumping into the table.

"Where I've been, when I'm not at work." He wrung his hands. "I've been going to a gentlemen's club."

Her blood turned to ice, sending shivering ripples down to her fingers and toes. This wasn't at all what she expected to hear. If ever she'd heard a misnomer, it was the term "gentlemen's club."

"There's a girl there," he continued. He glanced up at her face. He must have seen the shock she felt. "It's not what you think. I promise I'm not having an affair. But she does sit and talk with me, and…a few times…lap dances. But that's all."

…to have and to hold, till death do you part? He said I do, she thought, fighting tears, determined he would not see her cry. Her heart fluttered around her chest, trying to pump the liquid frost that clotted her vessels. *A girl, a girl, a girl*, it seemed to pound while her desiccated veins murmured, *'til death, 'til death, 'til death*.

His admission of guilt swept relief through her shamed soul even as it stabbed her heart. How could she feel betrayal and relief at the same time? Drained and inflamed, two sides of herself warring with the other. She wanted to be angry, wanted to scream at him — except, she was glad.

Her mother always taught her two wrongs don't make a right. But maybe in this case, his wrong evened out hers. Maybe they could call it a draw, move forward together. Except —

Did this mean he didn't love her anymore? She pictured another woman grinding on his lap, breasts in his face. Her stomach heaved, and she thought she might be sick. How could he?

"I don't know why I went the first time. But I went back because…it felt so good…to be wanted again."

"I want you. You're never home anymore. We never go out anymore."

"You've been drifting away. Instead of pulling you back, I guess I let go and reached for something else. I'm so sorry."

She'd been drifting away? She thought of all his long hours at work over the past year, explained away by his supposed stress to advance his research or to finish a grant. Had he been to the so-called "gentlemen's club" all those nights? Had the girl listened to him griping about his wife all those times, listening to his excuses for not going home, grinning and running her hands over him? And how much money had he thrown away on her? Did he really think a simple "I'm so sorry" could fix this? Could she ever trust her husband again? Jealousy won out over relief, flooding her heart with black thoughts.

"You're just like the men who visit the brothel. Why did you bring me here?" Her clenched hands longed to strike him. She held them tightly at her sides. "If you want to be with her, why not drag her along with you? Go rescue her from that nasty place and see how long you two last."

"I don't want to be with her! This was supposed to be our fresh start." He stepped toward her, but she backed away, edging along the table. She couldn't be close to him now, not with images of him entwined with another woman playing through her mind. "But it didn't happen. You pulled farther away. Now you're talking about divorce." His voice caught in his throat.

"You brought up divorce. You're making me choose between you and Raveena."

"And I think we both know you'll never choose me over the girl."

"Especially not now."

"Then it sounds like you've made your choice."

"Well, that makes it easy for you. You can spend every night at the strip club. Or run off and make a new life with your dancer."

She turned, needing to get away from him, wanting to hide the tears burning her eyes before they streaked her face. There was no place to retreat but the bathroom. At least the door locked.

He grabbed her arm, spun her around. "But I don't want

her. I'm never going back there. Rhea is right. The heart wants what the heart wants. And, goddamn it, I want you."

He leaned into her. Catching her off guard, the weight of his body fell against her, knocking her backward. She slammed against the table, throwing her hands back to break the fall.

He tumbled along, sprawling over her. She stared up at the fire blazing in his eyes, breathing heavily. He kissed her hard, knotting his fingers in her hair, clenching it in fistfuls. He'd never been rough with her. From their very first time together, when she wasn't technically a virgin but as inexperienced as one, he'd been careful with her. She suspected he held back, afraid of scaring or hurting her, handling her as though one wrong move would shatter her.

Not tonight. Mouth demanding, tongue insisting, his hands moved to her hips, kneading the body beneath him as if he could shape her to his will. His fingers were feverish, desperate, commanding her back to him.

The sharp, stale tang of his Kingfishers dove into her past, clawing up memories she wished she could purge. Dark eyes peered from her psyche like a beast waiting to spring. Fear—of betrayal, pain, the past—battled with the spark of desire he ignited.

Once you are married, then of course you may enjoy the gift of your body so long as it is shared with your heaven-sent husband and you have married him in the house of God. God! Even halfway around the world she couldn't escape the intrusion of her mother's dire proclamations.

No. Tonight was not about mistakes or anger, God or evil, shame or the past. Tonight was about her husband and the swelling warmth throbbing between her legs as he caressed her.

Tonight she wanted the passion she'd read about and heard of and longed for. She wanted forgiveness, and she would forgive.

"I want you. I love you," Tom chanted again and again,

running his tongue down her neck, his breath hot against her. "You are the most beautiful woman I've ever known. Hard-working. Faithful."

She shivered, her vision blurring as she tipped her head back, urging him on, the table hard against her back as he kissed her neck.

He covered her with greedy kisses, pressing a row of them down her cleavage and over each breast. Slowly he moved back up her neck, his tongue searing hot lines into her skin. When he reached the bandage hiding her wound, he recoiled, shaking his head as if remembering where he was.

He raised his weight from her, his biceps tightening as he propped himself on his arms, hovering over her, jaw clenched. Beads of sweat glistened along his brow, furrowed above eyes squeezed shut. "I won't—hurt you," he whispered.

She didn't want him to stop. The warmth he ignited radiated into her pelvis, which rocked against his groin with a mind of its own. She wrapped her legs around him, ran her fingers over his arms, entwined her arms around his neck, and pulled him closer.

He stood suddenly, lifting her with him. She clung to him like a vine, needing his support to sustain herself, curving around his strength.

Still kissing her, he stepped backward to the bed, tumbling onto the mattress. She straddled him, plucking anxiously at the buttons on his shirt. She stripped it from him and ran her hands over his warm skin, across his chest, over his shoulders.

She dragged her tongue along his shoulder and up his neck. She paused, bearing down, sucking hard and nipping with her teeth. His pulse quickened against her lips as he gasped.

"What—what are you doing?" he breathed.

"Shhhhh," she insisted, continuing over the curve of his ear.

He scooted toward the pillows, leading her. Yanking off her

shirt and tossing it aside, she lifted his hands to her breasts, pressing his open palms to her nipples. She cupped her hands firmly over the hard line straining against the denim of his jeans, impatient for release. He groaned at her touch. Something deep in her abdomen quivered in response.

She fumbled with trembling fingers, popping the snap, sliding down the zipper. He yanked the jeans off his hips while she wiggled out of her britches.

Sweat beaded across her forehead as she straddled him again and leaned forward, sliding her body over his chest. He seemed to thrum to the beat of her heart and shudder to the whoosh of the blood in her veins. The chill of his confession was gone. Heat flowed through her, fired by his desire, his hands, his mouth.

"Please, I can't stand it anymore." His hands shifted to her hips, lifting her weight easily. He guided her, sinking himself within.

She felt an ache deep inside, a pulling, longing sensation that swelled in intensity with each stroke. No admonishments shamed her. There was nothing but the feel of his skin against hers, the pounding of her heart, his hands holding her. Grabbing his shoulders, she ground against him harder, drawing him deeper still.

"Oh, God, woman," he rasped. "I can't wait much longer."

He strained against her, breath ragged, and groaned in the back of his throat, a deep, guttural hunger. The pulling sensation intensified, the pulsating wavelengths widened and grew closer in frequency.

With a sudden cry, he encircled her in his arms, crushing her so tightly she could barely breathe. He growled, straining and bucking against her, his fevered pitch setting off a rush of pleasure that built and swelled until it exploded through her. She cried out, wave after wave coursing through her, every muscle in her body tensed above her husband.

She collapsed on him, sweat running off her in rivulets,

soaking the sheets. Warmth radiated from her center, reaching all the way to her fingertips and toes. Still breathing heavily, he stroked her hair, caressed her face. She rolled over onto her side, trembling, shivering with the aftershocks that quivered through her body. This complete satisfaction was something new to her, something she'd never felt before.

Sleep tugged at her. Eager to give in to the peaceful contentment swirling around her as he nestled against her, she closed her eyes and breathed deeply, his strong arms tucking her close. Her last thought before she succumbed to sleep was of the women in the brothel, who knew only pain and suffering at the hands of men, and who might never feel as she did this moment, safe in her husband's warm embrace.

CHAPTER 35

The morning sun reached around the heavy hotel drapes, plucking at her eyelids, teasing her from a night of nearly catatonic sleep. She curled around the delicious satisfaction that infused every muscle in her body, clamping her eyes closed, savoring every last moment.

Her wobbly limbs still tingled with the lingering electricity she'd sparked with her husband the night before. She'd connected with him on the most basic level, carnal rapture as she'd never experienced it. She hoped it was as exhilarating for him as it was for her—the fresh start he'd longed for. And maybe she'd succeeded in obliterating any thoughts of another woman.

They'd both made mistakes, both admitted them. They could forgive each other and move forward, the marriage stronger than ever now the secrets were confided.

She'd triumphed over her guilt. Finally.

The next time her mother called, Leslie would challenge her to explain how that raw, open sharing with her husband could possibly be wrong in any way. If that wasn't enough to silence her chirping, she would go on to explain that Darren didn't electrify her the way Tom did, didn't make every fiber of her body ache to be touched, to move closer and closer and merge into one. That would shut her up, Leslie thought with a decadent stretch.

Last night she'd been completely unhinged and pieced back together.

She could do it again. She wanted to do it again, she realized, her body responding, warm and ready.

She rolled over to reach for her husband.

He was gone.

She noticed how silent the room was and sat up.

The bathroom gaped open, dark, empty.

She jumped from the bed. Why would he leave? How could he leave after what they'd shared last night?

A cold shiver reminded her she was naked. She was suddenly aware of his dark, musky scent all over her. She lifted his shirt from the floor and pulled it around her body like a robe, breathing him in. He should be wrapped around her like this, holding her, basking in the morning sun of their new beginning.

The note propped against his books on the table answered all her questions: *You're right, I'm no better than the men who visit the brothels, forcing myself on women who don't want to be with me. Sorry about last night. Drinking too much was no excuse—I was completely out of line. Went down to breakfast. Meet you at the jewelry shop.*

It wasn't enough. She wasn't enough. The thoughts rained down on her as she stood in the shower, thinking how foolish she'd been to imagine that one night of amazing sex was enough to save their marriage.

The floral-scented soap she lathered over herself was not enough to erase his scent from her skin, no matter how hard she scrubbed. They had melded together and nothing could completely separate them.

CHAPTER 36

*L*eslie was so familiar with the route to the brothel, she thought she could drive it herself. But she was glad Prajit was in the driver's seat. Maninder sat in the front seat beside the driver, chatting and laughing in what she assumed was Hindi. Prajit periodically glanced back at her in his mirror, making her wonder if she was the topic of discussion.

Tom sat beside her, staring out his window, refusing to look at her or talk to her. He hadn't said a word all morning. She'd smiled at him in the jewelry shop, tried to get close to him, hoped he would see she wasn't upset with him. But he remained withdrawn, and she didn't know why. Apparently, last night wasn't everything she thought it was.

She needed to focus on what she could fix. She caught herself about to lift a prayer for help today, about to ask God to be with her and help them bring Sanjana home. *Allow your daughter rescue.*

She decided to leave the prayers to Maninder. Nothing was going her way.

Sanjana could have walked away from the brothel years ago, if she'd had anywhere to go. Now that she had family willing to support and help her, nothing should stop her from leaving. Assuming she was Maninder's sister.

His light step and excited voice told her he believed it already.

"The owners never let them go without a fight," Rhea had told her over steamy cups of pungent tea in the jewelry shop. "We hope no one will be there today."

"What if Shardul is there?" Leslie asked, shuddering at the thought of his black eyes boring into her.

"He won't be, *bhagwaan ki kripa se*," Maninder replied.

"Bhagwaan ki kripa se," Rhea murmured, casting her eyes to the ground, then explaining for the Americans, "It means by God's grace. God willing, we will bring Sanjana home."

How could God not be willing? Even the angry, vengeful God from the sermons her father gave during her youth couldn't be against them, could He? In fact, He should stand with them, righting the wrongs committed against children. "Vengeance is mine sayeth the Lord," she remembered her father thundering from the pulpit. So where was He in this? Where was the vengeance, the justice? Her mother brushed aside the questions with her answer to everything confounding: "Not in this world but the next. Heaven is where we receive our just rewards."

Was that, perhaps, why her father shriveled in the wake of the loss of his little daughter? Did he, too, wonder how He let such things happen? Did he watch for the sky to split apart, for lightning to strike the offender? Did he feel as though part of him was ripped out that day, that the wound never completely healed? And though he continued to serve and preach, though he still professed to believe, did he feel lost without the surety he'd felt before? She should have talked to him. Strange how easy it was for two people living in the same home to drift apart. How easy it was, then, to lose touch.

The taxi clattered to a stop across the street from the brothel. With any luck, she would walk up to the door, lead

Sanjana away, and return to the hotel without incident. It would take just a few minutes. Easy.

So why was her heart a jackhammer chiseling at her chest cavity? Why did she wish Tom would take her in his arms, forgive her, and kiss her like he might never see her again? That's how you say goodbye to people you love and want in your life, not the people who disappoint you and drive you away.

He turned to her, his eyes churning. A chill ran through her. She reached for him just as Maninder turned around.

"I cannot thank you enough," he said, one hand over his heart.

"Of course." She returned her attention to Tom, but his back was to her, the stony wall erected between them firmly in place. Though she longed to draw on his strength, he was no longer there for her. She had to do this on her own. She opened the door and stepped out. As she closed the door, she thought she heard a whispered, "I'm sorry," but when she twisted around, his back still faced her.

With a deep breath, she turned her attention to the building.

She hesitated only a moment before tapping quietly on the door. Her eyes wandered up and down the street, and though she tried to pretend she wasn't looking for anything in particular, she was relieved she didn't see the black R8 they'd chased through the streets. Her ears strained for signs of movement inside. Nothing. She knocked again, more forcefully this time, insistent.

What if no one answered? That was one thing they hadn't considered. She turned back to the taxi, looking for guidance.

The bolt scraped as it disengaged. Her head snapped around to face the door. The knob turned. The door creaked open, dragging on the concrete floor.

In the thin crack between the doorjamb and the flimsy, warped door, Sanjana's face appeared. She wore no makeup, and her unruly hair escaped its braid. Blinking in the bright afternoon sun, her weary, suspicious eyes registered first recognition and then dismay.

"Not here," Sanjana said. She began to close the door.

"Wait," Leslie said quickly, leaning toward the shrinking gap.

Turning over her shoulder, Sanjana spoke quietly with someone out of sight, her voice little more than a low hum, then opened the door a bit wider. Tarla appeared, disheveled and groggy. She lit up at the sight of the American woman. She rubbed the sleep from her tired eyes before she spoke.

"You must go," Tarla said, sadly but firmly. "We cannot let you come inside." She dropped her voice and leaned forward. "Please, Shardul is here."

Leslie's stomach dropped. Images of Shardul pounding down the stairs and wrenching the door open ran through her mind. Her eyes shifted, straining to see past the women blocking her view into the building.

"He's here now?" Why? The timing was terrible.

"Yes. Asleep with one of the girls. Please, if we wake him..." Tarla trailed off.

There was no need to complete the thought. Leslie knew firsthand what reaction they could anticipate. She couldn't put these women in danger again.

But what if he had Raveena with him? Could she catch him by surprise? Was the girl here, perhaps on her cot, instructed not to make a sound? She imagined herself pushing past the women, scurrying up the stairs quiet as a whisper. Could she sneak the girl away while he slept?

What if he caught her? What if he called the police to report trespassers? What if he beat these women senseless?

She forced herself to focus on Sanjana. She would quietly convince her to leave and sneak her out.

"We came to get you," she whispered to the older woman. "That's all."

Sanjana looked confused. She looked at Tarla. Both women waited for more information.

"I have someone with me who thinks he is your brother." Leslie tried to keep the explanation as short as possible while keeping one ear open for footsteps on the stairs. "He has been looking for his sister many years. He wants you to come home with him."

The elder woman's face remained blank, revealing nothing of her thoughts. Leslie couldn't even tell if Sanjana understood what this meant. The look on her face wasn't so much incomprehension or disbelief as it was passivity. She might as well have been reading a grocery list.

Leslie wasn't sure how to proceed. She remembered Sanjana's comment that she wished someone had come looking for her, come to rescue her. Was this simply shock? Maybe she was afraid to even hope for rescue after so many years of captivity and maltreatment.

"Your family never stopped loving you or missing you. One of your brothers has been looking for you more years than he can remember. He and his wife are very kind people. If you let them, they will take you away from this."

She gestured to the brothel, knowing it was more than the crumbling building they would rescue her from. They would take her away from isolation, from harsh treatment, from a constant struggle to survive on the fringes of society, from being used and discarded. She remained quiet a moment, allowing Sanjana to absorb and process.

Before she responded, however, a harsh voice, one that would haunt her nightmares for years to come, called out from inside the brothel.

Tarla drew in a sharp breath, looking to her for...what? Guidance? Direction? Or was she warning her silently to run while she could?

The brothel door wrenched open and there stood Shardul,

his face contorted into an angry scowl. His eyes traveled over Sanjana and Tarla and came to rest on her.

Bare-chested, he shifted his loose trousers, barely tied around his waist. His dark eyes narrowed as if to say, "I know why you are here." He licked his lips, running his eyes up and down her.

Unable to look at him, remembering his hands all over her, she dropped her eyes to the ground, sure the same thoughts played across his mind.

He grabbed her by the arm and pulled her inside the building. Caught off guard, she stumbled along beside him. For a moment she didn't react. Until she realized he was dragging her upstairs—to one of the bedrooms.

She planted her feet and refused to budge, trying to wriggle free of his grasp. He dug his fingers into her arm, smirking at her distress, jerking her toward the stairs like a rag doll.

"Let go of me," she demanded, prying at his filthy fingers with her free hand, struggling to stop her feet as he manhandled her. "Stop it!"

He whirled to face her, yanked her close, catching both wrists easily in one hand no matter how she thrashed. His other arm circled her waist, pulling her against him.

His shadowy eyes stared into hers. For a moment, she searched them for clues. What made a person strike out against others? What horrific presence caused one human to harm another without remorse? How could someone tear apart a life, wipe out an existence, then carry on as if nothing had happened? Meeting his gaze, she looked for the demon she knew her mother would say possessed this man's soul. She saw no indication of an evil presence. No gnashing devil peered out of those human eyes. She saw nothing save the storm cloud of anger brewing.

He wrapped a leg around hers, scissoring her to him. Mashing his pelvis into hers, he pressed his lips to her ear. "You will like," he breathed.

The door crashed open, half-torn from its hinges. Tom and Maninder burst into the room. Tom's eyes fell on them and his face clouded over.

"You bastard." Tom crossed the room in a heartbeat and took hold of Shardul, landing a fist on his jaw before she could disentangle herself. The force of the punch resonated through her.

"Oh my," Maninder said, offering a hand and ushering her to Sanjana's waiting arms.

"Are you okay?" Tarla asked, looking her over for injuries.

"I'm fine," Leslie lied, unable to stop conjuring images of what she would be enduring had no one stopped him.

Still shaking, she watched her husband—the man she thought ready to divorce her—as he lashed out. Shardul lay on the ground, his nose bloody, one eye bruised.

"Don't ever touch my wife again," Tom bellowed, blow after blow punctuating the words, a muted smacking sound reverberating through the room each time his fist connected. Red-faced, sweat dripping down his face, he showed no signs of stopping. He was the one who appeared to be possessed by a demon, unable to control his actions.

Maninder stepped forward at last, resting one hand on Tom's arm. "Why not let cooler heads prevail?" he suggested. He lifted Tom to his feet, where he stood panting, staring down at Shardul.

She'd never seen her husband in such a state. Certainly she'd never seen him strike anyone. She eyed him carefully as he joined her, breathing heavily, eyes wild.

"Are you okay?" he asked.

She nodded. Glancing down, she saw blood on him and lifted his hand to inspect it. His knuckles were shredded. "What about you? Are you okay?"

"It's nothing," he answered, wiping his knuckles against his shirt.

Sanjana stared at Maninder, as if searching her memories

from years ago for the features now staring back at her. She reached for him, placing one hand on his cheek.

"Manu?" Her eyes widened as something clicked into place.

He nodded, pressing his hand against hers. "Finally, I have found you."

She fell into his arms. He curled her close, rocking her gently as she cried. She imagined the same thing but the roles reversed, decades previously, little Sanjana cradling and comforting her younger brother.

Shardul rose to his feet, dabbing his face, gingerly inspecting his injuries. He spat on the floor, the discharge tinged red. He fished a pack of cigarettes and a lighter from his pocket and lit one. His left hand—with nothing as important to do as shuttling a roll of tobacco to his face—twitched spasmodically, as though he wanted to pick up something heavy and lob it at his unwelcome visitors.

He glared at Tom. "I should call the police to take you away," he growled, "for bursting into an innocent man's home and attacking him."

"You deserve worse for assaulting my wife, stealing our money, and kidnapping Raveena."

Shardul shrugged. "I did nothing."

"Nothing? Where's my ten thousand dollars, you asshole?" Tom appeared ready to lay into Shardul again. She leaned against him, willing him to be still.

Shardul shouted back at Tom in Hindi.

"He claims he's never seen you before today. He's threatening again to call the police," Maninder told them.

"These women saw us here talking with you," Tom replied, pointing to Sanjana and Tarla. "They saw you steal the money and take the girl. Go ahead and call the police. We have witnesses."

Inhaling deeply on his cigarette, he said. "No." He blew a

cloud of smoke into the room. "They say nothing against me. The police will not listen to you."

Leslie believed the police would be no help. Of course they would listen to him. He brought them money every month from his boss, one of the most feared men in the city. They were on their own.

Maninder cleared his throat. "Sanjana will gather her things and leave with us," he told Shardul.

He turned his angry eyes on Maninder. "No. She is mine."

"She is free to go," Maninder stated simply, his tone remaining calm and collected. He didn't even raise his voice. "You cannot keep her here against her will. That is against the law. If you attempt to detain her, we will call the police to intervene."

He had rescued women before, Leslie knew that. It made sense that experience would instill confidence. Still, she couldn't help but be impressed by his cool, unflappable presence, stalwart in the face of his unpredictable adversary.

Shardul threw his cigarette butt to the concrete floor and stamped on it.

He glared at her, concluding correctly that she was somehow responsible for this unexpected turn of events. His dark eyes were no longer amused. They no longer lingered on her as though he would like to devour her body. Now he looked like he wanted to wring her neck.

Karma was not something she thought about much, but today she sincerely hoped it was a real force and that when it balanced out and Shardul got what he deserved, she would be nowhere near what ought to be a nuclear blast of justice.

"Sanjana should be with her family," Maninder asserted. "No one is forcing her. We are only returning her to the family that lost her. And misses her."

With an attempt at nonchalance, Shardul slowly extracted another cigarette and lit it, breathing deeply, staring at the ceiling.

Sanjana stared at the ground, refusing to meet anyone's eyes. Her passive face gave no indication what she was thinking. Leslie wanted to say something supportive, anything to encourage her to make the right decision and assure her she would be okay.

Shardul spoke, his voice soft and low, a timbre she had yet to hear from him, the silky tone a cross between seduction and guilt.

Tarla interpreted in hushed tones. "He says, 'Would you leave your family here? Your home? Your girls?'" Shardul glanced angrily in their direction before he spoke again. Tarla resumed translation. "'Where will you live? Where will you work? We need you here, where you belong.'"

"She belongs with family," Maninder reiterated, this time more forcefully. "She was stolen from us, mistreated, abused." His voice caught in his throat as his emotions broke through his surface calm. He turned away from Shardul, addressing Sanjana only, in their native language.

For her benefit, Tarla translated, "He says, 'Please, my sister, come home.'"

Sanjana fell into his arms, into his waiting embrace, into another chance at life.

Shardul, his face contorted into a vicious promise of violence, lunged toward his former gharwali, shouting angry words, pointing, gesturing manically. Leslie knew he wanted to get his hands on her, hook his claws, shake her into submission.

Maninder clutched Sanjana protectively, yelling back at him. Startled, Tom placed himself between Leslie and the escalating argument. He watched Maninder carefully, as if waiting for another excuse to wade in and pummel Shardul.

In the midst of the chaos, Tarla grabbed her arm with both hands and leaned close, bringing her lips so close to her ear she could feel the woman's breath.

"She is here," Tarla said urgently, barely audible above the angry shouts.

"I don't understand."

"Please, just listen. Raveena is here. She is in the alley somewhere outside. I saw her only once when he returned with her." *He* was a curse word in the woman's mouth. "I have not seen her since, but I know she is there. If you can still take her away from this, do. Go quickly. While no one watches and these men can protect you. Before it is too late."

CHAPTER 37

*L*eslie couldn't see much beyond a few feet of pollution-diffused sunlight. The alleyway was much too dark. She pressed past the smoldering garbage heaps, hands clamped over her nose and mouth in a losing attempt to block the fetid stench.

She knew her window of opportunity would not exceed a few minutes. She'd snuck out unnoticed in the midst of the commotion over Sanjana, but her absence would surely be noticed quickly. She couldn't hesitate. Shardul couldn't have any idea what was happening, and she didn't know how long she had before Tom turned around and realized she was no longer behind him.

Something scurried over her sandaled foot, squeaking a shrill protest to her disruption. She gasped, trying not to squeak in reply, inhaling too deeply and choking on the smoldering smoke that rushed into her lungs. She paused to catch her breath before proceeding.

Ignoring the ooze squishing under each step, the shattered glass grinding into her flimsy soles, and the scurrying, many-legged somethings she didn't want to identify, she forced herself forward.

Where was Raveena? She saw no sign of the girl. Tarla admitted she had seen her only once, when Shardul returned with her. Had he moved her since then? Was she hidden elsewhere? She wasn't sure what she was looking for. Where would a person hide a little girl?

The sunlight bleeding into the alley grew dimmer the farther she advanced. Sudden movement off to her right caught her attention. Her head snapped around.

It was only a piece of fabric, one corner flapping feebly, lifted and toyed with by a stray breeze wandering through the cramped space.

Droplets of sweat beaded at her temples, pooling together and trickling down her face. She stood still, eyes searching out anything that could conceivably hide a child.

Another errant breeze wafted through the stifling space, offering little relief but once again flapping the corner of the fabric.

She stared at it blankly before resuming her search for anything that could hide a child. She didn't see anything...

She turned her attention back to the fabric. Why did only that little corner flap idly in the breeze? Stepping closer, she found broken pieces of brick and an assortment of junk weighting down the lower edge. Unlike the rest of the alley refuse, these pieces formed a deliberate line. The opposite side of the fabric draped over jumbled piles of refuse. The result formed a very small, low...

Tent.

Her heart pounded as she reached forward and caught the flapping corner of fabric. With a firm tug, she freed the edge and pulled it to the side.

Raveena.

She stood absolutely still, stunned, and fought the urge to scream. Raveena lay on the filthy, rough concrete amidst shards of broken glass, wrists and ankles bound, mouth gagged.

The girl was on her side in a fetal position, completely still. Was she too late?

Raveena shifted slightly. The girl opened her eyes, squinting against the light, and then realized who stood above her. Tears leaked from the corners of her eyes, streaking the grime that darkened her face.

Leslie fought off images of Shardul crouched over the tiny body, handling her roughly, forcing a filthy cloth into her mouth, and binding her wrists together. She pushed the thoughts from her mind, unable to cope with the swell of fury. Raveena peered up at her, waiting for help.

Stay focused. Bending quickly, she placed a hand on the trembling girl's shoulder. "I'm taking you out of here." She spoke quietly, hoping to convey a modicum of calm that she did not feel. Raveena needed strength right now.

Leslie's trembling fingers struggled with the knots, starting with the gag in the girl's mouth, careful not to pull the strands of hair tangled in the tied fabric. When the cloth loosened and fell away, Raveena gasped, coughing and choking as she drew air into her lungs.

Leslie worked on the bonds around her ankles next, gritting her teeth at the raw wounds where the fabric cut into her skin. When the child's ankles were loose, she fought with the wrist restraints, wiping nervous sweat from her brow, ears straining for footsteps or voices—anything to warn her that discovery was imminent.

The moment the fabric fell away from her wrists, Raveena launched herself into her arms, knocking her over backward, grasping her neck so tightly she could barely breathe.

"Shhhh," Leslie comforted, patting the girl's back. "Shhhh. Let's go quickly. Before anyone finds us."

Little fingers ran through her hair, clutching and releasing over and over as if reassuring herself this was real.

A shadow fell over them in the dim light of the alley, like a cloud had drifted in front of the sun. Or someone had stepped into the alleyway entrance.

Without turning to look, even before Raveena gasped and quaked violently, she knew it was Shardul. The demon came to snatch away her chance for salvation and happiness.

Please, no. Why? Why couldn't he come two minutes from now after she'd safely hidden the girl in the taxi, retrieved Tom, and sped away? Why was he always there derailing her? Where was God? If she called out to Him now, would He hear and answer? He gave every appearance of turning a deaf ear on the suffering of helpless children.

Dressed now, Shardul carried a briefcase and looked like he was leaving. He also looked stunned to see she'd freed his prisoner. Anger quickly replaced his shock. He came toward her, each quick step crunching whatever lay in his path.

She twirled around, confirming what she already knew — they were trapped. No doors, no paths, nothing to squeeze through or escape into. Shardul stood between them and the only way out.

She glanced around for anything to use as a weapon. Nothing. Perhaps someone more resourceful might have found something, but she had never used a weapon in her life. She didn't know what she was doing.

Beside her, Raveena cried as she watched the man approach. She suddenly understood why Tarla believed herself fated to life as a sex slave — escape was impossible.

"Give me the girl," he growled, so close she could see the bruises on his face and the blood trickling from his nose.

Leslie shook her head, pulling Raveena behind her, shielding the girl the only way she could. She expected him to pull the knife on her and had no idea how she would defend herself.

He didn't bother. Tossing aside the briefcase, he grabbed her shoulders and shoved her. She slammed into the concrete wall, her head snapping back and cracking against it with a dull thud. The last of her bangles shattered from her wrist. She paused, stunned.

Raveena screamed as Shardul grabbed her arm and dragged her forward. Leslie thought she heard distant sirens. Or was that just ringing in her ears?

She shook her head to clear it and launched herself at the man. She caught him by the arm and dug in with her fingernails, a guttural sound escaping her throat.

He pulled a gun from a pocket, backhanding her across the face. Pain exploded across her cheek as she wheeled back into the wall. She stumbled, dark haze clouding her vision while points of light flickered in front of her. She hunched over, blinking rapidly, shaking her head.

"Auntie!" she heard Raveena shout as he pulled her away. "Help me, Auntie!"

The girl's plea drew her like a magnet. Her feet fumbled through the alley, following the girl's cries. She ignored the ache in her jaw and the pulsing throb in her cheek. Raveena struggled against her captor, alternately pummeling his arm with her little fist and prying at his fingers.

Where was Tom? When would he notice she was missing? Would he even find her in the alley? He had no reason to look for her here. And were those sirens she heard? She thought they grew louder.

She heaved herself forward, grabbing Raveena. "You can't have her," she insisted, as if saying the words would make it true.

He pointed the gun at her, snarling. She stared at it, contemplating her choices here. She wouldn't give up. No matter what he did. That much she knew. But of all the possible outcomes racing through her mind, she never suspected what really happened.

Raveena's hand moved to grab the gun from Shardul.

Before she could scream a warning or move to intervene, Shardul turned on the girl, slamming the gun across her face, sending her sprawling to the ground. She lay absolutely still. For a split second, the crazed man looked startled by his own actions.

"Oh, God, no!" Leslie cried, crouching at the girl's side, her back to her captor. Her head had landed on a broken brick, the jagged edge opening a gash that now pooled blood on the ground below her. She leaned low over the prone figure, watching for any sign of movement. "Raveena? Can you hear me?"

What could she do? All she saw was blood. She remembered hearing that head wounds always bled heavily. But this looked bad. There was a lot of blood.

Noise from the street filtered into the alley. She no longer heard sirens. But she heard voices, and some of them seemed to be shouting.

She would go get Prajit first, to watch the girl. He could keep an eye on her while she went back inside. Surely Maninder could call for an ambulance or something—whatever they did here for emergencies.

Standing, she brushed the dirt from her hands, willing the little girl to hang on. *Please, God, please*, she prayed, *whatever you think of me, please let Raveena be okay.*

A rough, dirty hand clamped over her mouth, stifling her scream.

CHAPTER 38

*S*he'd forgotten about Shardul. She tried to pull away, to run for the street, to cry for help, but he overpowered her too quickly. He pulled her close, held her against his own body, and dragged her to the wall. He pressed his back against the barrier as if trying to disappear into it.

"Shhhhh," he hissed in her ear, staring toward the alley entrance.

She didn't have time for this. Raveena still lay motionless on the ground. She needed medical help. Clawing at the hand sealing her mouth, she thrashed against her captor.

"Shhh!" He jerked his arm, yanking her head backwards. The gun dug painfully into her side.

In the silence, the voices from the street grew louder, but she couldn't distinguish words. Were they looking for her?

When she heard her name, she easily identified the speaker as Tom. He was loud and sounded agitated. Maninder's calm cadence responded. They must be wondering what happened to her.

Her mind raced. She had to get free of Shardul's grip. If only she could call for help, let them know where she was. Her face throbbed where he'd struck her with the gun. She was sure her cheek was puffy and bruised again. One eye felt like it was swelling shut.

"Here, here!" She recognized Prajit's voice as he spoke the words she longed to cry, words silenced by the gun bruising her side.

The voices moved closer. They must be searching the street for signs of her. Would they pass right by Shardul's hiding place? Could she draw their attention if they did?

She looked down for something to kick. Instead, she saw Raveena, motionless in a thickening puddle of blood. As if he could read her thoughts, Shardul wrapped a leg around her, pinning her against him, and adjusted his hand to cover her nose and mouth.

"I will shoot," he murmured, his lips beside her ear. He rocked the gun against her ribs, like she could forget its presence. Cheek pressed to her head, his quick breaths ruffled her hair. The lingering stench from the constant string of cigarettes pervaded his clothing and seeped from the fingers clamped to her mouth.

She held perfectly still, not sure what might provoke him to pull the trigger. Laboring to breathe, her airway obstructed by the silencing hand, she fought the alarm rising in her chest that clawed at her throat, longing for escape.

The heat of the day seeped into the dank alley, already squalid with decay. Closing her eyes, her pulse thumping painfully across her bruised face, she concentrated on the voices. Maninder spoke again, and she realized the reason she couldn't make out the words was because he wasn't speaking English. She didn't recognize the voice that answered. Who was out there with him?

The alley pressed against her, the shadows crept closer. She felt dizzy. When she opened her eyes, the world swam out of focus. Her lungs burned. She couldn't draw a breath. She tried to gasp, tried to soothe her aching body with great gulps of oxygen.

How had Raveena survived like this, alone and choking? Panic set in, and she clawed viciously at his hand despite the danger wrenched into her ribs.

"Why would she go in the alley? You're sure you saw him?" She heard Tom a moment before Prajit led him into the gloom, both men blinking while their eyes adjusted to the dim light.

Prajit, bless him, looked horrified at the sight before him. Of course. From his taxi, he must have seen her creep from the brothel into the alley. When he saw Shardul take the same path, he must have gone to get help. If she got the chance, she would have to remember to thank him for coming to her rescue again. She'd lost count of how many times he'd rendered assistance when things seemed hopeless.

His hiding place discovered, Shardul dragged her roughly from the wall.

"Let her go!" Tom started forward, fists ready.

Shardul held the gun out, halting him immediately. He dragged her, still silenced and suffocating, to his discarded briefcase. "Pick it up."

When she hesitated, unwilling to do anything he wanted, he trained the gun on Tom.

"Pick it up!" he ordered.

She stared at Tom, his hands in the air, rage contorting his face. Chest heaving, his eyes darted to her cheek, no doubt dismayed by the fresh injuries inflicted on her. She wanted to tell him how sorry she was that she had failed yet again and dragged him into this mess. Would she ever have the chance now?

Slowly, she stooped, stretching out her arm and grabbing the briefcase handle. Could it be used as a weapon? She tried to picture herself knocking the gun from his hand, whacking him over the head with it. Eyeing the gun, she decided anything she attempted was certain to backfire. She opted not to fight. If Shardul hurt Tom, or

God forbid, shot him...no, she couldn't bear to be the cause.

Shardul pushed her toward the street. She didn't understand why he didn't just take the briefcase and run. He was the only one with a gun. Why was he holding onto her?

Sweat trickled down her brow. Shardul edged her along, pointing the gun at Tom, then Prajit, then ramming it painfully back into her side. He muttered incomprehensibly while he dragged her forward. She thought he might be losing it.

She had to get back to Raveena.

Shardul waved the gun toward the two watching men, directing them back into the street, presumably so neither could get close enough to assist her. Dragging her with him, he stepped from the shadows, the gun held before him.

A police car was parked by the brothel. The sirens had not been her imagination. Two policemen hovered by Sanjana who, she was glad to see, clutched a bag. Tarla stood by the door, arms crossed, watching Sanjana leave. How would losing her surrogate mother affect the woman? Maybe they could convince her to leave too, with the help of POW.

Maninder must have been the one who called the police. The way Shardul hid in the alleyway did not suggest he had the upper hand in this situation—which also explained why he held her. Things must have gotten crazier inside the brothel after Tarla sent her after Raveena.

"That's my wife!" Tom yelled. "Do something! Please!"

The police stepped forward, raising their batons. They spoke rapidly, loudly, and as she looked closer, she realized she recognized one of them. It was Officer Verma, who had helped them—or rather not helped them—the day Tom dragged her to the police station.

Shardul laughed as he replied. She thought he was probably pointing out their batons were completely useless against his gun. She had to agree with that and wondered how she would get out of this. Her eyes swept over their faces, Sanjana and Tarla dismayed, Prajit stricken, Tom helpless and terrified, Maninder and the policemen somehow still calm and collected.

The police yelled something unintelligible. Shardul replied, waving the gun in the air before pressing it to her temple.

The noise attracted attention. Heads peeped tentatively around curtains and corners, ready to snap back to safety. A few people even ventured over thresholds. They jumped and disappeared as Shardul bellowed threats. No one would intercede. She closed her eyes, wishing she could wake up and discover this was all a nightmare.

Maninder called out, "Leslie, he says he will let you go if we allow him to get in his car and leave."

His car? She'd looked for his car earlier. She strained to catch a glimpse of the R8, but still didn't see it.

At dinner last night, Maninder had dismissed the possibility of danger with a wave of his hand. *Bhagwaan ki kripa se, Shardul will not be there. Bhagwaan ki kripa se, Sanjana will trust us and leave quickly. Bhagwaan ki kripa se, we will smuggle her away without incident.* And she couldn't stop from adding her own: *Bhagwaan ki kripa se, Raveena will be there.*

God willing.

That was the hinge upon which the entire plan hung. And that was the problem. Her entire life she waited for God to be willing to allow her to make amends.

Now her life hung in the balance.

$\mathcal{U}$nchallenged, Shardul changed direction, dragging her away from the others, moving with more purpose. Out the corner of her eye, she spotted a gleaming white car—a boxy thing, maybe a BMW? With a sinking feeling, she realized how very likely it was he owned numerous vehicles.

What did God want from her? Sacrifice? Was He the Old Testament God of Wrath that dominated her father's sermons before they were eviscerated by his devastating loss and centered around forgiveness and appreciation?

An eye for an eye, a tooth for a tooth? A life for a life?

She closed her eyes again and made a last ditch effort. The one thing her mother had told her she must never do.

She tried to bargain with God.

Make it one life for two, and it's a deal. See Sanjana and Raveena safely home. They've suffered too much already.

They stopped suddenly beside the white car. Would he really let her go?

"Open it," he said.

Bewildered, she looked for something to open.

"Open the door!" The gun barrel pressed painfully against her side reminded her why she should follow his orders.

He meant the car door. But she stood by the passenger's side, not the driver's. He wasn't letting her go at all. He meant to force her inside.

And girls who were taken rarely made it back home. *The slightest deviation changes the trajectory; the path is altered forever.*

She sought Tom's eyes. He stood by the police but no longer pleaded with them to intervene. She understood the helpless horror he felt, knew the look on his face matched her own when she watched a man steal her sister away. Now she was in Trisha's place, hand clamped over her mouth, eyes wide, watching her future change in a moment, one thought screaming through her mind.

That one thought was not, "Help me!" It wasn't the frantic plea that haunted her memory of Trisha's abduction—the plea she thought she'd failed to answer.

In that last moment, locking eyes with Tom, knowing this was the end, all she could think was, "I love you." And then she prayed. She prayed he would understand and would be free of the coat of guilt she had worn ever since her sister's abduction. She prayed God would be with her in these final moments. And she prayed that if there was a heaven and she was deemed worthy to enter, Trisha would meet her at the gate and lead her in, and the two sisters could enjoy the childhood they were denied in this life.

She prayed, knowing she would never get inside that car. She would take a bullet before she would go willingly into the nightmare.

Her fingers grabbed the handle and lifted.

She swung the door open, ready to fight until the gun ended everything.

Voices cried out, Tom's loudest of all. He seemed to be waving.

Shardul relaxed his death grip on her, just enough to push her into the vehicle.

Gritting her teeth, she prepared to push past him and flee, knowing the bullet would catch her no matter how fast she ran.

She glanced back at Tom one last time and realized he wasn't waving. He was motioning down, wildly gesturing again and again.

As her captor pushed against her, she stopped struggling and dropped to her knees. Shardul, accustomed to rancorous resistance, was unprepared for the limp form that slid easily from his loosened grasp.

Something whizzed over her head the same instant she heard a loud pop. Shardul jerked backward and collapsed in the street, as warm, red specks spattered over her and dotted the car.

The world around her swam out of focus. She wobbled on her knees, afraid she might pitch forward. Through her hazy vision, she could make out Officer Verma's rigid form, gun still leveled. The police were armed after all.

A flurry of movement and voices blurred about her, a watercolor painting of pale, broad strokes, the artist caught by a sudden storm whose angry droplets distorted the image.

Tom reached her first, pulling her to her feet and into a crushing embrace. "Oh, my God. Oh, my God. I thought you were gone. I can't believe it." He cradled her, pressed his face into her neck. "I can't lose you. Ever."

She couldn't believe it either and simply held onto Tom, dazed and shaking, catching her breath and trying not to look at Shardul as Maninder and the policemen assessed his stability. Alive, unharmed, she somehow managed to escape. The briefcase was still in her hands.

And Raveena was still in the alley.

"Raveena!" Leslie extricated herself from Tom's grip and shoved the briefcase into his hands. She dashed back to the alley, each step clacking on the paved street but muted as she picked her way through the refuse, oblivious to what might be beneath her feet.

She sucked in her breath. Raveena still hadn't moved. Her little form lay motionless where she'd fallen. Kneeling beside her, she placed a hand gently on her back, her own heart thumping as though it could beat for them both.

A shadow passed over them. Tom caught up and knelt beside her. "That's a lot of blood. Is she..."

"She's breathing. I think." Leslie prayed this wasn't wishful thinking.

"Here, let me." He moved beside Raveena and looked at the gash split open across her forehead. "I think it's okay to move her."

He lifted the tiny frame easily, carefully picking his way into the street. Leslie shivered at the congealing blood left behind, marveling that one small girl could lose so much.

The police waited beside Maninder, who blanched at the sight of the wounded child.

"Oh, my," he said. "This must be your Raveena."

"She's hurt. Shardul—"

"Yes, we must see her to hospital right away," Maninder interrupted. He raised his eyebrows, looked at her meaningfully, trying to communicate something to her without words.

"What has happened here?" asked the policeman she didn't know.

Maninder kept his eyes on her as he answered. "The child has been hurt. Please, allow her to go. I will finish giving a statement."

"We have taken your statement," the policeman said. "You came for your sister. But what about the child? Why is she here? With these Americans?" He eyed her suspiciously.

"She found my sister and led me to her. That is what brought them here today." He sounded so sure of himself. And why not? He spoke the truth, even though he left a lot out. He was silently instructing her to do the same—don't volunteer anything that didn't need to be said.

"Please, just let me get help for her," she pleaded.

The policeman looked at her skeptically. "You are the mother of this child?"

She knew it was fruitless to lie—Officer Verma knew for a fact Raveena was not hers. He'd heard the entire story of her first encounter at the brothel. She looked to him, remembering how she chided him for looking the other way for the brothel owners. And now here she was, wishing he would do the same thing for her.

Verma's dark eyes traveled over Raveena and clouded. Was he thinking of his own daughter? His eyes met hers, and she held them with as much silent intensity as she could, pleading with him wordlessly.

He was correct. She had no business trying to move in the shadows of his country. But no child belonged there either.

"Who else but the child's mother would risk her life in this way? Of course this is her child," he said. "You should take her to hospital now."

The slightest deviation, one kind act, a helping hand. They made all the difference in the world and changed the trajectory of a life forever.

Still skeptical, the other officer did not challenge his partner's assessment. "You can take." He pointed at Tom. "But you will stay to give your statement."

She worked her hands between Tom's arms and Raveena's body then hoisted the girl into her cradling grip.

Sirens sounded in the distance.

"That will be the ambulance we summoned for the gentleman you shot," Maninder said. He gestured her to go. "You should take the girl now. Would you prefer to share the ambulance or take the taxi?"

She wouldn't share anything with the man who had attempted to abduct Raveena and nearly killed her. Prajit would get them to the hospital just fine and as quickly as he could. She would trust him with her life.

Officer Verma stood aside to let her pass. She wanted to thank him but thought it best to keep moving and nodded instead. He wobbled his head in a figure eight and winked at her, patting Raveena gently as they walked by.

"Take care, madam, and I hope your daughter will be okay."

Prajit scurried forward to open the door of the taxi. Leslie stopped, considering this man who'd rescued her time and again, for no other reason than she chose to ride in his taxi and he was a good person. "Thank you. Again. So much."

He wobbled his head and waved her into the vehicle. "Okay, lady. Okay."

She embarrassed him, but she didn't care. She wanted him to know how she felt and how much she appreciated him. And she couldn't wait—because you never knew when you would have another chance.

CHAPTER 40

*S*he felt useless from the moment she raced into the hospital and watched the girl whisked away, surrounded by medical staff. Wondering where they were taking her, she allowed a nurse to lead her to an office. What else could she do but follow her and sit in the indicated seat? An admissions specialist attempted to take a medical history and general personal information from her. Saying "I don't know" over and over again left her feeling numb. Did she know anything anymore?

Finally, an easy answer. Amidst dozens of pages of fees and charges—hundreds and thousands of rupees each—she was asked room type request—general ward or private. The admissions specialist advised her she would not be allowed to remain with the child in the general ward. Private rooms came air-conditioned—something else to distinguish them from the wards and to contribute to their three-hundred-rupee-a-night fee—but her only concern was to be close to Raveena.

Her mind wasn't functional enough for basic arithmetic. She didn't know what three hundred rupees was in dollars and didn't ask. She didn't know how she would pay and didn't care. She pretended she was Raveena's guardian and signed every form pushed at her, agreeing to anything to get medical attention for the girl.

Eyeing her wounded face, the specialist asked if she would like to see a doctor too. She'd stared at her dumbly, forgetting about her own injury, then shook her head. All she wanted was help for Raveena.

The nurse instructed her to take a seat in the emergency room waiting area. Dark eyes peered at her curiously. Worry gnawed at Leslie's bones. Just a bump on the head, she told herself, ignoring the blood that soaked her clothes and contradicted that conviction. She longed for Tom, needing his familiar presence and strength to help her through this. But no matter how many people joined her, walked by, or left the waiting area, no matter how hard she willed each face to belong to her husband, he didn't appear.

Shardul did, however. They wheeled him in on a gurney, a dark crimson flower blooming over his shirt from the chest wound. He thrashed and moaned, and though suffering gave her no pleasure, she wasn't sorry for him as the medics crashed through swinging doors and out of her sight. He deserved what he got.

Where was Tom? What was he doing? Why didn't he come?

What was taking so long with Raveena? Why wouldn't they let her back with the girl? Couldn't she sit helplessly at her side instead of in the waiting area? Maybe she was even more hurt than they thought.

Weak with fear, she watched for Tom, waiting for an update.

Hours later, a nurse called her name and escorted her back to meet with a doctor, who happily spoke English.

The deep laceration required stitches. They wanted to keep Raveena overnight to watch for signs of concussion. She was severely dehydrated and malnourished. They would push IV fluids. They would transfuse blood overnight and run labs in the morning to make sure she didn't require another transfusion. "If all is well in the morning, we can probably let her go home tomorrow." He smiled, but she wondered where exactly home would be.

By the time they transferred to a room, it was late and Raveena was sound asleep, assisted with pain medication and a sedative. She needed the rest so her body could heal.

Leslie had never been in a hospital. She wondered if the buildings were always so cold. As she rubbed her arms to warm herself, she thought it must just be her. Then she noticed Raveena shivering in her sleep and requested blanket after blanket to tuck around the girl. Finally, the smiling young nurse stepped to the window and turned off the air conditioner. Feeling foolish and helpless, Leslie murmured her thanks.

She dug at her gritty eyes, forcing herself to stay awake. She kept vigil, unable to tear herself away from the girl's side. She couldn't bear the thought of the child waking alone in the dark, unfamiliar surroundings. She wondered what had happened to Tom. She expected him to follow her as soon as possible. What could possibly keep him away all night?

Raveena remained stable, the beeping machines assured her, as the morning sun crept through the window. They would scream a piercing alarm if any vital readings fell outside the programmed parameters.

The day nurse entered the room with a wide smile and what Leslie assumed was a greeting. The young woman carried a plastic basin that sloshed as she settled it on the bed beside Raveena. After removing blanket after blanket, she submerged a cloth into the sudsy basin and gently wiped the grime from Raveena's face.

The nurse smiled again and offered the cloth to her. Leslie took the soft fabric but only stood numbly, staring at the bandage hiding the stitches from view.

The nurse took her hand, guiding the cloth over Raveena's arm. Leslie nodded her understanding and continued the bed bath with gentle strokes, rinsing the cloth to refresh and warm it. The wash water smelled of baby soap, and she swallowed the lump that formed in her throat. Now that she wanted a child of her own, her body refused to cooperate, and circumstances kept her from adopting this little girl she'd grown to love.

The nurse lifted the thick bandage from Raveena's head to check the wound then pointed at the red line. "Okay," the nurse said with a smile, nodding and dabbing a cotton ball in something pungent.

The sharp, black ends of the stitches stuck straight out from the skin. They looked like angry wasp wings, but it was an improvement over the gash that gaped before, bleeding away the girl's life.

The nurse dabbed at crusted blood, carefully working the antiseptic around the raw area.

Raveena stirred again. "Mama," she murmured, reaching out, fingers grasping at the empty air.

Leslie stopped swabbing the dirt from the girl's hand and waited for her eyes to open, but Raveena slept on. And apparently she dreamed of her mother. Of course. Who else would a child cry out for when scared and in pain?

The nurse nudged her. "Mama," the young woman said, pointing to her.

Leslie shook her head sadly, trying to figure out how to explain. "Not Mama. Ummm." She placed her hand over her chest. "Auntie. Well, Auntie Mama," she amended, remembering she had signed the hospital admission forms as the child's guardian.

The nurse nodded, but understanding did not dawn in her eyes. She applied a fresh bandage and left the room, carrying the basin with its dirtied water.

Leslie pushed Raveena's dark, thick strands of hair away from her forehead, careful not to snag the pieces caught in the bandage. Maybe she could ask the nurse for a brush later, if Raveena woke.

Who was she exactly to this child? A stepping-stone to a better life? It wasn't the future she had spent the last few days hoping for. The guest room of her home could remain a guest room instead of blooming pink and frilly with a little girl's treasures and hopes. She could go back to teaching, pouring her efforts into the lives of many surrogate children as she had always done. Couldn't she?

She had no way to take her home. No guardianship documents. The best she could do was leave her in a safe place in India, if she could keep her from the brothel owner. If she could get her into an orphanage safely, would Raveena at least write to her, once she learned to read and write? How long would she remember her American Auntie? Could they maintain a distant connection, occasional letters sharing the important milestones in their lives? She pictured the letters, tucked into a drawer, fading and crinkled with time, a flimsy substitute for real moments spent together. Would Raveena eventually tuck her away into a forgotten corner, a faded memory, more imagination than real? Or, as she wove together a new life, would she try to forget about the foreign woman twined together with her memories of a childhood in a brothel and push her away completely?

This was never supposed to be about her. Leslie came to India for Tom. She fought for Raveena because the little girl reached out to her, asked her for help. Everything was crumbling now, her life a sandcastle in the rising waves the last few days wrought. It left her empty, questioning every decision she'd ever made.

She wanted to take Raveena shopping with friends. She wanted to learn to cook Indian dishes for her and help with homework and braid her hair. She wanted to take her to the zoo, to movies, for picnics in the park. She wanted to be present when Raveena decided what she wanted to be when she grew up and to help her plan how to make it happen. Someone else would get to do all those things now. Or no one, if she languished in an orphanage until she came of age. Surely, she would be a better parent than none at all.

So she wasn't perfect. She was human with all her faults and sins and mistakes. But some people were far worse. And Rhea was right, she'd done good things in her life. Didn't that count for anything? Why was she being punished? She wanted to shake her fist at the sky and demand answers.

Was anyone listening? Her mother would cringe at the blasphemous question and remind her she must trust in the Lord in all ways and always. But what if her mother was the one who had it wrong? What if everyone was just tumbling along on a big rock hurtling through space and when we die, we're just gone?

The thought left her physically ill. No good or bad. Just here, existing, breathing, doing. Which meant no justice or reward either.

So what was the point? She lived frugally and tried to help people and do the right thing, and, in the end, she wound up no better or worse than a dirtbag like Shardul? Or her sister's kidnapper?

What was the point of it all?

Her lungs heaved like a wet sponge, sopping up the pain and frustration and squeezing it out her tear ducts. She swiped at the tears that would not stop, wracked with quiet sobs. Staring down at the sleeping girl, time ticking by to the consistent beep of the vitals machine and the IV dripping into her arm, Leslie knew the point.

She bent low and kissed her soft cheek, sweet with baby soap. "Just wake up and be okay," she whispered.

Seeing her to safety, giving the girl freedom, would have to be enough, even if her life would be spent with others.

CHAPTER 41

"K nock, knock." Her eyes flew open at the sound of the whisper. That voice could wake her from a coma. She jumped from the chair she'd dozed off in and threw herself into Tom's arms. He carried a bag in one hand, a teddy bear tucked in the crook of his arm.

"Where have you been?"

Bloodshot eyes searched her own as she drank him in. Stubble roughened his face. He looked like he hadn't slept. "Oh, goodness," he sighed. "All over. How's Raveena?"

She led him to the bed. "They gave her blood last night, and we just kept an eye on her. The doctor might let her go today." She rested a hand on the girl's skeletal arm. "I wish I knew where she'll go, what will happen to her."

He nodded and settled the bear above Raveena's shoulder, away from the IV and oxygen tubing that snaked over her bed. He set the bag on the rolling table by her bed.

"We need to talk," he said with a sigh.

She braced herself. The teddy bear seemed like a good sign. But his haggard appearance concerned her. The last thing he'd said to her was that he couldn't lose her. She hoped he hadn't changed his mind.

He scrubbed at his hair, already at odds with itself in hard angles and crazy tufts. On a deep breath, he plowed ahead. "I guess there's just no easy way to say this. I'm sorry I haven't been treating you right. I've always worried I'll turn into my dad. And no matter how it sickens me, I've been acting just like him, out at clubs at night, ignoring my family at home. Then last night, drinking and coming after you like a caveman. You deserve better. I'm sorry."

She had mentally prepared a rebuttal for each imagined argument he might lob at her. Completely unprepared for an apology, she had no response. Her mouth hung open while her mind frantically tried to prepare a statement.

"Even my dad managed to keep my mom with him all these years," Tom continued. "I thought I could do better, but I understand. If we want different things out of life, if you aren't happy, it would be better to end it than —"

She grabbed his hand. "I don't want to end it. I want us to work through things and move forward."

"You're sure?"

Tears brimmed her eyes. "Just thinking about it hurts. I know we've both done things we aren't proud of. But I can't imagine my life without you."

He threw his arms around her, pulling her close, crushing the air from her lungs. He kissed the top of her head. "I'm so sorry about last night. Forcing myself on you like that. I never want you to feel pressured. I've been so selfish lately. I'll be patient from now on, I promise."

She pulled away to look in his eyes, startled by the tears leaking from the corners. "I was never upset about last night."

"You weren't?"

"Not at all. It was…fantastic." A nervous giggle crept into her voice with the admission.

He blinked. "You thought so too?"

She heard the hesitation, the desire to believe. Was it so difficult to accept she'd enjoyed his burning mouth drinking her in, his demanding hands pulling at her, unable to get enough? Yes, of course it was.

She took his hands and ran her thumb over his scabbed knuckles. "Best ever. I really enjoyed it."

"I just told you about..." He stopped himself before he repeated the words. His voice dropped to a whisper. "I felt like I forced myself on you."

"I didn't feel that way at all. After what I told you yesterday, I thought you wouldn't want me anymore."

"Well, I was shocked. And I didn't handle it very well. But that was a long time ago. We were kids. You were raped. Scared." His face clouded over as the weight of what he said sank in. She could see the ugly images his mind produced for him.

"You must've been drunk if you can't remember how much I enjoyed it." She grinned, hoping to distract him.

"Not drunk. Just scared to believe it. I remember how much I enjoyed it." He cupped her face in his hands. "You've done so much for me. I love you. I always have. Beautiful woman."

Warmth radiated from him, confirming her theory that he'd soaked up so much sun he could release it back into the world. Heat flowed into her, shocking her system like paddles to the chest. Her heart hammered as he leaned closer. He smelled earthy, as if the sun had baked right into his flesh, toasting it ginger.

His soft lips found hers, and for the first time in her life, she tasted forgiveness—spring rain, yellow-green meadows bursting with new life, lavender, honeysuckle, and rosebuds ready to bloom. Fresh. Sweet. Delicious.

He let her go and as she smiled at him, she knew something was different between them. Searching his eyes for the change, she realized it wasn't him. It was her. She felt whole. Clean.

She could look him in the eye without shielding secrets from view.

"I got you something," he said. "Just in case you didn't... you know...want a divorce. I was hoping."

He lifted a little velvet jewelry box from the bag he'd carried in and held it out to her.

Her fingers trembled as she accepted it and rocked back the lid. Sitting on a silver band, two round, black stones gleamed side by side.

"It was Rhea's idea," he told her. "Maninder made it. The stones are Indian black star. They're only found in India. Here, look." He led her to the window and tipped her hand so that the sunlight struck the milky surfaces of the smooth, polished stones. A four-pronged star appeared on each gem, forming a glistening, silvery X over the black surface. No, she decided, not an X...a cross.

"I never got you anything for our tenth anniversary, so I thought this would be a good time to make up for it. Rhea says the stone represents love and commitment. The ring represents you and me in India."

Let go and let God, her mother liked to say. Leslie thought of the moment before Officer Verma fired on Shardul, ending the standoff and saving her life. Tom had been signaling to her to get down. He'd seen the gun, she was sure.

Was God with her in that moment, orchestrating the timing, manipulating the outcome? Or was it simply a random string of events whose outcome this time favored her?

She glanced at Raveena, still asleep in the bed. Nothing this past week had happened the way she wanted it to. But if Shardul had given Raveena to her in exchange for the money, Sanjana would still be in the brothel and Maninder would still be searching for her. Perhaps this more difficult road was necessary to help them too. Perhaps divine intervention wasn't out of the question. Despite the silence for the last decade, was He sending her a sign? She wanted to believe He was. She closed her eyes and offered a prayer of thanks—for Raveena's life, her life, and another chance with Tom. It felt good to nestle back into His warm embrace after a long absence.

"I love it. It's beautiful." She lifted the ring from the box and slid it on her finger, tipping her hand back and forth to admire the crosses illuminated in the light.

He cleared his throat. "After you left yesterday, we had to go to the police station to give our statements and file reports. Sanjana and Tarla came too. They corroborated our stories and told them what happened the first time you went to the brothel. Officer Verma said he'd add their statements to the complaint we filed against him already. They want you to come today to give a statement as well, but it's just a formality. They have enough to charge him. If he leaves the hospital, that is."

"So they're free of him. Finally." Another blessing.

"Maninder says he'll be better off if he doesn't leave the hospital."

"Because he'll go to jail?"

"No, because the brothel owner showed up and found out what Shardul's been up to."

"Bikram? You saw him?"

"Yep. He looked crazy, and he has two big thugs that follow him around. It was pretty scary."

"But if Sanjana was free to go, why was he mad?"

"It wasn't that. Although he wasn't thrilled she left. He had to respond to the police and the shooting at his building. Then we opened that briefcase Shardul carried. It had almost ten thousand dollars in it."

"Our money?"

"Yes, almost all of it. Along with the guardianship papers and two train tickets to Mumbai. Maninder thinks he was going to take Raveena and the money and start his own brothel."

Leslie's stomach churned. She looked again at the injured girl, tiny and weak, completely defenseless. She shook her head, at a loss for words. How could anyone hurt her in any way?

"There's more," Tom said. "Turns out Bikram really did agree to let us pay off Raveena's debt, but for only three thousand dollars. Shardul got greedy and decided to scam us both. He told Bikram we took the girl. That's why he hid her in the alley like that. But he hadn't paid Bikram yet and it looks like he planned to run with all the money. Maninder says Bikram is not the sort of person you cross, and I believe him. So we paid him the money he was promised. It's a done deal. Maninder says Shardul will be better off dead at this point. He says Bikram will find him, even if he runs, even in jail."

"So Raveena is truly free now? She never has to go back to the brothel?"

"Never. You freed her."

"We freed her." She fell against him, appreciation swelling in her chest, tears of relief brimming in her eyes.

"There's still the question of what will happen to her. She could go to the orphanage. Rhea and Maninder considered adopting her, too. But they decided not to."

She raised her head from his chest to look in his eyes. "Why wouldn't they want her?"

"I told them we want her."

She stared at him, afraid to believe. Only moments ago she forced herself to let go of the future she dreamed of, and now he offered it to her again. She got a second chance with him, and now Raveena too? "You said you didn't want to adopt. You didn't want children at all."

"I know. But I was scared and being selfish. I really care about her. And you. I know this is important for you. Watching you at gunpoint—afraid I was losing you forever—I guess it put things in perspective."

"I can't believe you agreed to adopt her."

"I shouldn't have spoken for you, I guess, but after watching you fight for her yesterday, risking your own life...I don't know. If you want to take her home, we can make it happen."

"Yes. I still want to take her home. So badly."

"I thought you might. Maninder and I went to the embassy yesterday hoping for an emergency visa extension. They said tourist visas are never extended except in the case of death or illness. We argued that Raveena is sick in the hospital and obviously she isn't ready to travel. But the adoption process isn't even started yet, so they don't consider her our child. We have to leave the country the day after tomorrow. I called the airline to confirm our seats. I'm sorry you have to leave her here. I tried."

"And I wondered what kept you away yesterday. Thank you for this." She leaned in to kiss him, slow and lingering, ripe with her gratitude.

He looked very pleased. "Maninder is at the orphanage right now trying to make arrangements. He says they'll go see her every day and keep an eye on her. And then we can come back for her once the adoption is complete and her passport and visa are in place. It'll take some time, but it's doable. At least we got it started."

"It's a great start," she said, thinking of the years to come, now filled with her own little girl.

"And I emailed my dad." His voice took on a harsh edge. "I thanked him for sending some of my trust fund money to help us adopt our daughter. I told him I'd like to start receiving regular disbursements from my trust fund, and we will visit when my job allows. So I'm glad you still want to adopt her. Otherwise I'd look pretty silly." His hands drifted to her hips and squeezed.

"Do you think she wants to go to America? You said it might be too hard on her. What if she wants to stay here?"

Rustling sounds from the bed brought their attention back to Raveena. "Mama," she murmured, thrashing.

Tom looked surprised. "She's calling you Mama? How does she know?"

"She's been crying out in her sleep like that periodically. I think the concussion left her out of it." *She hasn't called for Auntie at all*, she thought, feeling selfish for even wishing she had.

She went to the bed and lifted the girl's small hand into her own. Raveena's eyelids fluttered and opened.

"Tom, call the nurse! They want to know as soon as she wakes up!"

He nodded and hurried to the door.

Raveena blinked, staring at her surroundings, slowed by the lingering effects of the medication.

"Hey, there," Leslie said. "It's good to see you awake."

Raveena turned her eyes on her, recognition dawning. "Mama," she croaked, reaching with both arms for her.

Mama. The girl no longer thrashed in a semi-conscious state. She was coherent, reaching for her, recognition in her eyes.

Leslie had overheard enough descriptions of infants moving their mouths to form the word for the first time to know she was not the first to experience this feeling, when the floor dropped out from under you and the world turned you upside-down in a barrel roll. Her breath caught in her chest, a lump formed in her throat, and she smiled knowing nothing would ever be the same again.

Only yesterday, she'd shed the stifling coat of guilt. Now a silken jacket draped about her shoulders to take its place, and with it, she was properly dressed. And she had a new job.

She'd always known life could change in a moment. Bad things happened to good people for no reason whatsoever, and in the blink of an eye, one future is scrubbed away, erased forever, replaced by something completely different, whether you want it or not. Watching her life shift was nothing new to her—rejoicing in the alteration was.

She leaned down into the gentle embrace, careful to avoid the IV in Raveena's arm.

A new nurse entered the room with Tom and smiled warmly at Raveena. "Well, hello. Do you know where you are?"

The girl looked around. "In hospital?"

"That is right. Very good!"

"With Mama and Uncle," she added.

"Well, Mama and Uncle, recognizing her surroundings is a good sign. Let me contact her doctor." The nurse turned with another smile and left the room.

Tom handed her the teddy bear. "I brought you something to keep you company while you're here."

"Thank you, Uncle." She hugged the bear to her chest. "I am glad you are here."

"That was pretty scary yesterday. Are you feeling okay?"

She wobbled her head in a figure eight.

"Raveena," Leslie said, closing her fingers around the girl's hand. "We need to tell you something. Uncle and I have to go home to America the day after tomorrow. And we won't be able to take you with us right now."

The girl's face fell, resignation clouding her eyes as though she expected to hear this. It reminded Leslie of the numb look on her face when Shardul stuffed her into his car and stole away with her. This little girl was accustomed to disappointment.

Raveena stared at the bed, lower lip quivering. "I will miss you."

"But you never have to go back to GB Road," Leslie continued quickly. "Uncle made sure of that." She watched her face closely, hoping to cheer the girl.

"Where will I go?"

Leslie glanced at Tom. "Well, we want you to come home with us. We can't take you right now, even though we want to, but we will come back for you."

"Our friend is at the orphanage getting things ready for you," Tom said.

"Just for a little while," Leslie added quickly. "Until we can fill out papers to adopt you."

Raveena looked up quickly, eyes wide and bright. "I will go to America?"

"If you want to."

"I want to go with Mama and Uncle!" Raveena smiled, finally. "I will wait, Mama."

Tom picked up the bag he'd brought with him and grinned. "I have more presents."

He brought out two more jewelry boxes and handed one to each of them.

Raveena accepted hers reverently, holding the flat, hinged box between her hands like a frail bird. Her hands shook, and she stared at them with wide eyes. "What is it?" the girl whispered.

"Want me to open it?" Leslie offered.

When the girl nodded, she took the box, glanced at her smiling husband, and lifted the lid. Inside, an elephant charm hung from a silver necklace. She held it out for Raveena to see.

"This is for me?" Raveena asked, looking from one face to the other.

"Rhea says elephants never forget," Tom said. "You can wear it every day to remind you we're coming back. Okay?"

"It is...so pretty, Uncle."

"We will come back for you, understand?"

"Yes, Uncle. I will wait."

Leslie opened her box next and found another ring—a little diamond in the shape of a heart mounted on a gold band.

"It's a mother's ring," he explained. "Diamond is the birthstone for April. Sanjana doesn't remember the exact date, but she does remember that Raveena was born in April. We won't ever know her exact birthday, so we'll have to make our best guess when we start filing paperwork."

She slid the ring onto her little finger, right beside the black star. They shone together, radiant and stunning. She held her hand out for them to admire. "I love them both," she said, and she wasn't referring only to the rings. "I can't wait for everyone back home to see."

THE NIGHT before she left India—temporarily, she had to keep reminding herself to fend off the tears—Leslie checked the stuffed, zipped luggage one last time. She was exhausted and ready to crawl into bed with Tom. They would sleep only a few hours before leaving for the early-morning flight. There was one last thing she needed to do, so she opened the laptop and brought up her email.

DEAR MOM,

I know this email will probably surprise you, but I wanted to let you know we leave India tomorrow.

I'll save you from asking—no, we didn't do any missionary work while we were here.

Remember the song we used to sing in bible study every summer? "Jesus loves the little children, all the children of the world." It's been on my mind a lot this past week. I'm bringing home one of God's children from India. It will take a few months to complete the adoption, but I wanted you to know so you can be prepared. Her name is Raveena, and I hope you will get to know her because she's precious in my sight as I know she is in His sight. Her mother is in heaven, and so is my unborn baby who never got a chance at life. I'm sorry I never told you. I was ashamed and afraid you wouldn't love me anymore if you knew about it.

I truly believe God sent me to India to rescue Raveena. I'm so excited to come home. Tom and I will see you soon. Hugs to Dad.

Love,

Leslie

ACKNOWLEDGMENTS

I owe thanks and gratitude to so many people for this book. Bill, your generous support and instruction helped this passion project develop from manuscript to novel. Thank you Betty Ridge, Faith Wiley, and Elton Williams for your initial support as this novel developed from first draft to end result and for your continuing support as trusted beta readers/critique group. Thank you Sri Shankar for proofing my manuscript for content. Whole-hearted gratitude to my agent, Dana Newman, for believing in this work.

And of course, thank you to my family for repeating "You can do this" until I believed it, and then graciously understanding the many hours required to make it happen.

SIGN UP FOR MORE

Did you enjoy *Shadow of the Taj*? If so, please leave a review wherever you purchase books.

Sign up for Lara's newsletter to be the first to know of upcoming releases, chances for contests, and to receive previews and insider information http://www.larabernhardt.com/contact

MORE BY ADMISSION PRESS

Looking for your next great read?
Visit www.admissionpress.com

ABOUT THE AUTHOR

Lara Bernhardt is a Pushcart-nominated writer, editor, and audiobook narrator. She is Editor-in-Chief of Balkan Press and also publishes a literary magazine, *Conclave*. Twice a finalist for the Oklahoma Book Award for Best Fiction, she writes supernatural suspense and women's fiction. You can follow her on all the socials @larawells1 on Twitter and @larabern10 on Facebook, BookBub, and Instagram.

ALSO BY LARA BERNHARDT

The Wantland Files series:

The Wantland Files

The Haunting of Crescent Hotel

Ghosts of Guthrie

Made in the USA
Monee, IL
24 September 2021

78157033R00194